MW01120245

The Peony Season

CONTENTS

There's a divinity that shapes our ends,
Rough-hew them how we will.

—Hamlet

THE SCHOOL CYCLE

1. GLASS

THE SUMMER BETWEEN GRADE ELEVEN and grade twelve Alice paints every window in the house. She dips the narrow brush into white paint and draws it precisely, like a knife, along the narrow wood frames. By the end of the first week her mother, coming home from work, finds scarcely a speck of paint on the glass.

It's an old neighbourhood—some of the houses still have sash windows with storms and screens that need to be taken down or put up according to the seasons. "Practise on the screens before you try the windows," her mother ordered. "What I don't need is spattered panes. Or broken glass."

Beginning of July, Alice spends hour after hour alone in the dim, cool basement, painting screens and storms, acquiring a sure touch, an economy of motion, learning patterns and rhythms of movement that become familiar as breathing. She believes she's being leeched of colour, growing pale as the white paint, becoming transparent as

1

glass. When she holds a window against a dark wall, her reflection, framed in a rectangle of freshly painted white wood, startles her.

After the first few days she no longer stops for lunch and refuses to run up the stairs to answer the telephone. "Where have you been? I've tried all day to get hold of you." Marcia sounds concerned when she calls evenings, after Alice has cleaned her brush and washed her fingers clean with solvent.

When she finally finishes the storms, she emerges, a reluctant chrysalis, from the basement into light so dazzling her eyeballs ache from it. She has forgotten how violent the sun can be. Up here the days are hot and stifling, her body always damp, her mouth dry, but she doesn't allow herself to stop for a drink of water except once every hour. Neither does she permit the sound of her mother's voice to invade the room she's working in. Or the memory of her father, who might be wandering without purpose in Vancouver or Edmonton. Might be here in Winnipeg as close as the next street.

Alice is painting a kitchen window that faces the street, a bus route with sidewalks on both sides, a kaleidoscope of constant movement and colour. She deliberately blocks out the particulars of rushing people, the roar of white or red or orange delivery trucks, the progress of bicycles and buses. She allows only an abstract blur of colour—blue, yellow and the green of trees and grass—to enter her vision. By determining what she will see, she creates a world in which she can work with the least possible distraction, least shift of the body. This strategy is a necessity as well as a comfort, but she knows that in the end it will wear her down. She longs for the cool, dim basement.

Mid-July Alice moves from the kitchen to the living room, also facing the street. She is limp from the heat and the terrible strain of shutting out the street. Afraid she can't keep this up, she permits the movements beyond the window to become specific. Through the lower right-hand pane of a window she sees a figure on a bicycle. Jason, riding an old ten-speed, occupies the white-framed pane just long enough for Alice to comprehend with a shock: he's wearing the purple t-shirt.

"ALICE, WHAT'S GOT INTO YOU?" her mother, warming stew for supper, said on the April evening of the day Alice first saw Jason wearing his purple t-shirt. "Grass needs cutting and who do you think's going to set the table, the butler? Time you realized that in the real world it's work, not dreaming, gets you from A to B. What are you staring at, a mirror?"

Alice wasn't staring at a mirror, wasn't held fast by tantalizing reflection or deceptive hope, though she could have been thinking of the futility of those curved mirrors set up in shopping malls to spot shoplifters. She often went to K-Mart in her spares, stopping to examine pendants at the jewellery counter, reading the labels on tapes and CDs, pretending to choose. It was something to do, somewhere to be seen to be occupied the way any normal person might be occupied.

That day she saw a hand moving with the stealth of a weasel along a row of tapes. The fingers, young and tight as springs, touched the tapes, picked up one, two of them, moved beyond Alice's vision and returned, empty. Alice moved her eyes up along the hand, the arm, to the purple sleeve.

"Hey, Alice." The words were not a greeting, they were a declaration, an announcement. Jason's hand resumed its motion. The fingers found a Pink Floyd tape.

"Nice shirt, Jason," she blurted out, it was all she could think to say, but her eyes took in everything from his purple football shoulders to the bulge of his jeans pocket to the annoyance in his eyes. Or was it hate? Or fear? Without her willing it, and without being able to prevent it, Alice's hand flitted to the tapes, hovered hesitantly over them, a pale, fluttering moth.

3

"Not like that. Not now." Jason's voice was a razor-sharp, threatening hiss. He took a step toward her.

"What?" She withdrew her hand, shocked at its errancy. And terrified by the fierceness of Jason's voice, his dark, flaming eyes.

"You're making it fucking obvious."

"I'm not taking stuff. I wouldn't. You're crazy, Jason." Her voice was a fragile whimper.

"Sure." As he moved to walk past, his purple shoulder slammed viciously into her body. She was flung against the tapes. Some of them fell to the floor. Jason disappeared behind a wall of pocket calculators.

When Alice took her place in Mrs. Dexter's English class, a shadow appeared beside her and a huge fist moved in front of her, opened tauntingly close to her face, revealing a digital watch with a black strap. The fingers of the fist closed like a trap around it. The fist withdrew.

Jason rarely sat in his assigned place near the front. Today he slid into the empty desk behind Alice, who knew Mrs. Dexter was too nervous about Jason to say anything. Instead the teacher asked him to read the part of Tom in *The Glass Menagerie*, which she had introduced last class.

I won't be able to read today if Mrs. Dexter asks, Alice thought, knowing perfectly well she didn't have to worry, Mrs. Dexter never asked her.

"*I'm a hired assassin, I carry a gun in a violin case,*" Jason read, spitting the words like splintered glass into Alice's ear. "*My enemies plan to dynamite this place. They're going to blow us all sky-high some night! You'll* be ripped to bits, vaporized, dead meat. *And I'll be glad!*"

The class cheered Jason's exaggerated interpretation and his ad-libbed embellishments. The stale air in the classroom sparked. Mrs. Dexter said nothing. She's nervous, Alice thought. Afraid Jason's act can't keep the attention of the class until the buzzer goes. There'll be an explosion.

When the buzzer sounded, Jason slammed his book shut. His face was so close Alice could feel his breath on her neck.

4

"You talk and I break your neck, bitch." He was first out of the room, his purple shirt a blatant banner filling the doorway.

Marcia was waiting for Alice at the door. "God, you look awful. Anything happen?"

"You're not coming down with something, are you?" her mother asked, serving peaches from a can. "I'm really counting on you to cut the grass today, the radio's saying there'll be rain." She sipped her coffee nervously. "I've had my fill of living with someone you can't count on. Your father always promising, but did he ever keep one promise? The only thing for sure was a good supply of booze and broken beer bottles littering the back yard."

ALICE HAS FORCED BACK INTO ABSTRACTION all colour, all movement beyond the window, though not before she's seen the figure of a man walking uncertainly along the sidewalk. Could be a stumbling, daytime drunk, or just an old man, weak with age or helpless with arthritis. Three more sections to paint on this window. Tomorrow she'll move to her bedroom. It faces the back yard and the quiet lane that's always vacant, though mornings on the way to school she will sometimes find the odd beer bottle. She'll pick it up, throw it in the garbage bin.

She's aware how empty the house is, empty as the space inside her. The hand she depends on to hold the paint brush steady trembles like a leaf, and yet she knows it could easily crash through the window, and her mother, coming home from work, would find the carpet stained with blood and littered with broken glass.

2. WATER

JULIA HAS FALLEN IN LOVE WITH BLAINE and thinks of nothing else. She no longer calls Karen to say, "If you can skip geography let's go jogging in Fraser's Grove Park, the trail along the river's worn smooth. It's shady and perfectly dry." She no longer tells her brother Derek he's lopping years off his life eating those greasy onion rings and burgers soggy with mayonnaise. She no longer notices that her mother brings home TV dinners and soup mixes with monosodium glutamate added, and candy with glossy, non-recyclable packaging. But she notices the clouds, the way they drift or coil, and at night the constellations. *Ursa major. Ursa minor.* Looking up, she feels dizzy, as though she's falling, falling. Or spinning into dream.

Blaine's hazel eyes, deep, mysterious as stars in the night sky, his sandy hair, sun-bleached to almost blond and riffled by the wind, his perfect shoulders, his masculine chest, these are the things that fill Julia's days and nights. The way his arms hold her close, the strong warmth of his body, the pleasure of their hips touching as they walk down the street, arms entwined or curved around each other, the afternoon sun through the leaves of elm trees throwing dappled patterns of light and shade on the hot pavement. Blaine's lips move over her hair, over the rim of an ear, along her neck, his breath melts flesh and bone. His mouth presses hard on hers. She marvels at that, at the way his hand slides hot along her thigh, moves up, up, along her burning, eager skin. She loves it when they walk beside the river and their reflection in the water is not two but one.

Julia's mother says she'll get over it, but she's not as confident as she sounds. She watches her daughter move around the house as if in a dream, as if she is surrounded with light, her movements like music, violin and flute. When Julia forgets why she entered a room, her mother says, sometimes firmly, sometimes gently, "Darling, I'd finish that sandwich, if I were you. Can't go to school on empty." Or: "Darling, will you help me shop for fabric for curtains this afternoon? This room needs a lift, don't you think? A change? Green, do you think, or ocean blue?" Sometimes she just says "Julia, Julia, Julia," as if she's thinking, what else can a mother say? Her anxious eyes follow her dreaming daughter across a room. Across spring and into summer.

ON SATURDAY JULIA WALKS ACROSS THE BRIDGE to Osborne Village. She leans over the railing and gazes down at the dark river water, dirty, flecked with debris. Her joy and her hope transform it, render it crystal clear. She feels light and buoyant. If she fell from the bridge she would float like a feather or like the seed of a dandelion west through the prairie. The water would bear her up as it bore dead Ophelia in Mrs. Dexter's English class last winter.

The traffic is a pleasant blur that she can shut out easily; it doesn't exist. She continues walking, steps inside shops, caresses softly flowered rayon dresses, denim jeans, a blue silk blouse. Everything, everything has her approval, her love, as she feels sure, very sure, she has Blaine's approval, his deep, deep love.

If someone had said to Julia, *Love bears all things, hopes all things, believes all thing, it never fails*, she would have said impatiently, "I know, I know."

KAREN THINKS IF ONLY she could get Julia to go with her on the next fine weekend to West Hawk Lake with Karen's family. It's early for swimming, but the two of them can walk along the water's edge, dip their toes in. If it's sunny they can bury themselves in the warm sand and laugh like children, like they laughed last year when they named every boy in class, finding one, two or three things wrong with each one: too skinny, too stupid, too eager. If only they could leave everything behind. School, all this business about Blaine, this dream. Exchange all the bother and the uneasiness for ice-cream cones. Vanilla for Julia, butterscotch for Karen.

Late evening they will build a fire on the beach and look for sticks to plunge into it, and when the sticks catch fire, they'll withdraw them, twirl them, laughing, till the flames die, and with the incandescent tips trace quick, glowing patterns against the blackening sky. They will hear the water lapping on the sand. And in the morning everything will be fresh and clear. Everything will then be real. For both of them, but especially for Julia.

BLAINE IS AT MCDONALD'S, serving burgers and grilled fish sandwiches with tartar sauce, making strawberry and chocolate milkshakes and handing cup after cup of McDonald's coffee across the counter. His movements are quick and confident, the supervisor says he doesn't miss a beat, the customers consider him amiable. If this were a regular restaurant, he'd get good tips. Blaine smiles at the customers, listens with interest to everything they say, glances at his wristwatch. His hands itch for the curved surface of his football, the reassuring firmness of his car's steering wheel. He thinks about Fraser's Grove Park and longs for the river bank, where kids go to relax and smoke or do dope. Mid-afternoon his sturdy shoulders slump, his hair goes limp from heat and humidity, his face is greasy and flushed, his damp shirt rumpled. Whenever he turns his head he notices the hair of the girl beside him. Karen. It shines softly copper. He'd like to touch it, touch the skin of Karen's white arm, her face.

"Do you like Julia?" Karen asks when there's a brief lull in the flow of customers.

Blaine turns to her with pleasure, glad of a chance to stop for a moment. "Julia," he says, puzzled, searching his mind for a face, a smile, a gesture to go with that name. Julia.

"Do you like her?" Karen asks, her voice insistent. She wants to say, "Do you like the way her eyes crinkle and narrow when she smiles, do you like it when she turns and looks at you in English class, do you like her creamy skin, her slenderness, her pale hair, do you want to touch her? Hold her? Do you *like* her the way she likes you? Do you *know* her?"

Blaine tries with the utmost good will to remember Julia, to pick her out of a swirl of faces, faces that swim around his desk in the classroom and spill into the corridor and out the door. His own face goes tense with trying. He is puzzled. His eyes look dull and tired. The shapes and colours in the swirl become more blurred. "Sorry," he says. "Sorry. No, I don't."

Karen thinks sadly of Julia. Her eyes. The way she will float through the summer in a fragile dream, holding with rapture something that can't be held. Karen feels a heaviness she hasn't asked for.

JULIA LEAVES THE SHOPS and clambers down to a rock at the river's edge. The light cannot glance silver from such yellowish, opaque water. A branch, a bottle, a clutch of soggy, rotting leaves come bobbing by. Flotsam. She bends over the murky surface, believing she sees her eyes reflected there, bright as stars in the night sky. She believes that any moment now Blaine's reflection will appear beside hers, his happiness rippling on the water's smooth surface, blending with her happiness. She believes this, hopes it. Knows it with her whole heart and body and doesn't see the sluggishness of the grey water.

If Julia were not giving her whole attention to the dark water that she believes is crystal clear, she would hear, swelling above the sound of traffic on the bridge, the raucous laughter of teenagers leaning out the open window of a car crossing the bridge. Their names might be Josh or Jason or Marcia or even Blaine. A tailpipe or metal moulding, something, has been jolted loose. It drags and scrapes along the concrete and clangs on the metal grillwork of the bridge. The jarring clatter and the young, derisive voices rise above the ordinary swoosh and hum of the traffic. Already the car is roaring off the bridge toward downtown. But Julia has not noticed it. For her it isn't real. From the receding car a radio blares, "Crazy About You

Baby." She continues to gaze into the sluggish river as if it contains the perfect and impossible reflection of a star.

3. JONQUILS

THE MORNING AFTER DENISE HAD SEX for the first time—with Jake in the back seat of his father's black Honda Accord at four in the afternoon, she was home in time for supper, no unsettling questions—she's walking down the corridor at school, the beige scuffed tiles newly mopped like they are every morning, the doors to the classrooms already open, the stains on the ceiling no larger, no smaller than they were yesterday. She stops in front of her locker, as if poised on the uncertain edge of a new world and who knows what it might contain. Her slender fingers work the lock and pull open the door. There's the timetable—it's day three, math first, then French, a spare, then history, in English they are reading *The Glass Menagerie*, and so on through the day. Should she leave the locker open for Marcia, who is always late? A voice over the PA warns: "Students are reminded to leave their lockers locked at all times for security reasons."

Should she tell Marcia she's been transformed, she is really a woman now? Should she mention love?

Jason, from French, wearing his Blue Jays baseball cap and his purple t-shirt, strides by, filling the corridor. He turns, swinging his football shoulders neatly around, and retraces his steps. "Hey, Denise. Lend me your French translation, you know, that paragraph? Didn't have time to get it done."

Denise wants to say no, wants to say she didn't finish, either. But she did, in the living room after supper—lasagna, her favourite, and hot garlic toast. "You're not eating, Denise," her mother scolded but without paying attention. Her father was nervous because after months without a job there's a nibble from Edmonton. Her brother Stevie begged her to make popcorn for TV. "No, Stevie, I've got tons of homework."

Denise pages through her looseleaf binder, Jason towering over her. She can smell him, feel his demand pressing down on her. His hands are massive, capable of violence. She removes the neatly written French assignment, holds it a moment with tendeness and regret, then hands it like a sacrifice to Jason, who mutters words that may or may not include the word "Thanks." She is certain he won't return the page before French class.

Marcia comes hurtling down the corridor, calling "Hi" left and right, dancing her body around to speak to someone she's already passed. She seems to be shimmering in colour and light. Marcia is always sure, Denise thinks, always confident, but that isn't the quality she wants to take hold of this morning. It isn't the essence she wants to name. *Carefree* comes close. Marcia is *carefree*.

"Denise, I'm having a party this weekend," she says, "My parents are going to Grand Forks. I need you to help me. We'll have chips and pop and maybe get pretzels. Some guys are bringing beer. My parents know, it's okay. What do you think?"

Denise doesn't know what to think. She wishes she didn't feel a need to reinvent yesterday afternoon, to refashion place and circumstances, to readjust time. Wishes she didn't feel this panicky urge to alter that strange entering of flesh into flesh, that *clumsy coupling*—she's read that expression recently in a novel. She regrets the cramped awkwardness, the way she bumped her head on the handgrip. She wants to remember it as soft and tender. Romantic. She wishes it had been splendid, that she could proclaim, "I am beautiful now, I am filled with amazed knowing." She wishes she didn't feel so hollow.

"Good morning, Denise," her homeroom teacher says. "Here's a note from Guidance. They want to see you before class."

Guidance! What do they know about her and Jake? What can she say to the always warm, always efficient, always on-the-run women in Guidance? Karen, from French, said it was rape, when it happened to her. Yesterday wasn't rape, although that startling explosion of need—Jake's, not hers—took forceful hold of the afternoon, determining everything. But she can't remember saying, "No, stop! Stop!" She's sure she didn't, although she may have wanted to.

There should be some way to start over. To try again.

The counsellor is only concerned about sorting out an exam conflict Denise reported yesterday.

Yesterday!

On her way to math Denise bumps into Jake. "Hullo," he says. What else is there to say, on the way to math the morning after? What does Denise want? Does she want him to stop, turn toward her, look her full in the face? Does she wait for his brown eyes to smile warmly into hers?

Yes, that would be enough for now. That is all she wants. She has no idea what Jake wants as they walk without speaking into class and take their separate places, Denise third row from the windows, second seat from the front where the sun turns her light brown hair to fire, Jake at the very back.

On the bulletin board there's a poster with a silver unicorn, the grey horn circled with light. It stands on a jagged cliff that juts out from a mountain peak where clouds swirl sullenly. If she looks only at the unicorn, everything appears luminous and very bright against a blue sky. Beside the unicorn poster there's one of Elvis Presley and next to it one of Albert Einstein, all put there by the math teacher.

Denise can't bear to look at the posters, not at the silver unicorn, not at Elvis, not at Albert Einstein. She can't bear the loneliness. Instead she fixes her gaze on the large calendar beside the chalkboard. Under the picture of Winnipeg—Portage and Main in summer, everything green—the month of June is neatly laid out. Someone has marked the exam days with a red felt pen, French on the nineteenth, math on the twentieth, the last day of June is the last day of school.

By the end of the month she will know whether her marks are good enough—whether she's won the prize for French, whether she's passed math. She will know if her father gets the job in Edmonton and she will have to move away from this familiar school, from her best friend Marcia, from Jake, from the unicorn and Albert Einstein.

She will know if she is pregnant.

The buildings on the calendar are immaculate, the Bank of Montreal gleams in sunlight, the thirty-four storeys of the Richardson Building push up, up into the cobalt sky.

"I've got my dad's car today," Jake said yesterday. "Wanna go for a ride?"

The trees in the park rushed by on either side as Jake drove, maybe with a fixed purpose, a destination already in mind. Maybe not. The warm scent of summer, of dust and pine, filled the car in a way she could not have anticipated. Yesterday.

Yesterday, less than an hour after Mrs. Dexter gave her the part of Amanda to read, the part about summer in the south. About jonquils.

Denise wishes she had turned then to Jake, laughing and carefree. She wishes she had said, *Stop! Stop! I see jonquils.* She wants her empty arms filled with yellow jonquils.

4. THE UNICORN

ALL DAY GRACE DEXTER HAS BEEN saying things like, "Don't panic, Denise, *of course* you'll pass English. You'll do *fine*." Or: "Julia, Julia, you've been dreaming, my dear. You've been floating like a lost star in a distant galaxy. *All class.* Come back to us, Julia. Come back." Or: "Blaine, do you *have* to work so many hours at McDonald's? I'm worried you won't get your assignments in."

At teachers' college Grace was taught to see each student as unique; she didn't know then how much easier things would be if they weren't. At the end of the school year she is exhausted by their uniqueness.

Exhaustion isn't unfamiliar, nor is the anxiety that blossoms in June, filling the hallways and classrooms, cramming the hours of the lengthening days. Alone at her desk in the empty room, Grace thinks it can't be only worry over students that wears her down, or the accumulation of ten months in the classroom, test papers to be read and graded, results to be tabulated and reports completed by the deadline marked in her day book. But she is incapable of saying what it is, what's gone wrong. If anything has. It might be just a mood. And now the silver unicorn is missing from her classroom, another niggling worry.

The deserted room is redolent with warm, adolescent smells. With effort Grace turns to next day's lesson on *The Glass Menagerie*. She'll get the class to read; they like that. Best voice for Tom Wingfield is Jason's, she thinks uneasily, remembering this morning's class. Intense, fortified with a thick shell of sarcasm, his voice can make the scenes with Amanda dramatic enough so the unwillingness or impatience of the class won't burst boundaries and erupt, as classes do at the end of June. Or go dead, which is worse. Who should read the part of Amanda? Should she choose Marcia? Karen? Denise again? If she chooses well, things take care of themselves, she gains a reprieve, a fifty-minute breathing space.

Grace would rather not admit she's afraid of Jason, the way he strides up to her desk, huge in his black jacket or that outrageous purple t-shirt he's been wearing this spring. She has to steel herself against the urge to edge back. This morning he held in his balled fist the grimed and crumpled sheets of his essay on the poetry of Robert Frost, graded D.

"I think there's been a mistake. I think this calls for a reread."

He towered above her, awkward and formidable. His

words were not especially sarcastic, not quite a demand. More like a proclamation made with a certainty that it would produce action. She didn't shrink back.

"I don't know, Jason, I think I've been generous. I could have justified an E, you know. Read my detailed comments." She gestured at the crumpled essay. "We can go over them if you like. Or we can discuss a rewrite."

The huge fist opened and the crumpled sheets covered with Jason's brazen scrawl dropped in front of her. He leaned forward and placed both large hands flat on the desk. His face moved in, hard as stone. Grace avoided his eyes and watched the way his mouth, a tight muscle, opened a narrow gash in the taut face.

"Hey, I'm not interested in detailed comments. I'm not interested in talking rewrites. I'm interested, *very* interested, in a C. You get my meaning, Mrs. Dexter?"

"D, Jason. Your essay is a D."

"I wasn't exactly afraid," Grace told her colleagues at the noon-hour department meeting. "I felt sort of wooden."

"Just keep cool. Just don't ever give in to the bastards," the department head said. "We've got to bloody well dig in and not give ground."

"Bunch of cretinous delinquents." Someone else.

"Did you report it to Hancock? You should."

Grace doesn't know, can't imagine, what Chad would say if she should begin telling him about her students. About Julia and Denise and Jason and Marcia. She can't imagine herself announcing into the silence of their evening meal, when they've come to the coffee, "I gave a student a D on an essay and he sort of threatened me. What do you think of that?" Chad is a family and marriage counsellor, and he holds seminars in churches and rural towns on topics like "A Pair That Prays Together Stays Together." "Deal With Anger, Don't Deny It." "God: the Unique Solution." "Honesty in Twos."

She doesn't feel right about inflicting her skittish students on Chad, the way they hang around the door at the beginning of class, as if daring her to make them come in and sit down. What would be gained if she described Jason's recent case of attitude? She might ask Chad, "What should I do?" But then she would be requiring him to share her weakness, her inability. She can't expect that of him.

When Chad leaves the house mornings, his briefcase is packed with neat notes and stapled handouts and brochures, his pants pressed the night before, his tie meticulously knotted. Evenings he brings his laptop computer to the dining-room table where she can watch him tapping out revisions to next day's presentation. He is so contained, so absorbed in his work. She studies his lean shoulders, groomed hands. His light hair has not begun to thin, he doesn't seem to be aging, though whenever he catches her looking at him, he clowns at her and his face turns comical, like an old man's. "Love you, Gracie," he'll say. "You're special," and she'll return to circling the run-ons, fragments, misspelled words in the essays she's grading. She underscores every cliché. Her students know she is conscientious. And critical. She likes to work in front of the TV, the sound turned down, the colour and movement of the picture a soothing presence whenever she permits her eyes a reprieve from the endless pages.

Whenever Chad pauses in his work, he stares out the east window, right into the branches of the mountain ash. What does he see in that mass of June-fresh, quivering leaves?

DRIVING HOME ALONG KILDONAN AVENUE, Grace thinks maybe she'll take a chance and assign the part of Laura Wingfield to Alice, even though Alice's voice is really too fragile for the classroom, always on the verge of breaking, like delicate glass. Still, Grace can imagine Alice reading beautifully, if she takes the courage: *Glass is something you have to take good care of.* Or that perfectly breathless line: *Oh, be careful—if you breathe, it breaks.*

Grace knows that the unicorn is hanging beside Albert

Einstein and Elvis Presley in Derek Bosco's room. She can see it whenever she takes the long way to the staff room. All available wall-space in the math classroom is covered with exuberant splashes of colour. Grace likes that, likes the energy and tries to breathe it in.

"Can I have it?" was the way Bosco put it. Teasing.

"Have it? Have what?"

"The unicorn. Not to keep, I just want to borrow it for a while for my classroom. Company for Elvis." There's something exuberant about Bosco's grin, something innocent that's out of sync with his middle-aged features, his old brown jacket. When he looks at her, Grace is sure he sees and understands something about her that she is unaware of.

Grace likes to move the unicorn poster up to the front of the classroom when she teaches *The Glass Menagerie* in early June, right after poetry and before exams, before commencement and year-end deadlines.

"There's a glass unicorn in the play we're going to read," she says every year. "It's a symbol I think you'll all understand."

Most of the girls in class, and even some of the boys, admire the unicorn in the poster, perched on a mountain ledge, silvery-grey against a brilliant sky. "Where did you get it, Mrs. D? Do you give away posters in June? Can I have it?"

But this June the poster is missing, relocated to Bosco's room. And her class is already well into *The Glass Menagerie*. Tomorrow she'll have to stop by and say, "Can I have it?"

Beside the driveway the geraniums are blooming blood-red. Grace wants to stay in the car and let the startling brilliance seep into the blood and tissue of her body, and then bubble up, pushing the heaviness out. She lets the crimson blaze blot out the drab sidewalk, the walls of the house. She pictures the silver unicorn surrounded with light and thinks of Bosco, his hands when he took the poster from her. Although she has never felt their touch, she imagines they have enough warmth and strength to call to life whatever they come in contact with. At lunch, Bosco likes to sit at the window table. He never brings papers to mark and she wonders if he is the kind of man who leaves education at the door when he comes home to the house he shares with a wife she has never met, in the new development that, according to staffroom authorities, curves around an artificial lake.

There's no lake near the house Grace shares with Chad, although the river flows near Kildonan Avenue. She seldom walks down to the shaded riverbank, there is never time. Her students like to come to the river, some for no reason, some for a variety of reasons like drugs and sex. She overhears them bragging to each other before class. When school is over for the year, she will take time to walk down to the river. She will walk along its banks and see the elm trees reflected in it. She will be refreshed.

Grace slumps behind the steering wheel a long while, not wanting to look up at the house. When she finally rouses herself and raises her eyes, she sees crude yellow blobs daubing the front wall and dripping grotesque patterns down the stucco. The large front window is shattered; splinters of glass litter the sidewalk and stick out of the junipers like needles from a pincushion.

The door is wide open, there's someone on the steps. Caught in the grip of fear, Grace feels her body go slack once more, her limbs turn to water. Somewhere on the periphery of her vision she sees Jason coming down the steps, walking toward her, a rock in each large fist, his face a cold metal slab. She is numb, unable to lift a hand, unable to scream or moan or even whimper. She waits helplessly as Jason moves without mercy toward her.

But it isn't Jason at all, it's Chad there beside the mock orange bush, a pail in one hand, scrunched-up rags in the other. He's taken off his suit jacket and loosened his tie.

Grace manages to open the heavy car door and lift out one unwilling leg, then the other. The effort leaves her drained, so weak she can barely take hold of her dog-eared copy of *The Glass Menagerie*. How young and innocent Chad looks there on the steps, squinting against the brightness of the sun. How awkward and irresolute. He comes down the steps in slow motion. Grace wants to shield him from the senselessness of the splattered house, from her own weakness. She moves toward him, stepping around the briefcase he must have dropped among the glass splinters. A shuffle of papers has spilled from it, each sheet proclaiming in a bold, ornate font: "God: the Unique Solution." One sheet is caught between green leaves and blood-red geranium petals. Grace bends to pick it up.

"Kids been flinging eggs. Nothing better to do, I guess." Chad sounds apologetic, as if he's to blame.

Grace doesn't speak. She's thinking how she'll never come home again without fear, without looking for a figure darting around the corner of the house or skulking in the shadows of the mock orange bush. From now on she'll be on the lookout for Jason—she's sure it's Jason, he's to blame—lurking near the door or striding defiantly down the driveway with malice in his hard features. She wonders if this should be reported to Hancock, the principal.

She remembers that tomorrow she must retrieve the silver unicorn from Bosco's room.

"You go on in. I'll clean it up," Chad says. "It's not that bad."

Grace wants to take one of the rags from him and wipe away the ugly yellow streaks. But she finds no strength. She is still holding *The Glass Menagerie* in one hand and "God: the Unique Solution" in the other. Chad sets down the pail and the rags, and takes the book and the paper from her. He puts his arm around her, and they stumble together up the steps and into the house.

5. THE FOURTH DOOR

JASON BENDS FORWARD ON A STRAIGHT-BACKED CHAIR in the school office, shutting out the conversation meandering between the two secretaries—the one with the straw hair who told him where to sit and the older, grey one. He's reading the last scene of *The Glass Menagerie*, the part where Amanda, the mother, says *Things have a way of turning out so badly.* Jason is not in the habit of evaluating his days: are they good, are they bad. Days come and go and he rarely thinks about his future, which the math teacher, Mr. Bosco, keeps telling him is spreading out before him like a clean page, or sometimes an open field. Jason pictures it more as a vague blur, or like smoked glass, opaque.

If Jason were to assess the past week that's come round inevitably to Friday afternoon he would rate it so-so. A new Pink Floyd tape—*Animals*—has been added to his collection. Yesterday the class broke up when he read the part of Tom Wingfield in *The Glass Menagerie*. They cheered and that was cool, not something that happens often to Jason. Wednesday could be written off as a downer because Mrs. Dexter gave him a D for his essay on poetry, but then he and Blaine Rebeck skipped Bosco's math class and cruised along Kildonan Avenue in Blaine's car. They parked it and walked down the oak-shaded trail along the river where they shared the dope that Blaine brought.

Jason isn't sure why the principal has asked to see him. If he wanted to be smart or cynical, he could call Hancock senile or just plain stupid, the way he likes to hassle students, but it's hardly worth the effort. He assumes he's been summoned because of skipping math, no big deal. He'll just let Hancock talk and won't say anything, and when the screws tighten he'll mumble that he was depressed about problems at home, personal things he really can't talk about.

It wouldn't be a lie, problems at home. His father absent three years, his mother silent. If his father should ever return, Jason will slam him against the door and kick him down the concrete steps, plant his fist in his father's face, he knows he can do it, physically, he's grown. Back then he was bewildered by terror, petrified by his father's huge presence, his rage. Not a drunken rage, Jason can't remember his father drinking. Rather, it was an animal rage that found expression in a flesh-on-flesh, bone-on-bone kind of communication. Sometimes there was blood. Jason learned to shut all of it out, shut out his mother's screams that came muffled through a closed door.

He is nearing the end of the play: *You live in a dream; you manufacture illusions!* Amanda is saying. *Don't let anything interfere with your selfish pleasure! Just go, go, go—to the movies!*

Jason doesn't go to the movies much, but sometimes when school gets tedious he hangs out at K-Mart, at the videos and cassettes. The tape decks and CD players. He has the ability to clear his mind and concentrate on one thing. His large hands move with amazing skill, carefully, stealthily if necessary. He is capable of deliberate patience and, if the occasion requires it, brutality.

Jason hurries through Amanda's lines, he isn't interested in them, can't imagine a mother who nags like that, his certainly doesn't. He tries not to think too much about his mother, her long silences. Day after day, coming home from work at the meat packing plant, tired. Eats a cheese sandwich or brings a hamburger from McDonald's. Yesterday he made macaroni and cheese, but she ate very little. Just sat there in the kitchen, under the picture of the two hands held vertically and pressed together, praying. The hands have been there as long as Jason can remember. He has no idea whether his mother was praying or not as she rested her head on her own work-worn hands. He doesn't know what he can do for her. It seems to him that she has always been unutterably sad, the house they occupy together pervaded with her sorrow.

He slows down for Tom's lines, rehearsing them noiselessly but with lips moving slightly. Maybe Mrs. Dexter will ask him to read Tom's part again next week. *The more you shout about my selfishness to me the quicker I'll go.* His lips move, he hears Tom's anger in his head. He likes the line. He reads the stage directions: *Tom smashes his glass on the floor. He plunges out the fire escape, slamming the door.* A satisfying kind of excitement, an arousal, moves through Jason's body.

"I hear they had a rock through the front window, and the door kicked in." It's the straw-haired secretary. Her voice, low and languid, intrudes on his reading. "And about a dozen eggs smashed all over the front. Egg yolk, that's not so easy to clean."

"A shame." The grey secretary.

"Kids are getting so damn violent."

The secretaries seem unaware of Jason, who pictures, with brief curiosity, egg yolk slithering yellow and thick down the side of a house, sliding over painted wood or filling the roughness of stone and stucco. He returns to Tom's last speech. *The window is filled with pieces of coloured glass, tiny transparent bottles in delicate colours, like bits of shattered rainbow.* Jason feels let down by the words. Where's the anger gone? It's anger he's hungry for. He tries to hold on to the excitement, but it diffuses inside him like a thinning cloud.

"Jason Flint. In here." The door to the principal's office has opened and Hancock beckons with an authoritative gesture of his close-cropped, reddish-blond head. He is medium in height and slender, the left side of his face scarred with a dull red birthmark, his dark slacks rumpled, his white shirt no longer crisp at the end of the day. He keeps his face deliberately grim.

"Tell me about that poetry essay, Jason." He doesn't bother to sit, doesn't ask Jason to sit.

Jason's head jerks up, his shoulders tighten. What does Hancock know about the poetry essay? About the D Mrs. Dexter gave him? Jason hasn't forgotten that he demanded a reread, banged his fist hard on her desk, but it seems unimportant now. He's thinking, poetry, that can't lead to anything serious. It's Friday and he wants to be out of here.

"To what extent do poetic techniques enhance the meaning in any one of Robert Frost's poems?" The words slide from his lips automatically, like a recitation. He might be parroting a teacher's assignment, but his voice is innocent of any sarcasm. Then he remembers.

"No, no, I mean, it was about rhythm. And rhyme. In Frost's poetry. Something like that." Jason can't say exactly what the essay was about.

"What mark did you get?"

"D."

"And?"

"And what?"

"Listen, Flint." Hancock is obviously impatient. "You threatened Mrs. Dexter and left the classroom angry. Where did you go?"

"Go?" He's not going to admit he skipped class, not when Hancock hasn't even mentioned Bosco.

"Let's not play games, Flint. You left school angry Wednesday, went to Mrs. Dexter's house on Kildonan Avenue, and for revenge you smashed her window and hurled raw eggs at her house. That's called vandalism, Flint, you got that? Vandalism."

Jason is caught off-guard, and doesn't know what to say. He didn't even know Mrs. Dexter lived on Kildonan Avenue. He stares at Hancock, whose face bears the assurance of victory, as if he's taken a chance, grabbed a hammer in his groomed right hand, brought it down hard and hit the nail on the head. Now he raises that hand to his face in nervous relief. Or maybe to hide the scar.

Jason feels as if he's on fire, his body aflame with resentment, his purple t-shirt damp. His hands, one still holding *The Glass Menagerie*, instinctively take the balled shape of weapons. In case of a physical encounter between principal and student, Jason would have the advantage: his limbs are young and fierce and every fibre of his body is charged once more with the raw excitement of rage.

The sharp, loud ring of a buzzer proclaims throughout

23

the building that the school week is toast. It is the moment both student and principal have longed for, each in his own way, and the strident signal interrupts the momentum building up in the warm, stale air of the principal's office. Jason can picture all the doors along the hallway opening, students streaming helter-skelter out of classrooms: he can hear a clatter of metal locker doors, an eruption of glad or defiant voices. The gush of colour and warm bodies and noise pushes to the doorways and is ejected into the open air, the freedom of a June weekend.

More than anything Jason wants to be part of that stream, wants to let it carry him into the street with its modest possibilities. He wishes for nothing else. As he forces his fists to open, he sees for a moment those other open hands placed carefully together, praying in his mother's kitchen.

"Well, you're wrong," he says and he almost adds, "Ask Blaine Rebeck. He was with me," but his brain has signalled "no." What's the point of dragging in Blaine and the dope? He can't do that to Blaine. This unpremeditated loyalty puzzles Jason. It was just a fluke, skipping class with Blaine, they aren't really friends, had spoken very little there beside the river.

"Phone my mother," he hears himself say, and this too puzzles him. How could she possibly help him, his silent mother?

"The number, Flint?" Hancock's hand has already lifted the receiver, his index finger is poised to dial.

It's possible, because it's Friday, that his mother will actually be home from work. She comes in the door and the phone rings. She dumps her worn cloth handbag on a chair and moves wearily to pick up the receiver. "Hello." Her voice is wooden and so crammed with exhaustion Jason feels compelled to shield her.

"Actually, no, my mom isn't home," he says quickly, thinking, what can I say now, what will work? God, how can I keep her out of this?

"I didn't do it, Mr. Hancock, I swear to God. I wasn't anywhere near her house." His passion, earnest and almost desperate, surprises him. It also surprises Hancock.

"Go on." Hancock sits and motions Jason to a chair. The receiver is back in its cradle. Has the hammer, after all, not hit the nail on the head?

A shaft of light pours through the narrow window. What a jail this room is, Jason thinks, what a bloody jail. He catches a faint glimmer of the irony that Hancock too passes the days in a prison cell. But now is the time to hint about problems at home, imply unspeakable things without giving anything away, without dragging his mother too far into this. He can't seem to begin. The noise in the hallway is already diminishing, the building is being emptied, and to keep sitting here in this alien place with a man who is a stranger is unbearable and ludicrous.

"Actually, my mother's out of town for the weekend," Jason says, proceeding slowly, deliberately. "She needed a break, she's..." He stops himself, wondering who there is in the whole world to trust, can anyone ever be counted on? He bends forward in the chair, elbows on knees, his forearms vertical, hands pressed together with *The Glass Menagerie* gripped between them, the fingertips almost touching his chin. His slumped shoulders feel tight as a steel spring. "I'll tell her when she comes back, she can phone you Monday. Or better Tuesday." How much does he dare stretch the time?

"I didn't do it," he says again. "Okay, maybe I was rude to her, but I didn't smash her window." His voice is becoming calm, the rage is there inside him, but he can handle it. By Tuesday, who knows, something will turn up. He looks up, looks at Hancock, who isn't looking at him but into the distance somewhere above the closed door.

Hancock has lost interest, Jason can tell. Lost that firmness of purpose he had when he opened his office door and motioned with a confident gesture of his head. Is he thinking he's being lied to about Jason's mother, and what sounds like sincerity is really fake? He keeps looking at his wrist-watch.

"Why can't you kids for once think of the bigger picture? I can't run a school without rules. Society can't be decent place unless everyone works together." The hint of whining in Hancock's voice rouses in Jason a flicker of contempt. He knows now there will be no phone call home and no detention. Not today. And along with the contempt and the knowing comes a rush of gratitude.

Jason runs a finger along the polished wood behind a row of books on the principal's desk. The finger picks up dust. On the other side of the door there is a scraping of chairs, a blur of voices: the secretaries are getting ready to leave.

Only a few students are still at the bus stop when Jason walks out into the warm June afternoon, shaking off the trapped feeling, the foreignness that inhabits the hallways and classrooms where he spends so many hours each week. He doesn't speak to anyone at the bus stop, cuts through the K-Mart parking lot where he slows his stride, thinking maybe this is a place he could hang out for a while. But he continues walking, neither in a hurry nor hesitant, and comes eventually to the low-rental housing where he lives behind the fourth door with his mother. Two or three children are playing near the large garbage bin. A woman is collecting toys from the steps, a red plastic airplane, a doll, a couple of dinosaurs. In this place Hancock does not exist, nor Mrs. Dexter, nor the two secretaries, nor Robert Frost. But this week Jason has imagined Tom Wingfield approaching or moving away from such a door as this, cradling his desires the way a mother might cradle a child, with fear and doubt and love.

Jason is aware of being hungry as he climbs the wooden steps, but he doesn't delude himself with the vain hope that his mother is planning fried chicken for supper. He thinks he should go next door to borrow a lawnmower and cut the small patch of grass that's going to seed in front of their unit. But the sun is still high and hot and he doesn't feel like it. His hands are relaxed now. One of them still holds his copy of *The Glass Menagerie*.

"Take it easy, Flint," Hancock said when he finally held the door open. "If your mother's away, just make sure she doesn't come home to..." As he groped for something to say, he let his eyes meet Jason's and Jason saw that they were deeply blue and held a glint of curiosity.

"Just give her a break, Jason."

Fishing for his key, Jason knows that this weekend Hancock's dull red scar and the curiosity in his blue eyes will follow him as he goes in and out through this door. But at night, when he closes his eyes for sleep, it's Tom Wingfield who will still be there, a mute companion in the darkness.

THE DIVINE VISITATION

IN A CROWD OF STRANGERS a person should have a companion, Lydia thinks, someone to stand beside and talk to. Like the two women ahead of her, mid-thirties she estimates, supporting between them a tiny scrap of a grandmother who can't seem to straighten her body and whose feet stumble on the worn path. The woman's back is bent in the submissive shape of pain and her eyes are lowered in fear, but at least she's not alone. Lydia thinks Doug should be here with her, but that's a futile wish. She would have asked Maggie McLeod to come, but on Saturdays Maggie's kids come for dinner.

The day is neither bright nor hopelessly dull. From time to time the sun edges out from behind pewter clouds, the wind is moderate, the air moist. Brown leaves sail indifferently to the ground. A few dishevelled sparrows flit from branch to branch in the not-quite-bare lilac hedge. It's the kind of day Lydia likes. But is it a day for healing? Isn't spring a more likely time for that? Maybe she's wasting a perfectly good Saturday, lined up the way drunks off North Main line up for the Salvation Army soup kitchen to open.

What possessed her to join this congregation of strangers in this neglected lot, along a path trampled in the grass by the feet of all those who have come here since the miracle? She tries to gauge the hope contained in this gathering. Or is it a convergence of despair?

"Door opens daily at three," according to the *Winnipeg Free Press*. Lydia would like it to be three o'clock right now. She thinks everyone's watching her, speculating why she's alone, pitying her awkwardness. She feels old and lumpish in her blue nylon jacket and scuffed running shoes.

When she gets up enough nerve to take cautious stock, she finds that the others look mostly normal: a wiry, bald man in a navy sweatsuit—she'll describe him to Maggie as fit and good-looking; a large woman wearing baggy, beige pants and a matching sweater, her wispy hair the colour of oatmeal; two women, one in a black, tailored coat and felt hat, the other in a long, print skirt and no coat but a blue shawl—how unmatched they are; even a few teenagers, hands shoved self-consciously into pants pockets, accompanied by parents whose faces reveal nothing. Are the teenagers the ones who need healing or the parents? Here and there she can see crutches and right in front of her a man is pushing a boy in a wheelchair. Father and son probably. The revolving metal spokes catch the subdued afternoon light. The boy is about twelve, same as Doug, but he's much smaller, shrivelled somehow. The thought of anyone as young as her own healthy son crippled and confined to a wheelchair sends a shudder sliding like quicksilver from the base of her neck down her back.

"You've got to be kidding, Mom," Doug said when she first showed him the story she'd clipped from the *Winnipeg Free Press*. "'A divine visitation,'" he read derisively. "'City Couple Claims Wooden Virgin Weeps Blood.' Mom, you're not gonna go and believe that crap? Somebody dumped ketchup on her is all it is."

But she's here in this ragged line with the others who have come. The congregation in the Mennonite Church she used to go to, at first with Abe and Doug, then alone, would be not so much shocked as puzzled. "That's what a faith community is for," Jean Dueck would say, her face gentle and somewhat helpless. "Don't you see? If you enter our fellowship, let us surround you, everything will be different. We all need each other." Pastor Funk would phone if he knew, and there would be sorrow in his voice, like there was after the police came looking for Abe. Any deviation from the expected left him wounded. And baffled.

The urgency that propelled Lydia here could be a residue of faith, though she's sure it's less than a mustard seed. Or it could be fear. Whatever it is, it's impossible to shake off. God knows she's tried.

Again she looks around her. What diseases have these people brought with them? Cancer, emphysema? Maybe someone has AIDS. Surely they are the ones who should be first up for healing and she is just in the way, increasing the length of the waiting queue, a parasite whose request will drain the wooden virgin of her divine power.

Lydia has no debilitated joints or atrophied muscles, nothing like that. None of the sharp, specific pain she hears other people complain of—there on the left side, or here just below the breastbone, or in the small of the back. Her arthritis is no worse than anyone else's. As far as she knows, her vital organs are sound. Heart and lungs and stomach. They never send her signals like Maggie McLeod's heart, thumping so frantically and hard she's forced to sit down and catch her breath whenever the two of them walk too fast, a pair of middle-aged women in jogging clothes, the skin around their eyes beginning to go slack, their mouse-brown hair tied back with scarves.

Then why is she here? An absence of tranquility has brought her. Sometimes this absence becomes a weight that settles in her gut; other times it triggers a dull buzzing that keeps her poised on the edge of headache. It forbids sleep, invites pain, pulls her limbs taut, her jaw so tense she catches herself grinding her teeth at night. When she wants to smile, to show that everything's all right, she has to force the muscles of her face into the right shape.

"You've got stress. The disease of the decade." That's the way Maggie McLeod dismisses it. "Everyone's got it, some more than others. You've got to attack it, Lyd. Think of your body. How it works. You've got to treat it half-decently, damn it. Take control. Of course, if you want to be rid of stress totally, that's like hoping to win a bloody jackpot. What do you expect?"

That's just it. Lydia *does* expect something. Always. She can't help it. Every year she expects her garden to produce tomatoes and corn, fresh asparagus that she steams to delicious tenderness, new potatoes she cooks in their jackets and serves with dill. Nurturing beets and zucchini and strawberries gives her pleasure that housework fails to provide.

Lydia expects to keep her modest job in the city office, even with cutbacks. Doug will grow up decent, not a lawyer—heavens, she knows a person's limitations—but maybe something with computers. She expects that she and Maggie McLeod will go on being friends, will go on arguing and calling each other up with news: "Fresh salmon's on sale at Food Fare." "Rita's Hair Place is closing. She says we didn't give her enough business." Twice, three times a week they'll walk, or even jog, together over the Peguis Bridge and through Kildonan Park. "Really, we should do it every day to make a difference," Maggie says.

One thing she doesn't expect is for Abe to come home. It's not likely he'll reappear, show up on her doorstep—she calls it hers now—and she won't be waiting for him. No, that's over and just as well. But in spite of that, she believes that what we are is not what we can be and that she, Lydia, will once more be surprised with that irrepressible elation bubbling up inside her the way it used to, and all the strain and heaviness will dissipate as if it's no more than a summer mist.

But her life is passing, ordinary and relentless as the Saturday afternoon traffic here on Bellevue Street. She can't wait forever.

IN HIS MOTHER'S UNTIDY KITCHEN, Doug is fixing a sandwich. Salami and cheese and ketchup. He's not hungry. He half considers taking a beer from the fridge, chooses a Coke instead. He pulls a chair around so he can see the small televison set on the shelf beside the telephone where he just called Ben, who said, "My dad'n'me are taking off to Lockport. Fishing."

At least his mother's not home, he consoles himself. Won't be for a while. If he can't hang out with Ben, at least he can occupy the whole house for a few hours with that sense of illicit permission his mother's absence gives him. He can do anything he likes. He wills the hours to be worthwhile, to be fun, to be crazy, but he can't think of anything he wants to do right now. A dreariness has descended on this Saturday. The weekend is slipping away.

He had counted on Ben. "Shit," he says. "Shit." He thinks for a split second that he should have a dad to take him fishing at Lockport, but no, he doesn't want his father. It's been over a year since the police came to the door, too late. His father's face appeared in the papers and on the evening news. "Abe Martens Pockets Company Cash," the *Winnipeg Free Press* said. "Corporate Thief Slips Town"— that was *The Sun*. Doug still finds the occasional "Son of a Thief" scribbled with a black marker on his locker or his books.

Doug doesn't want to think about being afraid, but a thin, hard border of fear constricts his gut, his chest. Every limb feels its constraint. It's with him always and nothing can lighten it. He's afraid to face Monday morning. Afraid one day even Ben will abandon him and hang out with the other guys. His father will come back, and that black cloud of disgrace that hovers constantly over him will descend and smother him. The front page of tomorrow's *Free Press* or, worse, the TV, will show his mother in her faded, blue nylon jacket, kneeling before a wooden statue, the worn-down soles of her running shoes facing the camera. Or her face, close up, filling the screen.

He glances quickly at the TV screen, but it's only a man and a woman walking along a golden, palm-fringed beach. The water is green-blue and the waves white-capped. The woman's eyes are the colour of sky, her legs long and tanned. Doug notices the man's perfect chest and thigh muscles. He has his arm around the woman and their laughter is buoyed by the beat of music.

"Shit." Doug gets up, his anger toppling the chair. He turns and grabs it with both hands and raises it. If he hurls it, the TV will explode, the telephone clatter to the floor. Instead, he brings the chair crashing down on the kitchen tiles and lets go of it. His hands are fists now, steel-hard. They descend on the table, jouncing the ketchup bottle and the plate with the sandwich over the edge. A pitiful, animal cry rises from somewhere distant and dark inside him. It swells, fills the room with its desolation, subsides and then dies, an eerie cadence.

When silence once again fills the kitchen, Doug lifts a hand to his face and finds a disgusting moistness there.

THE LINE BEGINS TO MOVE. Slowly. Lydia knows what comes next. This past week the television cameras have ushered her daily through the back yard and into the kitchen of the small, drab bungalow that shelters the virgin. The elderly man and his wife who live here, who own the wooden statue, the first mortals to witness the miracle of blood issuing from the divine, carved eyes, have opened their hearts and back door to the motley collection of suffering strangers. "Crazies," according to Maggie. The local priest interrupts his busy schedule every afternoon to sit in vigil beside the virgin and to maintain control of the traffic. The foot-high wooden statue that so amazingly, so graciously, exudes blood, rests on a table in front of the window, flanked by two potted geraniums blooming in profuse, crimson affirmation. Or is it alarm? A small plastic bowl for offerings sits near the statue.

And here she is, Lydia, a wage earner, a single mother, a woman of integrity and indisputable sanity, middle-aged, lining up for the virgin Mary. Am I a fraud? she wonders.

MAGGIE MCLEOD IS ADDING A TOUCH OF GINGER and a bit more lemon to the dressing for tonight's salad. She puts a pan of almonds into the oven to toast and sets the timer. Afterwards she'll grab half an hour to rake leaves in the back yard and then a brisk walk down to Safeway for extra whole-wheat rolls, in case one of the kids brings a friend. Maggie has arranged her life around exercise, fresh air, healthy food. "We're given brains," she tells Lydia. "And a body. Common sense is what we've got to use. Most people do bloody zilch to take care of their bodies. They just don't have a clue."

For Maggie, mystery doesn't exist, and if it did she'd be impatient with it. She believes that the recent irregularities of her heart only mean that she's got to take charge, exercise discipline, and in time this wayward organ will fall into line, resume its regular beating. And if it doesn't, you make adjustments and life goes on, modified, but still very much worth living. At least bearable.

The oven timer sounds. The almonds are fragrant and creamy brown. It's almost three o'clock and at this moment Lydia Martens will be over on Bellevue Street, waiting to see that bleeding, wooden virgin. She will come away unhealed, Maggie's convinced of that. She doesn't believe in miracles. She was annoyed when Lydia told her she was going.

"I know you think this is crazy," Lydia said. "That I'm crazy to take a Saturday afternoon to line up with all the most naive, gullible people in Winnipeg. But I figure it's a chance. And when a chance comes along, you grab it."

Maggie McLeod almost said, "You're nuts, Lydia, you've got that right. But what the heck, I'm coming with you. You shouldn't go alone." Instead, "It's your choice, Lyd." The idea was just plain stupid. Besides, her kids were coming home Saturday. She'd be busy.

About five o'clock they'll start coming. By eight they'll be gone. Some of them by seven-thirty. Maggie doesn't want to admit that the dinner she's preparing for them is an interlude at best, an inconvenient obligation at worst. Her children always have other plans for the prime of the evening—a Bomber game or a rock concert or just a session with videos and junk food. So far, though, they've all come, every Saturday, and everyone makes a decent effort to treat the event like a party, even while making excuses for having to rush off. Deep inside, Maggie knows that it's artifice, that Ruth is saying to Bob and Marcia, "Doesn't she ever twig on to the fact that we've got better things to do Saturdays?" And it's been a long while since any one of them brought a friend.

Tying her running shoes, Maggie wonders if she should, after all, be standing with Lydia this autumn day over on Bellevue Street in that assembly of the most foolish. Truth is, she can't claim to be free of folly herself, although, compared to Lydia, she believes her feet are planted on firm ground. She's the one who initiates the jogging. Prepares decent, regular meals even if she's living alone. It's common sense. Still, who is she to claim that there is nothing beyond human effort, beyond sensible living and routine? Beyond the here and now? To step out into a larger realm, is that any more foolish than all those experiments in space?

Time to get going. Attacking the brown leaves with firm swipes of the rake, she resolves to bite her tongue and listen when Lydia tells her about the virgin on Bellevue Street.

LYDIA IS ON THE PROPERTY NOW, on the sidewalk leading to the back door. Here the lawn is thick with fallen ash leaves, and a blaze of unruly giant marigolds glows against the yellowed stucco of the house. Lydia wants to walk over and pick off the deadheads among them and among the purple asters near the door. The place is forlorn, paint peeling from window frames, the eaves sagging at one corner. Abe never let their place get that dilapidated. He kept the exterior and the yard immaculate; the same could not be said of the inside, her domain.

The boy in the wheelchair is laughing at something his father said. The tiny ball of a grandmother seems to have shrunk and become even smaller. It's not too late to turn back. Lydia could just walk away from this alien crowd, take the bus to Polo Park, where winter jackets are on for half price at Sears. Doug needs socks for school. She should get home, see what he's up to.

"Mind if I just step in here, beside you?" A frail woman in a featherdown coat too warm for September has just arrived, late, and is cutting into line beside Lydia. There's a stiffening in the people nearest to her, an unwillingness, but no one says anything. The featherdown woman moves slowly, cautiously, though without a limp. Her face is yellow-grey.

"Liver," she says to Lydia, and as they approach the back step, "I've been to Lourdes. It was wonderful. I can't tell you how wonderful it was." Her voice is thin and bird-like.

"Were you... healed?" The word is awkward on Lydia's tongue.

The woman considers the question. "Healed," she says, and the word is neither affirmation nor denial, and not quite a question. She is on the verge of saying more but they have reached the steps.

The father lifts his son from the wheelchair and carries him into the house. And now Lydia, too, is in the hallway, with the featherdown beside her. The line becomes a single file as they enter the living room. A man stands with his head bowed before the table with the wooden statue. It looks very small. Someone is kissing the wood. Lydia cringes at the thought of how unsanitary that is. In front of her the boy's father kneels, holding his son. Both reach up to the statue with their hands. A young girl is trying to stifle a sob. Is it enough to look? Should Lydia touch the statue, kiss it? Will she have to kneel? Weep? So close to the miracle, she feels stupid and unprepared. She steps aside to let the featherdown woman go first.

The woman raises her arms. She wants to lift them above her head, but there isn't strength enough for that. All she can do is let them form a half circle in front of her, an opening. She begins singing in a quavery voice, "Amazing grace, how sweet the sound." The melody floats like spun silver through the room, exotic and unexpected.

Just when Lydia takes the step that brings her face to face with the wooden statue, the afternoon sun breaks through the overcast and its rays pour through the window. Dullness gives way to light so blinding she can't see the statue or the red geraniums. She has to close her eyes. Aware that she is keeping others waiting, she holds her ground, standing firmly in front of the statue, the sun warm on her face and shoulders. This is where she would like to linger. For a long while. But the impatient queue jostles her forward.

When she opens her eyes again, the light is gone. She turns and follows the sound of "Amazing Grace" out of the room.

And then the priest is ushering her to the front door and she emerges once more into the sunless afternoon. People are returning to their cars. A few of them stand around talking, their voices low. If Maggie were here, she'd be asking in her direct way, "Well, did anything happen?" and Lydia would be at a loss how to answer. Flustered, she realizes she won't be able to say if there really was blood. The five-dollar bill she intended to leave is clutched and crumpled in her hand. She is embarrassed.

"Want a ride?" It's the thin voice of the featherdown woman, calling from a waiting car. Lydia waves a "No."

"There's room," the woman calls. "Come. We can fit you in."

Lydia shouts back, "Thanks anyway."

"Room," the woman repeats. "And grace. Lots of amazing grace."

Lydia walks toward the bus stop.

"With a capital G," the woman calls after her.

Two women at the bus stop smile and tap their foreheads. Lydia recognizes them from the line-up and is embarrassed that they have overheard the conversation. They turn away and begin exchanging recipes for carrot casseroles. This reminds Lydia that she has a frozen pizza she can get out for supper. She's not fond of baking, but tonight she will make a chocolate cake. Doug likes chocolate cake and she can't remember when she last made one.

The bus is warm. Lydia unzips her jacket and settles back to take stock. She breathes in deeply and exhales gradually, attentive to every sensation. Turns her neck slowly, so as not to attract curiosity, to the left, to the right, and finds it no stiffer than it ought to be. She closes her fingers into a ball, opens them, tentatively. Hard to say if there's any difference. The warmth and motion of the bus leave her drowsy and comfortable.

She doesn't resist when her husband drifts into her consciousness. Abe's face floats before her, its vagueness not surprising, what with the silence of their last years together and her deliberate blocking out of everything about him afterwards. He's wearing a light shirt and dark tie, the way he always did when he left the bedroom in the morning, while she pretended to be still asleep. He came home late, too tired to speak. His coming and going provided a shadowy frame within which she and Doug moved, separate from each other, both of them separate from Abe. Eating and sleeping and thinking their own thoughts. Lydia going for walks with Maggie McLeod; Doug waiting for Ben to call. In the end, Abe moved too quickly for the Winnipeg police: out of the country, out of their lives.

Abe wouldn't approve of divine visitations, Lydia's sure of that, and her indiscreet stepping forward would draw his scorn. The whole thing so public, so open to fraud. But all those years when she knew nothing, but suspected everything, wasn't he trying to make his own separate miracle, planning to transform his ordinary life into something splendid? And how did he imagine she and Doug would fit into that contrived miracle, just supposing it had come to pass instead of exploding in his face, leaving all of them wounded? She would really like to ask him: where would she and Doug fit in?

As the bus alternately comes to a stop and surges forward, Lydia gives her thoughts free play. What if the featherdown woman was right, and there really is grace enough for everyone? For the old grandmother and the boy in the wheelchair. For Maggie McLeod, who doesn't believe in miracles and who keeps saying, "For God's sake, Lyd, forget about Abe." For Doug who goes off to school so joyless her heart aches for him.

Abe keeps moving in and out of her conscousness, his face averted. Averted, but she knows that if she were willing, his eyes would turn toward her and they would hold nothing but weariness and longing. She has always known that. She can no longer deny that the words to be spoken, the action that could have been taken, were not always beyond her reach. And where is Abe now? Settled and safe, or trapped in loneliness like she is?

Could there possibly be grace enough for her?

She looks out the bus window where snatches of life rush by and are left behind: children playing in a sandbox, a short woman restraining two German Shepherds, a cluster of boys halfway across the intersection before the light changes. Lydia turns from the window, closes her eyes and imagines she is in the Mennonite church, sitting near the back. As faces of the congregation and choir members she still recognizes come into focus, she is visited by a small rush of gratitude, and gladness. That she is here. That she is part of this imperfect gathering. She wishes Maggie were here beside her. And Doug. If they all moved over, there'd be room for Abe, too. Amazing. And now the choir rises to sing, but though their mouths move, the singing is soundless. It could be a Bach cantata they are singing, or something by Handel. Lydia could never tell the difference, but she found it comforting all the same. Pastor Funk steps up beside the choir, an unaccustomed expectation tempering the worry in his face. The featherdown woman is there, too, in the soprano section, her face pink and radiant as an angel's, her arms raised high in victory. She opens her mouth and her lips move. Lydia is certain it's not Bach or Handel the woman is singing, but "Amazing Grace," in a voice that is youthful and vibrant. The strongest in the choir.

Thursday, Friday, Sunday

By the time I reach the crowded foyer of the church, yesterday's numbness is wearing off, and there's a curdle of fear in my belly. A clutch of women crowds around the literature table; a man in a navy sports jacket greets newcomers. He hands me a bulletin, thicker than it usually is. I wonder if I should have come. Without speaking to anyone, I move with the stream of worshippers into the sanctuary and find a place halfway up. I slide down the pew to the centre where no one will squeeze past. The sonorous organ prelude wraps around me, sombre and comforting.

It's Good Friday. Last Sunday's palm branches are nowhere to be seen. Instead, there's a rough wooden cross, huge and spectral, to the left of the pulpit. Someone steps up to drape its outspread arms with a black cloth. I lower my eyes.

Yesterday, mid-morning, the police cruiser pulled up and Carla got out of the back. Two constables, one male, one female, accompanied her up the walk. From the kitchen window, squinting into the spring sun, I had a perfect view of the paunchy man's crumpled uniform, the woman's wiry height. Although I was expecting this arrival, had stood a long time at the window waiting for it, I was unprepared for the authority the uniforms announced. When I forced myself to look at my daughter, I saw defiance of that authority carved into every contour of her bruised and swollen face.

The vice-principal had already called to tell me about the fight. "Brawl," he said. "Your daughter was the instigator, Mrs. Kopp, no question. It happened in the lunch room. We've called the police and the ambulance. One student will be going to the hospital, I'm afraid, and I must warn you there may be charges against Carla. In any case, we'll be suspending her indefinitely." And after an empty pause, "I'm sorry."

In spite of the absence of harshness in his voice, I felt as if I had been struck by a whip wielded by some arbitrary, callous hand, and the lashing was vicious enough to cut through bone and tissue. But instead of pain, numbness.

The doorbell rang. Rang again. I pulled my hands from the edge of the kitchen sink and found my way to the door. For one hopeful moment I imagined Carla might walk weeping into my outstretched arms, into the comfort and shelter she would find there. But Carla's brown eyes were dry and remorseless, and my arms hung stiffly down at my sides. The officers kept their faces expressionless and said little, only that any possible charges would be deferred until Monday, after the Easter weekend. In the meantime, Carla should not leave the house.

"GOOD MORNING, KATE." The Schellenbergs have seated themselves beside me. Selma Schellenberg is wearing black leather pants. Her pearl-grey cashmere sweater brushes my arm; her face glows beneath a shiny black swirl of hair; blue and silver pendants dangle from her ears. Richard is

42

beginning to grey. Elegantly. I don't wish to deny that bank managers and their wives have worries too, though today I find it hard to believe. Billy Schellenberg has just won the national math contest for St. John's Ravenscourt. His sister Jen is in England, a Rhodes scholar.

Carla is detained in her own home. And still in bed. I would have stayed home too, but some absence in the familiar rooms, or was it my daughter's silent presence, made it impossible to stay, and out of habit I came to church.

Here in the house of God I find myself separate from everyone, excluded from the light of the sun, alien from God. I edge away from Selma Schellenberg's grey cashmere sleeve. Glenda Hoogstraten is singing: *Were you there when they crucified my Lord?* Her singing is nothing like Mahalia Jackson's on that old tape I play every year on Good Friday. But her voice is deep and confident and the melody weaves a mournful overlay to the fear inside me. Would Carla like the singing? The song? In junior high she joined the choir. Quite a good singer, the teacher used to say.

"This morning we remember the suffering of Jesus Christ." Pastor Schwartz has taken his place behind the pulpit. "We invite all of you to participate in the reading which you will find in your bulletins. Let us accompany the Saviour as he walks the cruel road to Golgotha." His voice is steady and upbeat. Glenda Hoogstraten walks forward to sing again.

When I was Carla's age, church was predictable. Two anthems. Prayer. A hymn or two. The preacher's sermon. Now there's a committee to plan services and every Sunday something is expected of the congregation, some involvement. Last Sunday I joined in with moderate enthusiasm when we were all told to shout: *Hosanna, blessed is the one who comes in the name of the Lord! Hosanna in the highest heaven*, while the children pelted down the centre aisle, zealously swinging their florist-shop palm branches. This morning I will only listen. I'll follow the part labelled

"Congregation" in the text inserted into the bulletin, but I won't read aloud. I can't.

A trinity of Easter lilies stands on the communion table near the base of the pulpit, silently trumpeting death and purity. Slightly to the right and three pews up, I can see the grey-blonde head of June Toews, who left a message on my answering machine, asking could I bring a jellied salad to the mother-daughter spring supper. What would June say if she knew how Carla, in anger, grabbed a pop bottle that became a weapon in her slender hand, and lashed out at a fellow student?

Glenda sings: *I saw one hanging on a tree, in agony and blood.*

Edmund and Betty Hudson and their three children have tiptoed in along the far aisle and are filling in the places to my right. Edmund sits next to me. He works for a relief agency and reports regularly to the congregation on Material Aid and Peace Issues. He knows all about The Year of Jubilee when wealthy governments are supposed to forgive the debts of poor nations. Betty volunteers at the local thrift shop. She's wearing her usual denim skirt and much-washed t-shirt with the word "Peace" stamped like a blue manifesto across the front. A dove-and-cross logo decorates the back.

"'Morning, Kate," Edmund whispers. When I turn toward him, I detect sympathy in his eyes, as if he knows about Carla. Betty leans past him, her eyes solemn, her mouth forming a silent "Hi." Beside her, their oldest daughter, Jacqui, waves to a friend, her hand kept chest high. I catch sight of her smile, a smile that turns her small, ordinary face bright. Isn't she in Carla's school? What does she know about what happened yesterday? And what has she told Betty?

A group of teenagers bounds onto the platform beside the pastor, where they become Roman soldiers and begin mocking the slender, blindfolded, straw-haired boy who is Jesus. He looks helpless, but also calm. Resolute. I am distracted, unable to give the words and actions my attention, though when June Toews's son yells out: *Prophesy! Who is it that struck you?* and raises a makeshift whip as if to strike the blindfolded stage Jesus, my whole body tightens, shrinks back from the blow that is never actually delivered. I open the bulletin and find the right place in the text.

Pastor Schwartz has stepped forward and begins reading: *So Pilate went out to him and said, "What accusation do you bring against this man?"*

This is the cue, and the dutiful congregation responds, its morning voice still tenuous, still ragged: *If this man were a criminal, we would not have handed him over to you.*

The volume of Edmund's voice catches me off-guard. I want to raise my hands to cover my ears, but instead, let the tense fingers of my free hand move back and forth over the smooth rayon fabric of my skirt.

The story of the crucifixion is familiar; years of telling and hearing have built up, and then flattened, its stark images. Last year I watched the video *Jesus of Montreal* with Carla, who sprawled on the carpet with her potato chips and Pepsi. I wondered if she was really watching, but when she said, "I expected the cross to be really humungous," and then, after a final sip of the Pepsi, asked, "Did you know they had to sit like that?" I knew that my daughter had been affected by the story. She picked herself up off the floor. "Death by crucifixion, that's gross."

Over the summer that followed and into the winter, Carla changed. I wouldn't say she became aggressive, but more distant. Cool. Sometimes she skipped classes on a Friday afternoon and refused to be repentant if I found out. Once she came home just before dawn and wouldn't say who she'd been with, no matter that she'd scared me half to death. Neither scolding nor threats could puncture her sullenness. I was afraid it might all end with a pregnancy. I never imagined assault.

Jesus and his Roman tormentors leave the stage. Is it wise to make the crucifixion story so visual? The images are painful enough read silently or aloud. Why intensify them with shape and colour and sound? All winter the TV screen has been glutted with scenes of gunfire, smashed bodies, limbs broken like matchsticks, spilled blood, the horror-filled eyes of starved and abused children—everything carried into your home and forced into your memory from where it surfaces against your will. When it erupts it leaves me baffled. I know that ordinary people harbour violence, people like Selma Schellenberg or Edmund Hudson. Or Reena Virk's friends who beat her up and murdered her. Or Carla, who would never go so far.

The pastor is still reading the words of Pontius Pilate: *I find no fault against him. Do you want me to release the King of the Jews?*

And then the reply: *Not this man, but Barabbas.*

This time the words erupt smartly from the congregation like gunfire. They are cruel and hard. A fearful thrill shoots along my spine as the passion builds. The congregation's getting into the mood; the worship planners will be pleased. Beside me, Edmund is tense, eager for the next cue, his voice and body poised to march out of Jerusalem toward Golgotha.

Then Pilate took Jesus and had him flogged. And the soldiers wove a crown of thorns and put it on his head and they dressed him in a purple robe. They kept coming up to him and saying: Hail, King of the Jews!

The congregation spits out the words, every mouth hurling scorn like missiles. I feel the collective loathing, so forcible it's a wonder the impact doesn't stun Pastor Schwartz. Knock him over. But he reads on: *Pilate went out again and said to them, "Look, I am bringing him out to you to let you know that I find no case against him."*

"There may be charges against Carla." The words of the vice-principal and the police, temporarily driven underground by the words of the gospel, now surface, reminding me that only Good Friday and Easter Sunday, and the blurred Saturday between them, stand like a buffer against those charges. I am not naive enough to think that Carla can be found innocent. But now anger grows inside me, not against Carla, but against life, the way it shapes and forms you. What control can anyone have? I didn't teach my daughter violence, I have never once struck her. Then why this brutality? It's unfair and uninvited.

Pilate said to them, "What shall I do with Jesus?"

The entire congregation shouts out with one vehement voice: *CRUCIFY HIM! CRUCIFY HIM! CRUCIFY!*

The savage demand fills the sanctuary, electrifying me. My tongue is loosened, and on the last CRUCIFY! I cry out with the others and my mouth stays open, as if for more. I am convinced a physical force, palpable and powerful, swells and explodes a split second after the congregation's outcry.

The shock of silence that follows lasts an eternity, as if Pastor Schwartz has lost his place in the text. As if an unseen stagehand has flashed an apocalyptic warning and now sheep and shepherd are struck dumb.

Finally he reads on: *And they led Jesus away to be crucified.*

I am shaking now. The exhilaration drains suddenly away, leaving me hollow. The bulletin trembles in my hands. The walls echo back, *Crucify, crucify!* and in the space above the congregation the words swirl and circle, looking for a place to light. I shrink from those words, words that I've spoken too. I hold my arms close to my body, knees, feet together. I want to be invisible.

Edmund is still tense, still waiting for more drama. Selma Schellenberg sits stiffly upright. I no longer follow the words. And then everyone is reaching for the hymn books and we all stand to sing "O Sacred Head Now Wounded." The benediction follows.

Other years the Good Friday service ended with communion, but today's bulletin makes no mention of it, and there's no bread and wine on the communion table, only the perfect white lilies. Maybe it's a good thing. My hands would tremble. They wouldn't be able to hold the piece of bread or lift the tiny plastic cup to my mouth without spilling the wine. And yet I want to protest, rage at being denied the elements, the symbols of grace that I'm unworthy to receive.

During the organ postlude everyone is seated again and afterwards I can't escape. Edmund is solid in his place, leaning forward to someone in the pew ahead. Selma's sleek head is bent over the bulletin.

"Look," she says, turning to me. "There's a mother and daughter supper Wednesday. Are you going?"

I shake my head.

"I wish Jen could be here."

There is longing in Selma's voice, yearning for a daughter who is far away, engrossed in studies and new friends and success and likely not thinking of her mother. I hate both of them. And now I'm shocked, as if I have actually spoken the hate aloud. I can't raise my face to Selma's or look into her eyes.

"I'm sorry," I mumble finally. "How's she doing?"

"She phoned this week. She hasn't been well. She's pretty much dropped her studies. For now. She's seeing a doctor."

Pregnant, I think, and say, "I'm sorry."

I feel stupid and helpless. Angry at Selma for dumping on me. I want to squeeze past the Schellenbergs, but I am incapable of that much rudeness. And equally incapable of offering help. Beside me, Selma's fingers worry the bulletin, folding and refolding it. Suddenly I want to reach out and hold those smooth, restless hands in mine, but instead I turn the other way, to where Edmund has finished his conversation.

"Want to join us for lunch?" Betty is leaning past her husband, her smile transparent as a child's. "Just soup and sandwiches. Come."

"I can't. I really have to go." I get to my feet, clumsy, as if I'm just learning to walk. The Hudsons press their knees to the pew to let me pass, and I can't avoid Betty's eyes. Their wistful concern leaves me more helpless than ever. I don't dare look at their oldest daughter, Jacqui, who probably knows all about Carla.

I push down the aisle and through the knots of conversation in the foyer. Pastor Schwartz is at the main door, waiting to greet his congregation. I escape through the side door into the parking lot. It hasn't been properly cleaned after winter; dried mud and leaves have been ground to dust by the traffic. I find my way between rows of cars, grimed or gleaming. A cat sits on the hood of a red Honda, its arched back glistening in the noonday sun.

The closed-in silence of the car is peaceful after the crowded church. There is little traffic in the street. All the way home I pretend that when I arrive I'll find my daughter still a child, innocent and glad to see me. I'll find a way to reassure her. I'll tell her that from now on nothing can go wrong.

Carla's door is closed. She'll be lying on her bed, headphones clamped to her head, the blinds drawn as usual. Is Jen Schellenberg in bed too, feverish, lonely, and probably pregnant, in her dormitory bed somewhere in England? TV voices seep through the crack below the door. I head for the kitchen. Carla has been here. She's left a sandwich, ham on brown bread, and a bowl of potato chips. I'm not fooled into thinking that it's for me, that this is a gesture of penance or appeasement. More likely Carla made the sandwich for herself and then lost interest. I wrap it in plastic before putting it into the fridge, wondering what kinds of sandwiches the Hudsons are making for Good Friday lunch.

Not so many years ago, following communion, the congregation washed each other's feet, a ritual of humility and service. Afterwards the pastor encouraged us all to fast for the rest of the day. Today I may as well fast; I'm not hungry.

What was Carla thinking, there in the lunchroom, armed with a pop bottle, in the company of other teenagers, children with whom she might have played in a sandbox? When things got out of hand, was she horrified? Or was she thrilled, high on blood lust? I haven't allowed myself to wonder much about the victim, who she is. Or if there was much blood on Carla's hands. Surely the harm couldn't have been so very severe or Carla wouldn't now be home in her own bed.

I put on the Mahalia Jackson tape, lie down on my bed, like Carla, and maybe like Jen Schellenberg. The words: *Oh-o-ooh, sometimes it causes me to tremble, tremble, tremble*, crowd out the terrible echo of *CRUCIFY, CRUCIFY!* I let the tape play over and over until the knots in my muscles ease and anxiety relaxes its stranglehold. I'll wait all day and, if need be, right through the grey Saturday that precedes Easter Sunday for Carla to open the door of her room, step out into the bright kitchen and break the silence.

IT'S LATE AFTERNOON WHEN I VENTURE FROM MY BED and find Carla in the living room, in the blue chair facing the window, a cushion filling her arms. The street is shimmering with colour. The blue birdfeeder hanging from the eaves, the spirea bush, even the sidewalk, everything glows and vibrates with light. Across the street our neighbour rakes his front lawn, while his toddler, a boy, crawls around in the piles of dead grass. Two girls I don't recognize ride by on bicycles. Wind stirs the branches of our mountain ash.

Both Carla and I jump when the phone rings in the kitchen. All day there's been no call, as if on Good Friday there's a law against it. Carla hurries to the kitchen. "Heard anything?" I hear her say. "About Meg? Is she still in hospital?"

Meg. I don't know any Meg, but even having a name gives me something to hold on to. Right away I want to phone the woman who is Meg's mother—she must be frantic. I want to explain to her, but how can you explain what you can't comprehend?

"Right. Yeah, okay," Carla says in the kitchen, and after a few more dead phrases like that she hangs up. I expect her to escape into her room once more, away from me, but she returns to the blue chair and the cushion and I take this to mean it's my move now.

"About Thursday, Carla…"

"I'd like to wipe out Thursday," she interrupts, her voice a blend of anger and anguish. "Just erase it from the week. But it keeps repeating and repeating like constant replay in my head and I can't put my finger on the 'off' switch."

I'm surprised at Carla's outburst and disgusted with myself for pussyfooting around my daughter all day.

"What happened, Carla?" I ask. "In the lunchroom." My fingers are locked together as if that can keep my voice steady, my heart from pounding. "Who was there?"

"I was having lunch with Meg and Twila. They're from my English class."

Twila. Another name. I wait, but nothing more is offered and I realize it's my move again.

"I used to dread lunch hour," I say. "Walking into a full room alone. I hated it so much I'd sneak my sandwiches into the library and eat them behind a novel." This is leading nowhere.

But Carla has turned toward me, curious. Her face, caught in the light, is more swollen than yesterday, the bruises darker. I gasp. She turns away then, and begins telling me how there was a disagreement about a boy Meg liked and said was out of bounds to Carla. Carla snapped back that Meg was welcome to him and then the kids sitting nearby egged them on.

"They kept yelling 'Fight! Fight!' like that," she says. "And then they were chanting, 'Go, Carla. Go Meg,' like they wanted something, anything, to spice up a boring lunch break."

Hearing them fling her name across the lunchroom tables infuriated Carla and she swung her pop bottle at Meg. "It didn't seem like it was me, just my arm doing it," she says. The weapon found its target, Carla swung again. The bottle clattered across the littered tabletop and landed on the floor. Meg screamed. Blood ran down from a cut in her jaw.

"Everything went dead quiet," Carla says.

"And what about *your* face?"

"That was Twila, with her fist and nails. Well, she had to. Meg's her friend."

I don't ask for more—the ambulance siren, the cops, the school administration. On the day before a long weekend, a lunchroom of kids can be volatile. I know that.

"Mom, do you know Jacqui Hudson?" Carla asks, and there's a small leap in my chest because she says "Mom."

"Was she there?" I ask.

"Jacqui's the mousiest kid in English class," Carla says, staring out the window. "But when she smiles it's like her face could split open. Like there's so much happiness inside it wipes out the mousiness."

There is a long silence before Carla continues. "We were reading *Macbeth* on Thursday morning. The last part where they fight it out. And the teacher got us talking about the violence. And some kids said it's just part of life, you can't stop it.

"Then one guy, Darren—he's always in the school dramas—tells us he's going to play Jesus in church on Friday. The crucifixion, that's violent too, he says, and I'm thinking about that video you and me watched last year. And Darren says the only way to stop it is not by fighting it, but by absorbing it. Jacqui looks like she's going to cry and Twila says we sure need someone to absorb all the genocide and child abuse. But who's going to do it? And Darren says it would have to be someone who isn't afraid to suffer. Then Meg—she's always so sarcastic—says, and who would that be?"

I have nothing to say, and can only wonder at what's been unleashed in Carla and made to spill out. But now, it seems, everything's drained away and she only adds, "Jacqui's not fake. I know fake when I see it."

"Was she there?" I repeat my question. "In the lunch-room?"

Carla tells me then how Jacqui yelled out just as the pop bottle was about to strike Meg, "No, Carla! No!" It was too late.

The neighbour has finished raking, lifts his little son in his arms and carries child and rake around to the back. The sun has moved west; the brilliance is gone from the street. Carla doesn't move and I wait.

"It just happened," Carla says finally. "I don't know how. This Meg, I don't like her, but I don't hate her, either."

Then she turns her bruised face toward me. "Mom, what if the botttle struck Meg's eye and blinded her? What if she was brain-damaged? Or in a coma?"

Or dead, I think.

Carla's one hand clenches the cushion, the fingers of the other trace patterns in the blue upholstery. I watch them move. I stare at them.

IT'S WELL PAST TWELVE ON EASTER SUNDAY and the service will be over, the resurrection unfolded without me this year. Pastor Schwartz reading how the women come early to the tomb, alarmed to find the stone rolled away, the angel telling them not to be afraid. Glenda Hoogstraten singing "I know that my Redeemer lives," and maybe the congregation shouting *Alleluja*. Tulips and hyacinths flanking the pulpit. Some stage-hungry teenager playing the drums. The worship planners' idea of the resurrection made visible and audible.

Selma Schellenberg in a chic new dress and maybe even a hat will leave the sanctuary with her elegantly greying husband. They will smile and exchange polite words with the pastor. The whole Hudson family will be there, Betty on the look out for someone lost and lonely to invite for lunch. My church attendance is far from perfect, but I've never before missed an Easter service.

Carla sits down at the table, her light brown hair wet from the shower, the bruises a shock on her fair skin. She waves aside the plate with toast, pours herself a mug of coffee and wraps her fingers around it. They are slender and strong. You have nice hands, I want to tell her as I've told her often, but this is not the time. After Friday, silence settled between us once again and remained there all day Saturday. It wasn't comfortable, but we both let it be. Maybe the misery we each carry can seep into the shell of silence we are careful to build around ourselves. This is our way, and who's to say it's good or bad?

A car door slams shut on the driveway. I go to the kitchen window and open the venetians in time to see Betty and Jacqui Hudson climb out of a rusty beige van. Betty's wearing her denim skirt and Jacqui a flowery summer dress unlike anything Carla would ever put on.

"Who?" Carla asks, and I tell her, expecting she'll disappear into her room, but she only mutters, "Oh, God," and stays put. The doorbell rings.

When I open the door, Betty is there, holding out a platter with a round loaf on it so large it obscures the "Peace" on her t-shirt. The white icing is decorated thickly with coloured sprinkles.

"We brought you some Easter bread," she says with a tentativeness that waits for my approval. I take the platter from her and we look at each other, reserved and uncertain.

"I've got coffee," I say. Betty and Jacqui follow me into the kitchen, where Carla's staring into her mug.

"Hi, Carla." Jacqui's pale, shy face breaks into a smile that takes me by surprise.

"Hey, Jacqui," Carla says, barely looking up.

I bring out two more mugs and a jug of milk—I can't imagine Jacqui liking coffee—and the four of us sit around the kitchen table. Betty cuts the Easter bread, hands it around and we all take a piece, even Carla. Betty and I try this and that to get a conversation going. All dead ends. And then she says, turning to my daughter, "Meg's doing fine, Carla. She'll be OK."

Carla's head jerks up, as if by reflex action, involuntarily. There's an appeal in her marred face so naked I want to cover it. I want to hold Carla in my arms, press her face against my body so Betty Hudson can't see.

"I spoke to Meg's mom," Betty says, her voice suddenly

strong and reassuring, as if Carla's need has given her confidence, as if she will now take on the responsibility for everything, and it's really not an overwhelming problem after all. Any minute now it will be sorted out. "I told her it was important you should know, Carla. Of course, there'll be plastic surgery, but she'll be fine."

Betty has laid her hand on Carla's arm and Carla hasn't pulled away, but her eyes have lowered again. The sun on her still-damp hair turns it gold. Can Betty Hudson see how beautiful it is? How it shines? Does she notice Carla's fine hands?

"You don't look so bad," Jacqui says, giving Carla's face a careful scrutiny. "That was pretty awful, Thursday."

She means no harm, but I'm shocked, as if she's put her small finger directly on the wound and bluntly named our misery with her soft voice.

Carla looks surprised too.

"We'll try to manage without you at school," Jacqui continues and there is no silliness and no awkwardness. Just an acknowledgement of what is.

"Yeah, right," Carla says.

And then we are quiet again.

"Good bread," I say, and it's true. Betty's Easter bread is feather-light and not too sweet.

"It rose beautifully, I have to admit," Betty says with pride. "I made it yesterday."

Yesterday: that endless stretch of time between death and resurrection. The friends of Jesus waiting, putting in the anxious hours, their hands idle, their movements restricted because of the Sabbath, though nothing can command the agonized heart and mind to keep still. Carla and me wrapped in our separate silence. The longest, bleakest Saturday in my memory.

"You'll be finished *Macbeth* when I get back," Carla says to Jacqui.

Jacqui lifts her hands from the table, rubs them together, brings them to her face, which has become animated.

What, will these hands ne'er be clean? she recites in her thin, breathless voice. She lets her face take on the torment of Lady Macbeth before she continues, *Here's the smell of blood still. All the perfumes of Arabia will not sweeten this little hand. Oh, Oh.*

I want to reach out and grab her hands, yank them down, tell her to stop. But it's not necessary. Jacqui, realizing, ends her recital with a final, piping "Oh." Her hands fall to her side, but her face is still racked.

"Go on," Carla says." I like how you do that."

"That's all I remember."

"It's cool."

My anger at Jacqui subsides. I pour coffee, and remember how we shouted "Crucify!" on Friday. Ages and ages ago. I wonder if Jacqui kept silent? I can't imagine her shouting anything so violent.

"Selma Schellenberg called this morning," Betty says. "Her daughter's been diagnosed with leukemia. She'll be flown home this week."

"Oh God, no," I say. And there's nothing now that can stop the rush of grief. I'm appalled at the news, appalled that death, not new life, as I wrongly suspected, has taken root in Jen Schellenberg's body. Indifferent to her youth, to her Rhodes scholarship, to her delight in friends and plans for success and happiness, unmoved by her parents' money or their frantic worries, destruction is staking its quiet claim on Jen Schellenberg's body and eating away her future.

"Her chances are good, Kate," Betty soothes. "She's young. They'll start treatment right away."

But my tears, more than sufficient for all four of us, keep pouring out. The others wait for me to finish, and then Betty carries our cups and what's left of the Easter bread to the kitchen counter.

"Maybe I shouldn't have said. You've got enough as it is."

"No, no. It's okay."

"Jacqui, we'd better go. We still have to drop in at the Schellenbergs'."

"It's good of you to come," I say. "I appreciate it." And as if I owe her more, a confession, perhaps, I add, "Carla and me, we've been fairly dreary this weekend."

Carla mumbles something I can't make out.

At the door, Betty turns to hug Carla, who doesn't resist. She no longer tries to hide her face. Then Betty turns to me, and there is no pity in her eyes, no condemnation, and no overwhelming sorrow, only a calm so palpable I want to grab hold of it. "Good-bye," she says.

She leaves, with her daughter. I am left with mine. And with the rest of the Easter bread. A measure of peace stays with us too. It will have to be enough for Carla and me. Enough for today and for the possible charges tomorrow. I close the door behind our guests and go in search of the telephone book so I can look up "Schellenberg" before I lose courage. At the kitchen window Carla is watching the beige van leave our driveway.

THE PEONY SEASON

THERE IS NOTHING to distinguish Tuesday Bay from any number of similar bays in Winnipeg, or in any other prairie city, for that matter. It curves without fanfare from Delta Road where the city is beginning to bulge toward the east. Five houses, let's say homes, face the concrete-curbed circle of clipped grass at the centre of the bay. Two bungalows, a modest multi-level, a split-level with a bright blue door. And a huge two-storey structure with Tyndall stone façade, gold canvas canopies on both lower and upper storey windows, and a double garage. This mansion asserts itself imperiously in that ordinary circle of houses, leaving you to wonder if its residents also dominate the bay.

Diverse vehicles are seen parked at various times of the day or night on the driveways belonging to the five homes. You might see a fiery red Grand Am tearing onto the driveway of the first bungalow and stopping a little too abruptly. Jean Tremont is in a hurry again. What's she always got to do that's so urgent? Is her briefcase crammed with history tests needing to be marked? Is there another meeting? Must she rush back after supper to teach an evening class at the university? You might wonder if her frantic activity is designed to drive out the loneliness of her childless, husbandless existence. Designed to drive out fear. You want to say to her, "Jean, look at the clouds piled like wool above the trees. Aren't they beautiful? Do you think it'll rain?"

Or you might see Jim Yaworski's tidy black van pull up to the steel-grey-with-white-trim multi-level. Jim gets out, walks around to the back of the van, opens the door. Amazing, the order you see there. He's a painter, and in the back of his van he's fashioned a raft of shelves with slots for his brushes, space for folded dropsheets, compartments for paint. A view into the van is a view into an astonishing pattern of discipline and planning. A place for everything and everything in its place.

His wife's car, small and manoeuvrable, flits in and out of the driveway. Rita doesn't care to work "outside the home," no matter what the other women of Tuesday Bay, or even the rest of the world, may think. She's content in her kitchen, out for coffee with friends, shopping in the malls of Winnipeg. Yet, she rarely misses what's happening on the bay. She could tell you that, although the driveway of the second bungalow is usually empty of vehicles, the black, polished Lincoln Continental parked in elegant solitude behind the closed garage door is not always idle. Old Adam Andrews brought it with him eight years ago when he retired and moved to the bay, and it's been wife and child to him ever since. Once or twice a week, well before lunch, he backs it out of the garage, and Rita Yaworski hurries to adjust the venetians of her living room window so she can watch the large car's sedate progress out the driveway, around Tuesday Bay and on to Delta Road. If she's at her post at the right time of the afternoon, she'll see car and driver return and glide into the garage.

The split-level is home to four children, the youngest an infant, besides parents, so you'd be excused for expecting another van. But in addition to the bikes and plastic dinosaurs and toy trucks and dolls the Emory-Dixon kids

59

habitually leave scattered across their lawn and driveway and in front of the blue door, a Ford station wagon of indeterminate vintage is what you'll see. Rusty and bent. "A disgrace to the neighbourhood," Jim Yaworski complains to Rita, but the Emory-Dixons always find it ready for an excursion to wherever.

And the mansion? Wanda and Bill Unger live in it. Not so long ago their youngest daughter, Susan, a third-year human ecology student at the University of Manitoba, still lived with them. Susan would leave early each day in her grey Tercel to pick up the others in her car pool and almost every day someone would have an evening class or a lab, or else they'd all decide to stay and do research, or go to the pub, they'd earned this little pleasure after a day crammed with classes. So although she lived in the mansion with her parents, she was seldom there.

"She was a damn good driver," Bill always says when he remembers Susan.

"And a very good student too," Wanda adds quietly, her fingers wanting to clench into fists.

Wanda and Bill each own a car, but let's not get bogged down with vehicles. Nor with landscaping and gardens (though it's a shame to overlook the Yaworskis' lilac hedge and Jean Tremont's spirea, and, in their seasons, bushes of white and mauve phlox, roses, blue monkshood, white and pink lupin).

The people in the neighbourhood are beginning to forget that just over a year ago Tuesday Bay was more elegantly named: it was known as Belvedere Bay. The reason for the change of name had nothing to do with any desire of the residents, none of whom had ever given a blessed moment's thought to the name of their bay, except for Jim Yaworski, who complained to his wife that twelve letters and one space took way too long to print into the blanks in all those forms he had to fill out.

City officials had discovered that, besides Belvedere Bay, the city map had a street named Belvedere Boulevard. They hadn't discovered this by poring over the map. There was no need. The post office and various businesses whose deliveries frequently arrived at the wrong Belvedere informed them of it in language that was accusatory, demanding and, as time passed, furious. Something had to be done.

Jean Tremont agreed. Racing home one Wednesday afternoon, she had to bring the Grand Am to an abrupt halt in order to avoid an immodest and unexpected pile of building materials dumped on her driveway. Wanda Unger next door had obligingly signed for the delivery in Jean's absence, failing to notice that though the address on the delivery slip said 28 Belvedere, Jean's address, the name on it was Smith, not Tremont. It took a week before the mountain on Jean's driveway was moved.

Apparently, a resident on the other Belvedere—and this is one of those hard-to-swallow coincidences—was also named Jim Yaworski, and keeping the mail rerouted was becoming a regular nuisance for Rita, though she always took the pleasure of opening the mail and reading it before she discovered her mistake. "Three this week," she'd complain to her husband. "The last one was from a lawyer. That Yaworski's behind in his child support, isn't that just like a man."

"Our street was first." That was Bill Unger's verdict. A building contractor, he regularly consulted city records. "They damn well can't make us change." His confidence spread easily around the bay and everyone relaxed, though no one knew the opinion of old Adam Andrews, who was rarely seen by his neighbours and was imagined by them to be senile, or at least slightly bonkers.

It was decided by Winnipeg's city officials that Belvedere Bay would have a new name, even though it was, as Bill Unger rightly pointed out, the older of the two Belvederes, and you'd think it would have the benefit of a prior claim. The memo that arrived at all five residences gave a reason:

To all Residents of Belvedere Bay: Since your
street has only five addresses, and Belvedere
Boulevard in west Winnipeg has fourteen, Council
has decided that changing the name of your street
will be least disruptive. You are invited to confer
with your neighbours and come forward with a
new name by May 20 at the latest.

"Isn't it just like them," Rita Yaworski yelled across to
Jean Tremont without further explanation of what she
meant. Jean had just parked her Grand Am on her driveway.
Ivy Dixon—she liked it if you used her maiden name—was
standing on her front step, in front of the blue door, looking wistfully at the first faint budding of the trees. Then she
began to pick up toys left lying around the yard last fall by
her three children. It was late March; spring was here.

"Think of all the address changes," Rita sighed and Jim,
thinking of his painting business, grew morose.

"At least our telephone number won't change." That
was Rita, trying to console him.

The Emory-Dixons were merely amused.

Jean Tremont was sure a "reasonable solution" would be
found. "We can have the meeting at my place," she added.
"Next Tuesday."

"What meeting?" Bill Unger asked, afraid that his
neighbours were caving in to the city. "Let me negotiate
this." Meanwhile, Wanda had decided it would be fun to
choose a new name.

If you had spent time in the various houses of the bay
in the days before the meeting, you would have noticed a
certain preoccupation with names—though in each home
the preoccupation took its own direction.

Jim Yaworski, who had heard of a park in Winnipeg
named after an Olympic athlete, pored over names of
medallists: Stojko, Rebagliati, Auch. Each one left him
unsatisfied. Susan Auch was a Winnipegger. She'd be a good
choice. But his favourite, really, was Wayne Gretzky, because

everybody would recognize the name and most people could spell it too.

Wanda Unger had a list of ten names worked out during coffee break with the help of her colleagues at the daycare where she worked part time. She refused to divulge the names to anyone, even Bill.

"I'm hopeless at names," John Emory-Dixon declared. "Three kids' names, that's about it for me."

Ivy had a friend in an area where street names had a recurring motif: Melon Lea, Autumn Lea, Summer Lea, Bramalea, Mornlea, Spring Lea. She loved the charming musicality of the repeated "Lea," and desired it for her bay.

Jean Tremont kept a map with all the streets of Winnipeg on her desk while she racked her brain for historic names. It would be futile to choose something like "Columbus Circle." She would have to look for some lesser explorer, some statesman not yet honoured with a street name. Some city out west had named a street after Ben Heppner, the opera singer, but she wasn't enamoured with contemporary celebrities; give her something tested and tried. She considered the leaders in the Winnipeg strike of 1919: Woodsworth, Russell, Armstrong, Pritchard—all taken. She didn't like Heaps. Ivens? Hmmm. Or what about early female activists: McClung. Beynon. There was still time.

The Tuesday meeting had to be relocated to the mansion because Jean Tremont discovered on her calendar a meeting on the same night and would regretfully have to arrive just a tad late. This was fine with Wanda, who had known all along that her newly renovated family room was the largest on the bay, and she had a superb recipe for chocolate cheesecake. Everyone wondered if Mr. Andrews would arrive and when he did, Bill directed him to the white and beige rocking chair with a good halogen light beside it.

"Well, let's get this thing resolved," Bill said from the entrance to the family room, an ideal place for a leader of such a meeting to preside from. He still believed they should insist on "Belvedere," but the others had come with new names.

"Not so fast, Bill," Wanda cut in. "Refreshments first. Who wants coffee? Beer? Don't rush this. I've got cheesecake. Susan's coming. Let's give her a chance to get here before we start."

Truth to tell, Wanda was worried. Susan had said she'd be there for supper and she had a great idea for a street name, a name to surprise everyone. But she still wasn't here and hadn't called. Wanda found herself moving frequently from the family room to the kitchen window where she'd be able to see the Tercel pull in at any moment.

"Mmm, great," Rita gushed, after the first forkful of cheesecake. "Wanda, this is scrumptious."

John Emory-Dixon, even before Rita's endorsement, had helped himself to a huge slice. He looked out the corner of his eye at his wife on the couch next to the rocking chair. Ivy was uncharacteristically silent. Her hazel eyes held a profound mournfulness that had nothing to do with street names. It had something to do with children, *her* three children, who had flung themselves, right after supper, into one full-blown war after another with a frenzy that would leave any parent limp and exhausted. For a pregnant woman—Ivy's pregancy had been confirmed just this morning—it was entirely too much. She found herself cringing at the thought of weeks of morning nausea and couldn't bring herself to contemplate the years ahead. She hadn't told John, who was puzzled by her pensiveness.

"Susan should be here any minute," Wanda announced into the room. She believed she could hear the motor of the Tercel, she really believed it, but the next person to walk in was Jean Tremont.

"Nothing's happened," John Emory-Dixon told her. "You haven't missed a thing." And then he added hastily, "The cake's great. I recommend it."

By the time the telephone rang, Jim Yaworski was restlessly folding and refolding the paper with the name Wayne

Gretzky on it. He would propose to his neighbours that they choose either "Wayne" or "Gretzky." Either name was nice and short and very suitable. Jean, for whom each minute was valuable, was itching to get to her feet and get the meeting going. She was head of the history department this year and accustomed to running things and running them efficiently. Small talk left her uncomfortable, but presiding over a meeting of her neighbours, she'd be right in her element. Old Mr. Andrews was dozing in his chair. Ivy Dixon had just called her babysitter on her cell phone and said, before setting it on the glass-top coffee table, "Well, just don't let the twins into Joel's Lego. He'll go crazy."

Then there was the kind of hush that falls strangely over a gathering where a moment ago everyone had so much to say that no one could say anything and be heard. It was into this sudden silence that the Ungers' telephone emitted its shrill ring. Wanda picked up the receiver.

"Hello."

She didn't sound alarmed, Jean would say later. Maybe a bit nervous. And Rita would remember that there was a plate of something in Wanda's hand, the one that wasn't holding the receiver.

Mr. Andrews, roused by the harsh ring of the phone, sat fiercely upright in the rocking chair and cleared his throat. "So what's it going to be? What have we...?"

Wanda's sharp gasp severed his spoken words from the unspoken, leaving the fragment dangling like a limp string. It cut across Ivy Dixon's sorrow over her pregnancy and side-railed her apprehension about bringing another child into the world. Her husband retracted the hand that was conveying a forkful of cake to his mouth. He set down the plate and glanced at his wife. How pale her face had become. Jean Tremont had a peculiar fluttering of premonition. Jim and Rita were blank. No one that evening asked for another coffee or beer or a slice of Wanda's chocolate cheesecake. Bill moved toward the telephone, toward Wanda, who had gasped once more.

Susan was a good driver; it wasn't her fault. The driver of the half-ton truck that smashed into her Tercel that Tuesday evening was also a good driver. He would have the rest of his life to live with this moment of inattentiveness, the ill-advised change of lane that changed everything. And he would drive again, a lifetime without another accident, whereas Susan would never again find herself behind the wheel of her Tercel, or any other model of car. The jaws of life were not used to extract her body from the wreckage; it wasn't that bad. But bad enough, and before Susan would learn to handle her wheelchair and prepare herself to consider exchanging the hospital room for a unit in downtown housing for the disabled, before the endless legal complexities had been sorted out, she would have time to contemplate the future. *Her* future. It stretched before her like a dismal uphill road. Her anger at the driver who carelessly, stupidly, no—criminally—changed lanes gave way to anger at everyone not afflicted with a disability such as hers and then it swung around and zeroed in on God, who should surely have prevented the catastrophe.

"She's going through dark valleys." That's how Wanda put it to Ivy, who instinctively put her hand to her belly, although it was too soon for anything to be different except that she had told John, and now everything *was* different.

"You don't have to go through with this, you know," he said, drawing her into his arms, not with assurance, but tentatively, as if she were fragile as a china cup. Ivy let her body rest against his, not that she was allowing herself comfort, no, she was testing, as if their two flesh-and-blood bodies that had made a pregnancy, that now curved cautiously into each other, could send her a message: *this is what you must do.* There *was*, of course, no such message.

"We still haven't named the bay," Wanda told Susan, who lay motionless on her hospital bed, and immediately regretted having introduced something so mundane, so fraught with the normal things of life, into her daughter's static existence. What did it matter if the street never got named? She had only mentioned it because that morning Bill had looked at the calendar and announced that May 20th, the city deadline for the naming, was only four days away. And he had only mentioned it because of the unbearable silence inhabiting the two-storey mansion with the golden canopies after the accident.

Ivy Dixon brought Joel, her oldest, to visit Susan. After his lightning inspection of the hospital room, he insisted they go home. "Right now, Mom." Embarrassed and helpless, Ivy turned to Susan's expressionless face and whispered, "I'm pregnant. Again." A flicker of something appeared in Susan's empty face and for a moment the two women gazed into each other's eyes.

"Tomorrow when John's home, I'm going to St. Benedict's," Ivy said. "I'm going to pray. For you. And about this baby. Whether to. . ." She stopped, perplexed. Tried again: "I'm going to pray to God," and then she rushed out after Joel, whose footsteps could be heard galloping down the hospital corridor.

Jean Tremont made room in her schedule for a visit with Susan on Monday. When she stepped off the elevator, she was still trying to line up topics for conversation with her injured neighbour in the white hospital bed. Fortunately, it had been one of Susan's better days—there are always those—and they spoke about how human ecology was a good discipline to get into, for one not completely mobile. Jean stayed longer than she had intended. Talking to a young woman who wasn't in a huge hurry to get away, like her history students, gave her unexpected pleasure. For once she had no meeting to rush to, no lectures to be prepared for the next day. There was a sort of rare companionship in this hospital room. Even when their sporadic conversation had faltered, leaving them wrapped in the late afternoon's soft stillness, she felt a reassurance. She would come again, she decided. Before she left, she asked, "Susan, what was your name for the street? What did you come up with?"

At the question, the face of the injured girl seemed to grow grey with weariness, or indifference, and she turned toward the window. "I can't remember."

The Yaworskis had to leave for Vancouver to visit their son, who was in the process of divorce and needed their support and their out-of-practice parenting skills while he made adjustments to his mateless life and arranged for child care. It wasn't easy for Jim to rearrange his careful work schedule, but Rita said, "We have to." Since they would be absent when the other residents met in Jean Tremont's bungalow to attempt once again to rename Belvedere Bay, Jim left his choices—"Wayne" or "Gretzky"—with John Emory-Dixon.

Wanda sent Bill to the meeting. "My place is with Susan," she told him, a world of sorrow in her eyes. He didn't have the heart to ask for her list of ten names. She hadn't mentioned them since the first meeting. "She's aged," he thought, taking in with a kind of shock her weary eyes, the slow shift of her shoulder.

Jean was pouring wine and Bill fidgeted, wondering whether he should call to remind Mr. Andrews, when John and Ivy walked in. They were holding hands as awkwardly as if they were teenagers for whom the world was not a good fit, and everyone in it, even husband and wife, strangers.

"We've got an announcement," John said, somewhat breathlessly. "We're pregnant." He dropped his wife's hand and put a clumsy arm around her. Ivy's hair hung untidily to her shoulders. The weariness in her features was under-laid by a kind of terror that made her face glow. Jean stared at Ivy, startled by the stab of envy somewhere beneath her own neat silk jacket.

Everyone lifted their glasses in a toast to Ivy and John. The tinkling and the cheers momentarily dispelled the stiff-ness that had pervaded the small gathering, replacing it with a tenuously festive mood. Into this celebrative interlude walked Mr. Andrews, more animated, it seemed to his neighbours, than they had ever seen him. He declined, then accepted, a glass.

Before the arrival of the neighbours, Jean had worried about whether she should mention the first meeting, acknowledge the accident that had interfered with their earlier efforts to find a new name for Belvedere Bay. She had decided that a few remarks about impermanence and change would be in order, but before she could make them, Mr. Andrews had set aside his glass of wine and now he was clearing his throat.

"I have a name for the street," he began, a shy but perceptible authority in his voice. "You'll like it. I consulted a friend and she. . .this friend"—here he seemed suddenly embarrassed—"she had this idea. You see, we took the first letter of everyone's name and found that putting them together you get *Tuesday*. It's very democratic, you understand, with everyone, well, everyone's represented. And it's simple too, you don't have to spell it out for people. Oh, the "s," that's for Susan. Because the accident happened, this tragic accident, on Tuesday, this friend—*my* friend, that is— thought it would be nice to include Susan. So you see, there it is: Tuesday Bay."

There was silence in the room. No one spoke or moved. Ivy was puzzled: she wasn't aware of any city streets named "Sunday" or "Monday," wasn't sure about "Tuesday" and anyway, didn't like to give up "Lea." John had no opinion, really. He had come to this meeting mainly to announce the pregnancy and anything else seemed unimportant. The origin of the letter "s" brought a hot rush of unaccustomed tears to Bill Unger's eyes. He looked at the old man as if he'd never seen him before, then walked over and shook his hand. "Thanks, Adam. Thanks." He sat down beside him and the two men remained uneasily side by side for the rest of the meeting.

Jean Tremont was outraged. What a ridiculous name, Tuesday. And the old man obviously didn't know the meaning of democracy, allowing the Emory-Dixon residence two letters in the name. She had no intentions of living on a street named Tuesday, but she was unable to find words, or nerve, to say so.

In due course the city put up a new sign: TUESDAY BAY. Jim and Rita Yaworski, utterly drained of energy by their two west-coast grandchildren, scarcely noticed it when they returned home and resumed their normal lives.

Despite her outrage, Jean Tremont remained a resident of the bay, though she dreamt one night that a city works crew was replacing the street sign with one that said NEL-LIE McLUNG WAY.

Susan died on a snowy Sunday in December. One day her body seemingly forgot its inability to walk, lurched forward as if to get up and fell awkwardly out of the wheel-chair. A bone in the left arm was broken by the fall, and while the doctors were setting it, Susan died. A renegade clot of marrow had come detached and entered the blood-stream, impeding the flow of blood to the heart. At least, that's the story that circulated around the bay, though it seemed improbable to Jean Tremont, like something she might have read in a novel. The doctors were taken off-guard, Wanda was overwhelmed with a loss too vast and complete to comprehend, Bill was stoic.

You might have expected, as Jean Tremont did, that John and Ivy would name their newborn daughter after Susan, but no, the baby was called Tara Lea.

ON WARM DAYS, YOU'LL SEE TARA LEA in her stroller in the Emory-Dixon front yard where the blue jays squawk from the leafy branches of the maple tree and cheeky red squir-rels chase each other furiously along its trunk. It's spring once more. Rita Yaworski comes over to appraise the baby and to assure Ivy, who needs no such assurance, that the baby is beautiful and that children are a fearsome responsibility.

Old Adam Andrews returns one day from his mid-morning drive with a woman in the seat beside him. A woman with greying hair and bright brown eyes, petite and

alert as a sparrow. She has come to inspect his small bungalow, with the option of moving in. You might expect Rita
Yaworski to notice Adam's wide smile from behind her
venetians and perhaps find her own face shaped quietly into
a smile. In fact, Rita is absent from her post and the last to
hear of Tuesday Bay's prospective new resident.

Wanda is poking around in her perennial beds. This
year, like every other year, she will add one new perennial
to her display. You might think that this year she'll select a
lily, but she already has several. And she's never been successful with roses. Maybe a peony. Not pink, not white. She
fancies something bold and red. The past year's sadness tugs
and tugs at her, maintaining within her a heaviness so enormous you'd think it should have weighed her down. But it
hasn't. Not entirely. True, her hair has a touch more grey and
she walks somewhat less confidently than she did a year ago.
But every morning she draws from an unfailing source sufficient energy for the day's demands. She looks up at Jean
Tremont vacuuming her red Grand Am on the driveway.
Jean's movements are purposeful, efficient. She'll soon be
done and then she'll pack up the vacuum cleaner, drag it
into her bungalow and shut the door behind her.

How quickly one spring follows another, Wanda thinks.
You barely blink and everything's changed. A robin on the
grass. The maple transformed into that delicate, translucent
green, as if for the first time in the world's history. The orna-
mental crab exploding into fuchsia blossoms overnight.
Tuesday Bay is a paradise she observes as if from a distance,
with longing.

The saleswoman at Place For Plants will help Wanda
select the red peony that she'll plant south of the mansion,
at the edge of the bay just where the Ungers' property
touches Jean Tremont's. Every spring Wanda's neighbours,
arriving home in their various vehicles, will see the peony
bush, resplendent with audacious globes of flame, proclaiming its transient glory on Tuesday Bay.

PICNIC AT LAKE SHARON

THE ROAD IS DUSTY AND VAGUE, and sometimes it disappears altogether in yellow grass and scrubby thorn trees. Only my father's familiarity with the countryside keeps us headed toward Lake Sharon. I close my eyes and try to forget that I'm being jolted relentlessly through this parched corner of the world toward a missionary picnic. I shut out the other passengers, the dust and the thick smell of sweat. It's the end of the grass-burning season and smoke hangs like a veil over Zaire. The July sun seeps through the veil and oppression settles on bush and grass, on every living creature. My blouse is damp under my arms, it sticks to my back. I'm sitting on a blanket-covered wooden crate near the back of the carry-all, the worst spot. The front windows are rolled down and the rush of wind makes conversation impossible, but it's an impossibility everyone except me is determined to overcome. From the minute we left Kenjiri, it's been the marvellous mango crop this year and the inconvenient breakdown of the hospital's power generator and the laundryjack's new baby.

"Lori, you still there?" Mrs. Bates shouts from the front

seat, raising her voice above the rushing wind and the motor. "How was school this year? Tell us about Kinshasa."

I pretend that I don't hear, but Mother has turned to look at me. I have to say something. "School was okay, I guess. I passed all my subjects."

"That's good, Lori. We were praying for you. I prayed that you would do well, really well, in your exams. And the boys too. Every day I prayed."

Some kind of answer is called for, a thank you or something. But I don't want to get into a conversation about prayer, it will only lead to Mrs. Bateses' next favourite topic, the Lord's will. I'll get enough of that next year, my last in high school. "Lori, what will you do after high school?" they'll ask. "Pray that you'll find the Lord's will for your life."

Find. As though it's lost, like a key or a passport. More than prayer was needed when the Bates's son came to visit last summer and lost his visa. I wonder how many bills slipped into black hands to get that quick replacement. They all refer to it as an answer to prayer.

If I set my mind to it, I can reverse the direction of the vehicle, creating the sensation of moving backwards, back to Kenjiri, back to the papaya tree overlooking the ravine behind my parents' reed-thatched cottage. From under the papaya tree I can see the water carriers emerge like phantoms from the misty ravine. First their black heads, granite patience etched in their faces, the whites of their eyes intense. Then their wiry torsos, naked to the waist, shiny with sweat. A pole balanced on one shoulder, a full pail of water in front, another behind. One after another they rise, as if out of nowhere, a human conveyor belt bringing water from the stream at the bottom of the valley. They never spill a drop.

When I was very small, my father took me down the steep ravine into the valley and showed me the narrow stream. Watching its frail trickle, I worried that it would dry up. One day there would be no water for me when I came in thirsty from playing. But the stream is still there, the carriers still haul it up, moving in slow, endless cycles, and even in the dry season I can drink all I want. We have never gone thirsty, never had to wear unwashed clothes or go without a bath, even if it's just a few inches of water. After watching the carriers for a morning, I don't need any reminder to use water sparingly. Those enduring forms, skin stretched tightly over ribs and muscles, have always frightened me. They are so awfully thin.

Not like Alice Bates. Alice completely fills the space between my father, who is driving, and Reverend Bates, who has the window seat. Even with eyes closed I can picture the sweat beading from the folds in the back of her plump neck. Impossible to shut out Alice Bates. The sharp insistence of her voice buzzes in and out of my consciousness like a pesky fly. She's telling the story of how the missionaries fled into Angola during the Independence upheaval in 1960. We all know the story; she tells it all the time. I know exactly when she will lower her voice dramatically or pause for effect. She has come to the part where the three-car cavalcade of missionaries leaves Kenjiri. The villagers, usually friendly and loyal, hold clubs in their hands and some bend to pick up stones.

"But not our houseboy," Alice says, and even though her back is turned to me, I can picture her mouth moving, her eyes bright with the telling. "Donatien had tears in his eyes. He was loyal."

In the end the cavalcade is allowed to leave. No one is hurt.

The dangerous flight from Kenjiri has worn thin with her constant reliving of it. For my part, I wish that all missionaries had been edged permanently out of Kenjiri, out of Africa, for that matter. But most of them came back, bringing new ones, like my parents and Miss Nafziger, who teaches at the American School in Kinshasa. She says missionaries should stop disrupting the natural rhythm and simplicity of village life. They shouldn't try to make

Canadians out of Africans. I haven't noticed any Kenjiri villagers becoming the least bit like Canadians, but if missionaries had kept away, *my* life might be normal.

Each vacation I feel more encircled, pushed into a centre position I don't want. They crowd me until I'm sure I'll suffocate.

"Are you with us, Lori?" my mother will begin saying soon, like she did all last summer and all the summers before, especially after Mame left for Regina.

I will retreat to the papaya tree. Establish defences. Claim breathing space.

Reverend Bates is almost as round as his wife and every summer they seem to resemble each other more. The same resignation is stamped on both faces and they harbour the same assured foreknowledge of fresh crises waiting around every corner, new tests of their faith and commitment. Their anticipation of hardships is seldom disappointed. Neither, come to think of it, is their serene assumption that whatever new calamity is visited upon them, they will endure and move on.

Reverend Bates wants to baptize me, I can tell. He's concerned that I'm seventeen and not yet baptized. I'm safe in the carry-all, he won't talk of it with the others around, but I must be on my guard at the picnic and never let him speak to me alone. "Lori, will we be baptizing you this summer?" he'll ask, using the royal "we." It's assumed that it's his prerogative to do all the baptizing there is to be done, of African or white. "So many missionary children before you have followed the Lord into the waters of Lake Sharon for baptism. Your sister Mame, two years ago."

Well, Reverend Bates, this is one missionary kid who isn't in a hurry to become another star in your crown.

The wooden crate isn't getting any more comfortable. Mother hands me a thermos of cold water and a cup. I drink without spilling even one drop and pass the thermos to my brothers. Carl and Matthew are playing Dutch Blitz a few feet away from me. Their voices rise above the wind.

Matthew is winning. Our grandfather in Regina always sends games and puzzles. He must think missionary kids are always bored. The twins are never bored. They are always on the point of breaking into laughter or cartwheels. If we stop at villages they grab handfuls of tracts and hand them out with as much exuberance as if they were playing soccer at the American school. I envy their carefree natures. They're like Mame. I find myself slipping more and more into the role of spectator, especially at Kenjiri. I'm not unhappy in that role; I choose it. But a seventeen-year-old isn't supposed to enjoy solitude and contemplation as much as I do. Will I be able to step out of this role when I've outgrown it?

Mother keeps turning her head to look at me. "How can we make Lori enjoy her vacation?" I heard her say to Father last night. By leaving me alone, Mother. It's that simple.

Mother is sharing the second seat with Calla Peters and Miss Hildebrandt, the single missionaries. All three are nurses in the hospital my father runs. Before I wake up mornings, they have already made rounds and attended to the serious cases. The hospital's always crowded, and if the beds are filled, the patients share beds or sleep under them like dogs, or on the ground outside. A superstitious mixture of faith and fear informs their attitude toward the hospital and toward white people who have magic machines that show how their bones are placed. Whenever I go into the hospital, which isn't often, I hold my breath and hurry through. The smells of bodies and antiseptic and vomit enclose you like a poisonous cloud. If I had to spend even one full day in that place, I'd lose my mind. How can it be God's will for anyone to spend a lifetime in such a dismal place? When I was small, I was afraid God might want me to be a nurse, like my mother, always ready to jump out of bed at night whenever there was a knock at the door. I still don't know what I'll do with my life, but whatever it is, it won't be nursing and it won't be in Africa.

The carry-all slows, comes to a halt. We've reached the ferry landing and everyone gets out, glad of a chance to stretch. The ferry is over there on the other side of the nameless brown river we must cross. One of the attendants waves at us. It could take half an hour to locate the other one. I look for a shady spot. Reverend Bates is moving downstream, so I head in the other direction. I will give him no opportunity to speak to me. Evading him is one of the bothersome necessities of summer.

At the river's edge I push both hands into the muddy, brown water. Lake Sharon will be cool and clean. The air is filled with the many-toned hum of insects, the sky is grey-blue. Through the smoke, the sun is a huge, indefinite egg yolk, but there is nothing indefinite about the power of its rays. There will be no rain for two more months.

I walk a little distance along the stream and let my thoughts go back to Kinshasa, to the American school my brothers and I go to. I'm not one of the popular students, but I have a few good friends, all of them dispersed like me for the duration. In Kinshasa there's a Wimpy's Hamburger and a chance of being invited to embassy socials. Last week was a parade of parties and picnics to celebrate the end of exams. The freedom we'd been waiting for grabbed hold of us and pulled us into a week-long, crazy whirlwind, even the teachers.

In Kenjiri there's nothing. Kenjiri is missionaries and villagers and mangy goats, and I'll never know why Mame cried when she left.

Reverend Bates has caught up to me; I haven't been watchful. He sees me alone. An opportunity to go after the stray sheep. I could walk further upstream, the ground is rough. He couldn't keep up. But that's undignified. I stand my ground, brace myself for the inevitable, predictable exhortations. He is red-faced and out of breath. He stops a little distance from me, pulls a large, white handkerchief from his pocket and wipes the streaming sweat from his neck and forehead. He looks around, helpless, as if he needs a place to sit down. It occurs to me that the heat is more intolerable for him than for me.

"Lori," he begins, "Lori…"

I don't say anything; he'll get no help from me.

"Lori," he begins again, and there's a sadness in his voice. "Is it this hot in Kinshasa?"

The question and his weariness catch me off-guard. I don't know what to say. The ferry has arrived and they are calling us. I follow Reverend Bates slowly back to the landing.

Father cautiously drives the carry-all onto the ferry. The rest of us find places to stand. There are no guardrails. Mother is still as nervous as when we were small and she would take our hands to make sure we didn't wander off the edge. I think she would like to do that still. I don't think she likes these missionary picnics, even though she laughs and chatters like the rest. It was Father's idea.

"We need a break," he said yesterday. "The kids are home, let's celebrate." When I asked if the picnic could be just our family, he wouldn't hear of it. "We're all one family," he said. "A missionary family. Besides, we can't burn petrol for a half-empty vehicle. The carry-all belongs to all of us."

Mother didn't contradict him, but she didn't support him, either. I think she'd like a day with just her family, but she'd never say so, it would be selfish. I volunteered to stay back, leave more room for the others, but she looked so hurt, I didn't press the offer. With Mame in Regina she wants to do things with me, mother-daughter things. I've decided, no confrontations the first week home. I'll give them that. But then, no more missionary picnics. After grade twelve I'm leaving Zaire. For good. Not like Mame, who's got plans to return. She and the twins are welcome to continue the missionary family if they want. I'm checking out.

We all climb into the carry-all for the last stretch to Lake Sharon. The road gets worse, the conversation falters, comes to a stop. After half an hour, the road ends at the fringe of a scant bush. From here it's a fifteen-minute walk to the lake through scratchy grass and underbrush. We fall into the familiar routine. Reverend Bates leads the way, carrying two folding chairs and an armful of *Christian Leaders*, all the back copies since Christmas. He rarely reads, but at the lake he "redeems the time," as he calls it. The wide brim of his hat flops up and down ahead of us, a limp banner. The rest of us are strung out behind. No one is empty-handed. Picnic baskets have been distributed evenly. I carry a basket of oranges and papaya and a bag of swimsuits. Mother has checked to make sure everyone wears a hat; Father has locked the carry-all.

The land rises slightly before it levels off to a plateau that drops unexpectedly down to the lake. It's always a game to see who will get there first that's why Reverend Bates likes a head start. But before he gets there the twins will pass him. They will be the first to see Lake Sharon. Reverend Bates will set up his folding chair under the lone palm tree, a decent distance from the water. The thin scattering of trees we are walking through ends before long, and it's an old joke that the only shade at the beach comes from that one slender palm. Not even a thin person can be covered by its shade. Someone will remember to say that we need a schedule so everyone can have a turn under the tree. Reverend Bates always gets more than his fair share. He thinks he's entitled because of his seniority and because he doesn't like swimming. Alice Bates loves swimming. She has to be coaxed out of the water when it's time to eat.

"Lake Sharon!"

Carl sees it first and now we all crowd forward to the edge of the rise for the first glimpse of the small, silver-blue oval resting in a broad depression in the landscape. Its surface is glass-smooth with here and there a shimmer of fine ripples. Mist blurs the far shore, obscuring the low hills that border it protectively on that side. I had forgotten how beautiful it is, how serene, how magical. Everyone is transformed and speaks at once. The boys dash down to touch the water first, and suddenly I'm glad, glad to be here. I can't wait to throw myself into the cool water, disturbing its perfection, letting it close around every part of me and hold me in its exhilarating wetness.

Amazing how quickly we descend the short slope and find clumps of grass tall enough to change in. At the water's edge an old woman is crouched on her haunches, soaking manioc roots. She pays no attention to us. She places the basket of roots on her head and stands erect. Her patterned skirt is the colour of seared grass and mangoes, her dried breasts rest on her stomach. She walks off, regal as a queen. We haven't passed a village, but Zairians appear out of nowhere. They keep their distance, staring with passive curiosity at the strange phenomenon unrolling before them: these peculiar white women who shamelessly reveal their legs while keeping their breasts covered. One of the Zairians has a transistor radio and the restless energy of the music comes to me, sharp and urgent.

The first cool shock of the water electrifies my body. I want to shout and laugh as I swim—long, clean strokes. I am graceful, powerful. Every movement of my arms, my legs is effortless and efficient and perfect. I dive down to the dark, cold layers of the lake. My hands find the bottom. I am as far away from the sun as I can be. When my body rises and breaks through the surface, I feel clean.

I have forgotten what a good swimmer Alice Bates is. She moves augustly out into the lake. Mother and Calla Peters and Miss Hildebrandt are more hesitant as they walk into the shallow part. They stop when they are chest-deep and just stand there, moving their hands like fins. The twins are halfway across the lake, Father trying to keep up. Reverend Bates is a pale blob under the palm tree, a safe distance removed. The music from the radio pulses across the water, clear and tribal. I close my eyes and float under the sun, dreaming a circle of black bodies dancing under an amber moon, beating drums and chanting to a deity. Their voices swell in the darkness of night and trees, then fade to a whisper.

I pretend that I am on a ship, sailing to Canada, home to Regina. The water around me is the Atlantic Ocean, there is no land in sight. I have finished grade twelve and won a huge scholarship, big enough to wipe out all worry about how I will live and study and travel. Big enough to wipe out Reverend Bates and Alice Bates and all of Africa, even the beat of the music.

"Lori, we're having a shampoo party. Come join us." Alice Bates's voice cuts like scissors through my dreaming. "Hold the shampoo bottle for me, will you?"

All tranquility is swallowed in the anger that rises in me. She is so transparent in her efforts to include me. Can't she see I don't want to be included? But I swim in the direction of the shampoo party anyway. At Lake Sharon I can wash my hair extravagantly and no water carrier needs to struggle up the ravine for my indulgence.

The four women are standing in a circle, Mother and Calla and Miss Hildebrandt with newly acquired white foam halos. Their raised hands are slowly scrubbing their heads. They are a circle of priestesses performing a ritual under the watchful eyes of Alice Bates. The water is flecked with suds that form a pale ring around the ceremony. I take the bottle from Alice. She sudses her hair, the sparse strands gain substance and she too wears a halo. She submerges her head to rinse and I watch the flecks float away on the rippled water. They recede quickly, leaving the lake clean.

Alice Bates holds out her hands, spreads her fingers. Is this still part of the ritual, I wonder, but I see a wave of shock and disbelief move across her face. She stiffens.

"Don't move, anybody, please don't move," she says and her voice sounds strangled. "I've lost my ring."

No one speaks for a moment, no one moves, as we absorb the information and try to think what to do. I want to say, "You'll never find it, it's gone," but the grief on her face prevents me.

"It's my wedding ring," she says, but we already know that. I've never seen her wear any other jewellery. "Can you help me find it?" Her voice is soft and frightened; I have never seen her so helpless.

No one moves, but the circle is electrified. Mother puts her hand on Alice Bates's shoulder and looks at me.

"Lori, you're good at diving. Can't you dive down and grab handfuls of sand? The ring must be nearby. It must have fallen straight down. Maybe you can find it. Try."

I almost laugh, the suggestion is so ludicrous. Any move I make will churn up the sand, and the lake has currents. We'll never see that ring again. But Mother's words have raised a faint glimmer of hope in Alice's eyes. I know I will have to try, even if my efforts are futile.

"I'm not moving from this spot," she says. "I'm staying right here. Right where the ring dropped. Try, Lori. Please try."

Pushing the water with all the strength in my arms, I dive down to where Alice Bates's pale legs are rooted firm as pillars in the bottom of the lake. I grab for sand with both hands, trying not to stir up the water any more than necessary. I flip myself right side up and surface. Holding my hands well above the water, I slowly release a stream of wet sand, first from one hand, then the other. The women stare at my hands, watching in vain for a glint of gold.

"I'm not moving. Keep diving."

I dive again. Flip up. Surface. The women stand motion-less as I open my hands and let the sand run through my fingers. Alice Bates has closed her eyes. A wet strand of hair hangs down along her nose. Her lips are moving. Prayer is her automatic response to any event, extraordinary or commonplace. This one is not commonplace.

I enter into a rhythm of diving and surfacing. The water becomes murky, I can no longer see Alice Bates's legs. When I bump into them, she stands her ground. I grope for sand, flip up and surface to the orange brightness of the smoke-veiled sun. The four priestesses are distressed but steadfast. Calla has tears in her eyes. When I return to the darkness of the lake I can still see Alice's pale face, her closed eyes, the strand of wet hair.

Gradually my movements seem less foolish, more

inevitable. I will go on forever, compelled to dive in a ritual that I share with the others. We are all doing what we must: me diving, Alice Bates praying, Calla weeping, Mother and Miss Hildebrandt encouraging me with resolute smiles whenever I emerge with more sand. It has become a liturgy. Dive. Surface. Release the sand. Slowly, slowly. The rhythm gains momentum and intensity. I am tireless. I wonder vaguely who has the authority to call a halt to this solemn choreography. The music from the shore beats faintly in some part of my brain.

I hear Mother's sharp gasp even before I see the quick, bright glint in the sand cupped in my right hand. I close my fingers over it, just in time, just before it slides back into the water. Mrs. Bates lets out a small moan, like a hurt animal. She snatches my hand and pries the ring from it.

"It's found!" she cries out. "Henry, it's found."

And then everyone is talking at once and laughing and hugging each other. I hear the words "miracle" and "answer to prayer" three or four times in the babble of relieved voices. Alice Bates's face glows with tears, it's completely overlaid with a kind of glory. I can't stop looking at her. I don't resist or hold back when she encloses me in a wet hug.

Past her shoulder I see Reverend Bates, waist-deep in water, walking slowly toward us. A smile shapes the folds of his face into the concentric circles of an ingrained halo. He doesn't speak, but I see him extend his hand, the way he extended it to Mame when he baptized her two years ago, right here in Lake Sharon. Drops of water from his out-stretched hand fall back into the lake. As I watch them, I raise my hand, slowly, hold it toward him, as if for a bless-ing. But it's his wife's hand he is reaching for. I am embar-rassed. And disappointed. I hang back as Reverend Bates and Alice wade hand in hand out of the water.

The group of Zairians has grown larger, and they have moved closer to the water. The radio is silent. They know that something out of the ordinary has happened, that we have been looking for something. Reverend Bates tells them in Swahili about the ring. He gestures with his hands. I don't understand Swahili but I can tell that he is giving them more than just the facts. Probably he is making missionary mileage out of the event, teaching them about miracles and prayer. They smile, nod their heads.

The old woman with the shrivelled breasts reappears, ignoring us with splendid aloofness. She has brought a fresh batch of manioc to soak. Father and the twins lurch like dripping walruses out of the water and have to be told about the ring.

"I bet I would have been the one to find it if I'd been around," Carl says.

Matthew looks at me with restrained admiration.

We all wear hats for the picnic lunch and sit on towels or clothes, except for Reverend and Alice Bates, who get the folding chairs. Alice and I are celebrities. Mother insists on serving us first. There are sandwiches and oranges and papaya and thermoses of tea and water. Miss Hildebrandt has brought her usual treat of candied peanuts. Father hands me and Alice bouquets of dried grasses, bowing with playful formality. After the excitement with the ring, everyone is giddy and quick to laugh.

Reverend Bates is coaxed into telling how he bought the ring in Toronto, thirty years ago. After that everyone wants to tell stories. About the herd of elephants that wandered into Kenjiri station who knows how long ago and demolished the old hospital. About the lion that attacked old Doctor Althorn. The boys tell about soccer games at school and about the latest pranks at the hostel where we stay during the school months.

I am surprised to find myself describing the antics of Bibi, the monkey the house mother let me keep the year I was thirteen and nothing was going right. That year I was the child of cruel parents who had abandoned me in this far-away cruel place, left me in the charge of cruel strangers who didn't like me. All the other girls ganged together to shut me out. And the dormitory kitchen produced the most inedible *fufu*. I might have drowned in resentment and self-pity if Bibi had not slept at the foot of my bed and comforted me. Mother is watching as I tell this story. I have never told her about Bibi.

When we run out of stories, Mother puts her arm around me, and I let her, because my resolve to keep aloof seems foolish and unnecessary.

On the way home, Calla insists on taking the wooden crate and I sit in front, between my parents. Reverend Bates and Alice share the second seat with Miss Hildebrandt. The sun is low, we won't be so hot now, but the dust won't be any less, nor the roughness of the road. We won't feel very refreshed when we arrive home in Kenjiri. I lean my head back and for a moment I want to be small again and cuddle against my mother, but I haven't done that in years. Miss Hildebrandt is humming "Bringing in the Sheaves."

"Lori, you've been a real blessing today," Alice Bates says.

I don't know what to say, but I raise my head and turn to look at her. In the dimness of the carry-all I see her slumped against Reverend Bates. Her hand is placed on her husband's knee and he has covered it with his. I can't see the ring at all.

I turn toward Reverend Bates. In the dusk his grey eyes contain an innocence, a guilelessness I've never noticed before. He leans forward, motioning with his free hand for me to listen.

"Bless you, Lori," he says. "Where did you learn to dive like that?"

Behind him the boys are playing one last game of Dutch Blitz before it's completely dark. They will be asleep long before we've travelled the long, bumpy hours that will bring us home to the ravine and the papaya tree.

INVISIBLE

IT IS NOT DIFFICULT TO BELIEVE that Wilma will appear, sudden as a sparrow, her frizzy brown hair showing first above the garden fence. She swings her slight body onto the thin wooden edge and walks the length of the garden, saucy as a squirrel, not minding the sharpness on her bare feet. She never catches a splinter. She leaps lightly to the grass, heads for the ash tree and scrambles up its thick trunk, testing with her toes for foothold in the rough branches. Halfway up, she parts her leafy ambush and grins down, a girl-version of Tarzan, but with more audacity, more freedom.

Elaine finds it reasonable to believe that Wilma will do all this and a lot of other things too.

"Wilma, for godsake, you'll break your neck, I haven't got time for that," Elaine's mother has been saying for as long as she can remember. And sometimes, "Aren't you getting too big for that?"

Not that anyone could call Wilma big. Elaine, three years younger, is wearing the brown shorts Wilma got new for spring. Her thighs are beginning to turn pink along the edge of the shorts. She wishes her skin would turn as easily and naturally gold as Wilma's. She likes the word *skin*, repeats it to herself, *skin, skin*, and finds her tongue can't let it go.

"Skin like yours, you have to look out," her mother says every summer. A sparrow flits from branch to branch.

Her mother doesn't like her to wear Wilma's clothes. "How about we get you new shorts? Blue would suit you better." She can hear her mother in the kitchen, rattling drawers, shifting pots on the stove top. The Good News Messengers are singing *It is well, it is well with my soul.* The sparrow has disappeared. She drags the tattered lawn chair, the glass of warm lemonade, the plastic pail of peas she picked this morning with the high sun beating down on her, and arranges everything in the shade of the ash tree.

"You almost done out there?"

Her mother's voice is as disembodied as the voices of the Good News Messengers. Elaine doesn't reply. She slides her thumb along a pod with just enough pressure to split it open. A firm movement dislodges the peas and they leap into the pail. Elaine knows that her mother intends to blanch and freeze this morning's peas before she changes into her sleeveless dress, flicks a comb through her brownish-grey hair, stops in front of the hall mirror to apply lipstick and hurries off to work. Elaine concentrates, forces her fingers into steady motion, and for a while the *pip, pip* of peas on the plastic bottom of the ice-cream pail is unbroken.

Do not be afraid of those who kill the body but cannot harm the soul. The voices of the Good News Messengers continue to float eerily through the screen of the kitchen door and mingle with the heat of the backyard. *Soul, soul.* Easy to picture her mother's body moving from stove to counter to cupboard, but how to imagine her soul? Bird-like, Elaine thinks, but not sparrow-like. A soul must be translucent, shining. Not brown. More like the blue shimmering wings of the dragonflies that hover around the drainpipe. Could it be that each soul is a different colour? If she had a choice, hers would be the cool colour of lakes. Her mother's mauve. And Wilma's?

It's easy to imagine Wilma, tanned and upright in a canoe, her arms in rhythmic motion, girl and canoe moving like a sleek fish on the green-grey waters of Lake Winnipeg, the silver spray around the paddle sparkling and then vanishing as she leaves the beach behind. Easy to hear her singing *Michael row your boat ashore* as she turns the canoe and steers it around the jutting point and disappears past a chaos of fallen trees.

"You almost done out there?"

Elaine looks down into her pail. The bottom is scarcely covered. Once again her hands have stopped moving, but now she grips the pail between her splayed thighs and gives her full attention to the green pods, ignoring the wetness that's collecting above her lips and in every hollow of her body. Moisture runs down her ankles, the crotch of the brown shorts is damp. Where, exactly, in a body does the soul stay?

Hidden by the garden fence, someone is coming along the lane on a bicycle. The crunch of thin wheels on gravel electrifies Elaine, a bright charge zaps her body, her fingers drop the pods and grip the arms of the tattered lawn chair. "Wilma!" The word bursts from her mouth with fearful expectation. The sound of crunching gravel moves like the exaggerated rustling of a snake down the sun-baked lane and fades. Elaine can no longer hear it.

"You almost done out there?"

THE MIND OF A WOMAN IN HER KITCHEN on a hot summer day is free to dwell on a variety of things while her hands lift a casserole out of the microwave or load the dishwasher or grate carrots for the coleslaw or, like Mildred Braun's, lower a net of garden-fresh peas into a pot of near-boiling water for blanching. Mildred is aware of the clock: her shift begins at three and she'll have to clean up first. She hopes there will be a dozen small packages of peas for the freezer, depending on how many Elaine brings in.

A fistful of newspaper clippings is wedged behind blue breakfast plates on the second shelf. Mildred resists the magnet-pull of those clippings. There is no time.

Do not be afraid of those who kill the body but cannot harm the soul. Mildred moves to turn off the radio, but the phrase *do not be afraid* prevents her. The speaker repeats it during the program: *do not be afraid, do not be afraid.* Mildred is torn between drawing comfort from the words the way she might suck juice from an orange, or shutting out the voice.

She rehearses the words she will speak to Elaine when the peas are safe in the freezer and she's changed into a dress and put on makeup for work. Will there be time enough to say what must be said? She moves her lips around the words, willing them to emerge from her mouth clear as a bell, ringing with authority and at the same time offering reassurance. Tenderness.

"Some things we have to accept, Elaine, those we can't do a thing about. Wilma's not here. And won't be, ever again. Still, every day I have to work at the drugstore. You have summer holidays now. Then school again. And that's how it is. We've managed for two months, haven't we? And God hasn't forgotten us. You'll see."

Should she say, "Elaine, *darling*"? Should she try to hold her silent, eleven-year-old daughter in her arms? Should she say, "I can get the weekend off if you want to go to the lake?" Or is it much too soon for that? She will not mention the brown shorts, how unsettling she finds them. Should she leave out the part about God? Should she say, "Don't be afraid?"

Mildred isn't sure how long she's been standing there, her face wet, holding the pot of near-boiling water in her hand. She puts it down, her arms suddenly powerless. She's been talking to herself again.

Mildred's hand moves toward the clippings shoved behind the breakfast plates. She pulls them out and begins unfolding, unfolding. There is no need to read them, the headlines are always dancing crazily in her head. *Treacherous lake claims victim... First canoeing fatality... Wind and sun prove deadly.* There is nothing to choose from. No comfort. Mildred looks at the clock and calls for the third time, "You almost done out there?"

There is no answer, although Mildred thinks she hears a voice, someone callling with unconcealed urgency: "Wilma." Or is it her own mind screaming? She shuts off the radio.

THE WARM KITCHEN FEELS COOL after the heat of the back yard. Alone in it, Elaine wonders whether she loves her mother, wonders what the word *love* means. Is there anyone who knows, who can tell her what it means? She opens the fridge door and thinks the kitchen isn't really empty, her mother is still there, and the evidence isn't just the oven mitt that's fallen to the floor, the pot not returned to the bottom shelf, the scattered newspaper clippings on the counter. She knows with certainty that although her mother is at work, her soul is still here, in this kitchen with her. Mauve. She takes the two-litre carton of milk, stares at it, pours a glass. No one could ever get Wilma to drink milk.

"Your bones won't develop properly."

"My bones will be just fine."

Fragments of conversations ring in her skull, playing over and over, embedded the way the voices of the Good News Messengers become embedded: *I've anchored my soul in the haven of rest.* Any minute now Wilma will open the door, fling off her sandals. Her body will be all colour and motion and she'll say, "Hi, what's to eat?"

Elaine leaves the glass of milk on the counter and walks into her mother's room, carefully avoiding the mirror. The room is pastel: pink and pale green. She moves toward the closet. Her hand gropes in the darkness of a shelf's far corner for the silky texture and pulls out a tangerine bathing suit. She peels off the damp, brown shorts and the navy t-shirt, and slips into the bathing suit. Then she forces herself to face the mirror, turns this way and that, in detailed appraisal. In the dim light of the bedroom her face seems pale, the grey eyes dull. Only the tangerine bathing suit glows like a stubborn flame. After a while she pulls it off and stuffs it back into the far corner where it can't be seen. She feels colourless. Invisible.

Wilma is never invisible. Her face is gold, like sand. Elaine can see it if she closes her eyes and waits, terrified, as her sister's features take shape. They emerge as she knows they must and suddenly the gold turns dark, darker than wet sand, dark as clotted blood, almost black. Wilma's face, swollen out of shape, grotesque against the white pillow. There is nothing in those features to be envied. Nothing to desire. The eyes are shut. The motionless body is covered with a sheet, except for the face and the hands resting like two black sparrows on the white fabric. Elaine stares at them. She believes she could draw those hands. Maybe she could draw the face of her sister, if she loved her. Really loved her.

Elaine opens her eyes and realizes she is still naked. She is not sure she loves Wilma, has ever loved her, but she longs for her.

She reaches for her shorts and t-shirt.

THE SUN APPROACHING THE SUMMER SOLSTICE is well above the birches that fringe the beach, and the sand, although it's late afternoon, is still hot under bare feet. Summer has come too early, everyone's saying. Anyone scanning the expanse of Lake Winnipeg might see a sailboat or two, or a ghostly freighter on the horizon. The usual gulls hover above the water, swoop suddenly or plummet. In the distance the smooth expanse is broken by barely discernible white-crested waves that dissipate long before they reach shore.

Mildred Braun is sitting on a towel in the shade of a beach umbrella, reading the latest *Chatelaine* and listening to a radio. From time to time she rests her eyes on the lulling motion of the water as it laps the sand. Behind her a girl in a tangerine bathing suit and carrying a paddle emerges from the birch trees that obscure a brown cottage. She walks quickly across the hot sand to the water's edge where a canoe is beached. The girl is about fourteen, slender, fine-boned, her hair dark brown, frizzy, her movements confident and sturdier than one would expect in a person so slight.

"Take a hat. Something with a brim." Mildred, looking up from the magazine, has noticed her daughter. "And while you're at it, a t-shirt."

"Don't need to, Mom. You know I never burn." Wilma pushes the canoe into the water and gets in.

"Wind's hard on the skin. And it's hot for June."

The girl turns laughing to her mother, but says nothing.

"Why don't you take Elaine?"

"She doesn't want to."

"Wilma, the wind's offshore. You know what that means."

"You worry so much." Impatiently.

"And don't head straight out. Keep to the shore."

"Mom, I'm not stupid."

Mildred says nothing more. Maybe she doesn't want to spoil her daughter's joy. Or maybe she's reluctant to summon the energy to cross wills with anyone on a free, unseasonally warm afternoon.

Girl and canoe move smoothly away from the beach. They are followed by the voices of the Good News Messengers repeating a line from their theme song: *I've anchored my soul in the haven of rest.* The woman returns to the *Chatelaine*, but not with the same attention as when the canoe lay beached on the sand, and her daughter was somewhere in the cottage, invisible. She looks up from time to time, shielding her eyes against the sun's brilliance, and gazes into the grey water. How well the girl guides the canoe. She paddles gracefully, and for a while her mother can hear her singing, *Michael row your boat ashore.* The canoe heads straight out, then turns left and follows the bend of the bay until it is out of sight.

Mildred wishes she hadn't spoken so sternly. Wishes there hadn't been the need. Later, she will remember how a sudden terror gripped her, and she prayed with all the fervour she could muster that the invisible canoe would continue to hug the shore. That the wind would die down or change direction.

WITH THE BIRCH TREES IN FULL LEAF, the brown cottage on a rocky rise can't be seen from the beach, but from inside the cottage, from the large window facing the water, it's possible to see large snatches of sand and lake and, intermittently, the movement on both. Elaine stands at the window. She sees her mother on the towel, sees her sister cross the sand, get into the canoe and guide it away from shore. The tangerine bathing suit is a flag, a beacon her eyes can follow until it rounds the point.

It's not difficult for Elaine to feel invisible in the birch-shaded cottage where it's cool even on a warm day. She doesn't long to be in the canoe with Wilma, heading away from their cottage, their beach. She's not sorry Wilma doesn't want to include her in late-night beach parties. *Sorry.* The word came from her mother's mouth at noon, Wilma still in bed, still sleepy.

"I just don't want you getting into things you'll be sorry for."

"Mom, it was just a beach party."

"Greg and Julie and the rest, they were drinking?"

"Mom, it was a goddamn beach party, OK?"

"You went canoeing after dark."

"There was a moon. It was bright as day."

Yes, there was a moon. Elaine remembers its huge and patient white face looking down on her where she lay in bed.

"I just don't want anything to happen we'll all be sorry about."

Elaine can't imagine her sister ever being sorry about anything. She imagines her moving through each day in a swirl of light, as if she's cheered on, even when she's alone, by an unseen, adoring crowd. Land or water, every element carries her where she wants to go and there won't be any trace of trembling in her, trembling that grows into fear.

There is no reason to fear. Elaine's mother is here, and her older sister. It's the first weekend at the cottage, she can sleep as long as she wants, she can wade in the shallow water and no one will urge her to go deeper, no one expects her to do battle with the waves. If she wants to, she can take the path through the birches to the beach. Her mother will make room for her under the umbrella so her pale skin won't burn. So hot this year. She's sorry she didn't bring paper and her coloured pencils to draw the birch trees and the lake with a small tangerine speck on the grey water.

"I'll be glad to get away from the drugstore, believe me," her mother said on Friday after school, packing frozen hamburger meat and iceberg lettuce and fresh towels with purposeful movements, as if purpose was the thing needed. "It's not likely to rain. I bet you guys could use a break from school before the last stretch."

Elaine doesn't like school. "Who does, at eleven?" her mother always says. "I didn't. It's normal." But Elaine knows it isn't. *Normal.* Elaine doesn't like the word. Sometimes she doesn't like her normal sister who doesn't mind school, never did, although she sometimes skips class—something Elaine would never dare to do—and goes with her friends to the park or the mall. It's unlikely that Wilma notices how classroom walls tower like stone cliffs over the desks, how windows refuse to let in light or air. In Elaine's classroom it's impossible to breathe when the students are all in their places, the teacher in hers and the chalkboard covered with endless words in neat handwriting. Do any of the students occupying desks near Elaine's ever feel the terror inside? Does anyone in the whole world?

In the windowless counselling office the airlessness is unbearable.

"Don't be afraid, Elaine," the counsellor always says and

her voice, cool and smooth as jade, comes from far away. "I'm here to help you." But although there is gentleness in her voice, it can't stop the walls from pressing in.

"We can get you through this, really we can." The patient, lulling voice holds kindness, warmth. But Elaine trembles with cold fear.

"You'll have to cooperate, Elaine. You'll have to let us help you. You'll have to speak, tell us how you feel." And after a silence, "I know you like to draw. A drawing can say what you feel."

Feel. Feel. In the art room Elaine feels nothing and her fingers are just as stiff and cold as in the counselling office. She tries with her whole mind, her whole body, to press the pencil to the paper the way Wilma might do it, but when she wants to move the pencil, she doesn't know in what direction.

All the birch trees are trembling; a breeze is setting the world in motion and Elaine wants to move toward the door. But first she looks once more, intently, for the tangerine speck, not sure whether she is straining for its presence or its absence. She knows the speck has moved out of sight around the point and is startled to find it still there in her mind, visible, as she walks through the shivering birches toward the beach.

IN THE AIR-CONDITIONED DRUGSTORE, Mildred Braun is busy at the check-out. Everyone lingers, wants to say something, anything, to delay going out into the sharp heat, into a parked car the relentless sun has turned into a furnace.

"Isn't it a beast out there?"

"No hope of rain, they say."

"I'm sweating like a pig. Look at me."

Some of the customers are regulars who have the right to ask questions, to offer sympathy, to demonstrate they have taken notice.

"How's Elaine taking it? She doing any better now?"

"She's fine," is Mildred's automatic, weary response, but

at coffee break with Ella from the post office, she admits, "The thing is, I don't know if I'm overreacting or not doing enough. I feel so totally helpless. She doesn't speak. Hasn't said one word about it."

Ella doesn't reply to that. The two women sip coffee and the cool silence of the room holds comfort that surprises Mildred. It seems to her that Ella in her blue work smock, her sensible brown shoes, is waiting for her. It seems as if sitting here with this woman drives out fear. She wants to stay in the cool, silent room, and not go back to the check-out. And not home.

"Maybe I should take her somewhere," Mildred says, finally. "Find a new doctor."

And again there is silence. Then Ella says, "I'm praying for Elaine," and her voice is not sweet and thin with goodness, but somewhat awkward and matter-of-fact. She finishes her coffee, throws out the paper cup. "And you too. What about you, Mildred?"

And then she's telling Ella about the hospital room where the body lay, the skin seared dark, the face swollen, unrecognizable. Not like Wilma. Not even human at all.

"What I can't get out of my mind is this picture of Wilma paddling, paddling, after the current pushed her into the lake, paddling and getting nowhere, just getting nowhere, and terrified, she must have been scared to death when she realized she was caught in the wind and the waves getting higher and she's all alone out there. The wind and the terrible sun burning her black. Trapping her out there. When they got to her, she was delirious. She wouldn't have suffered nearly so much drowning, but she'd never give up, not that one."

And then the two women sit without speaking, the afternoon wrapping around them.

"I shouldn't have let Elaine come to the hospital."

"You did what you thought best, Mildred." Ella's voice begins to wobble, as if Mildred's grief is gaining power over it. But it doesn't break.

"They never got along. So different, you know."

"I know."

"Sometimes I used to wish they weren't both there, you know, both in the same house. It might be easier."

"I know."

"Ella," and now Mildred's voice is thread-thin, scarcely a breath, "sometimes I ask, why *Wilma?* Why *this* one? I ask that." Her eyes, pale blue and haunted, search fearfully for Ella's.

Ella has nothing to say to this, but she raises her wet eyes to meet Mildred's.

"I hear those Good News Messengers on the radio," Mildred says, lowering her eyes. "They come on just before work. That theme song, do you know it? *I've anchored my soul in the haven of rest.*" And after a while she adds in a voice knotted with anguish, "Ella, where do you think she is?" She's not sure whether she means Wilma or Elaine and without Ella's arm warm around her, nothing would be possible.

Coffee break is over and Mildred walks slowly back to the check-out, clinging for a while to the solace of Ella's arm, Ella's words, but after half an hour of customers lining up, of constant, "Hi, Mildred," a rush of shame comes over her. Why did she say all that to Ella? Some things are best kept unspoken, some burdens meant to be borne alone. Why did she suddenly let everything out, bringing tears to Ella's warm eyes while her own remained dry? She couldn't prevent the words. Now, to prevent the tears that want to come, she thinks about her garden.

The season for picking peas will soon be over. She imagines the shrivelling rows beyond the ash-tree, the brown vines dry and ready to be pulled. A jay screaming across the garden, over the fence and into the neighbour's chokecherry tree. The trees shedding their leaves, the ash tree's gold mingling with the blood-red chokecherry leaves. Summer giving way as it always does to fall. Nothing remains forever as it is. There is both terror and hope in this.

She pictures Elaine opening the door and stepping out into the light. She is holding something in her hand. Mildred wonders what her daughter is doing.

The customers are waiting. With enormous effort Mildred pulls herself together. Shuts out Elaine. Shuts out the garden.

AT HER SMALL DESK ELAINE IS ARRANGING coloured pencils and paper for a drawing she is about to make. She is alone in the house and the afternoon light spreads a quiet glow. The picture she has in mind will not be large, but very precise. A butterfly or a bird or the cheeky red squirrel that scolds her from a crotch in the ash tree. When it is finished it will be a picture of a soul. *Soul.*

As she picks up the pencil to begin, she looks up and notices that the wall above her desk is swimming in light and she thinks of the way sunlight on water turns it brilliant, so brilliant no one can look at it. She is uncertain and hesitates to put the first pencil stroke on paper in case it is the wrong one. Beginnings are important. "Let's start over," her mother said again this morning. "It's the only way," and the Good News Messengers kept repeating *Don't be afraid.* She wanted to step close to her mother, touch her. She remembers how the school counsellor would speak sometimes about turning over a new leaf. The leaf, Elaine thinks, would be the pale, gentle green of spring.

The page before her is white as a white pillow. And empty. When it is filled she will offer it to her mother. If she has the courage. She turns inward, looking for what she is to draw, and sees, instead of a delicate hummingbird or the shimmering blue wings of a dragonfly, a face, charred and misshapen as an ancient ruin. It is there, an undeniable suffering, and it wants to be drawn. She shudders. Then she fits her fingers around the pencil and commands her hand not to tighten into a fist. Now she is ready to begin. If she draws the face, maybe she will no longer look toward the door trembling, waiting for Wilma to come. It will be a miracle. A miracle to offer her mother. To offer herself. "Don't be afraid," she says and draws the first line.

Days of Noah

EVERY SATURDAY MY MOTHER chased down and slaughtered a leghorn, the fattest she could catch, and by the time I was twelve I was expected to help with the weekly beheading. My part was to clutch the red comb with my reluctant fingers and pull so the neck lay stretched across the oak stump, which over the years had become dark and stained. My mother gripped the body with one hand, an axe with the other. A dull thud, and blood dribbled down from the severed head in my hand to the brown grass around my toes. My mother held the twitching, headless body away from her until the dripping stopped. The other hens raised their heads briefly in alarm. Then, as if they were afraid time was running out for them, they returned with urgency to their pecking.

We had chicken every Sunday. This Sunday, because my mother's friends, three sisters, were coming by bus from Winnipeg, the chicken would be stuffed with *bobbat*, the potatoes mashed, my mother would brew real coffee instead of *prips,* and we would eat in the living room. My father was gearing up, changing from greasy, barn-stained chore overalls to his brand-new pair. He didn't allow his denims to be washed, ever. "It takes the firmness out of them," he told my mother. "It fades them." His word was the law. My mother, I knew, would have wanted him to wear the pants of his only suit, dark blue, but she didn't suggest it. If he so much as guessed that there was an attempt underfoot to impress someone, that's when he was capable of coming to the table in his stained and stiffened chore overalls.

The Ford was temporarily free of carburetor trouble, there was gas in the tank and my father hadn't raised serious objections against driving out to the main highway to meet the Sunday morning Grey Goose run from Winnipeg.

"You can drive with your father to the bus," my mother told me early Sunday morning, potato peel flying from her paring knife. She made it sound like a privilege to sit beside him while the three visitors crowded into the back.

"Ellie can go," I offered quickly, but my mother paid no attention.

I knew with a dull, unwelcome knowing that I was to serve as shield and protection. Ellie was only five, and not protection enough. My father was scared of meeting three women he didn't know very well and this embarrassed me, the way I felt embarrassed whenever he asked for flour, raisins and sugar in his immigrant English at Tymchuk's store.

My mother was afraid too. She arranged and rearranged the geraniums in the window at least three times. Recipes and poems clipped from the *Free Press Weekly Prairie Farmer*, usually strewn here and there on every available surface, were gathered up and pushed behind plates in the cupboard or slipped inside the Bible or under embroidered, lace-edged runners. My Saturday dusting, usually accepted as being done if I said so, had been scrutinized and tested, and I had been ordered to cut a bunch of calendula and daisies for the table. This once, my father would do the midday chores alone—mash, oyster shells and water—and the dishes would be left for me, no use begging. The fussing and preparation left me irritable. I wanted to withdraw from it all.

My father and I never had what might be called a conversation, so the drive to the highway was mainly silent. That
morning he had read his favourite verses in our before-
breakfast Bible reading even Ellie had to sit through. He
didn't go out of his way to choose the verses; we'd been
labouring steadily through the gospel of Matthew for several
weeks and that morning we reached them, quite naturally:
*As it was in the days of Noah, people were eating and drinking,
buying and selling, marrying and giving in marriage, up to the day
Noah entered the ark, and they knew nothing until the flood came
and took them all away. So it will be. . . two women will be grinding at a hand mill. One will be taken and the other left.*

I was afraid my father was going to remind me of those
ominous words that hovered over my childhood like outspread wings. Knowledge of the Days of Noah had entered
me early and lay lodged deep in my consciousness. There
was no escape. While waiting for my father to mention
them, I tried with drummed-up daring to fill the silence by
imagining orgies of eating and drinking, a sort of Persian
feast with everyone reclining on Ali Baba carpets, devour-
ing chicken and fried sausage and pineapple and huge
chocolate cakes. Wine sparkled red in crystal glasses. The
feast was a shimmering kaleidoscope of colour and noise. It
was followed remorselessly by mysterious disappearances.
One taken and one left.

My father seemed to have forgotten the prophetic
words. He commented occasionally on the ripeness of the
wheatfields that rushed by and twice asked me for the
names of our visitors. He didn't mention Noah. That proved
how nervous he was.

"Elizabeth, Martha, Mathilda." The name "Mathilda"
intrigued me; it wasn't a common name for a Mennonite
woman, and it struck me as very modern, very sophisticat-
ed, very beautiful. With my whole heart I desired the name
Mathilda. It was one more wish to add to a string of
wishes—for a piano, for permission to wear pants like my
friends, for my parents to speak English like everyone else's

parents. With stubborn hope, I carried these huge, vain wishes around with me. Occasionally I put one of them into words for my mother's benefit, on the faint chance that she would pass them on to my father with that insistence she was capable of mustering if something really mattered to her. From me to my mother to my father—that was the chain of communication that prevailed in our household. My burning wishes, it seemed to me, mattered little to either of them.

My father parked at the intersection across from the Esso station, the regular Grey Goose bus stop, and we got out of the hot car. I looked down the highway for signs of a dust cloud that might signal a vehicle as large as a bus. There was nothing. I tried to imagine what these three women, my mother's friends from childhood, from an impossible village in Russia, would look like. Three. How would that work if the Days of Noah were to arrive today, now, while the yet-unseen bus was roaring toward us along the dusty highway? If Elizabeth is sitting next to Martha, who will be taken and who left? Or if Martha is sitting next to Mathilda—Oh please, no! Not Mathilda.

"It's coming," my father called sharply and a cold, damp chill raced down my spine and along my arms. But he only meant the bus.

The first evidence that Elizabeth, Martha, Mathilda had really arrived was the appearance of six shiny, black-patent shoes with high heels. They emerged one by one from the darkness of the bus and sank into the loose gravel at the edge of the road, each one the base for a sleek leg, and naturally the bodies followed. Not as tall as my mother, not as slender. Their pale, summery dresses were sprinkled with tiny flowers and adorned with strings of pearls and sparkling brooches. My father stepped bravely forward to help with a cluster of lumpy, fantastic packages that emerged with the women from the bus.

"So this is Hedwig. What a fine big girl you are. Blue eyes like your Papa. How old are you, Hedwig? Look at her,

Martha, so tanned, she's been helping Mama in the garden. What grade are you in? A few weeks and it's back to school, eh, Hedwig, that make you happy? Pretty soon boyfriends, yes? Where's the little sister?"

It wasn't necessary for me to reply, there was no room for that. It wasn't expected. They obviously couldn't think of things to ask my father, so they surrounded me with a buzz of questions and exclamations, like bees in the alfalfa on a hot day. Struck dumb with embarrassment, I endured the onslaught.

When we were all settled in the car, there was a time of silence while my father attended to the driving and the windows were rolled up to protect Elizabeth, Martha, Mathilda's hair against wind and dust. My blouse stuck damply to my back and sweat dribbled down my legs. Now and then I caught a trace of scent, perfume I was sure came from Mathilda. Although I had grudgingly looked forward to this visit, part of me wished I could hurry time and it would be tomorrow, a whole day open before me like a new book, a day fresh as the morning air after rain. A day unmarred by visitors and their relentless curiosity, their many words, and at the end of it piles of dirty dishes looming before me.

Although I had never seen them before, I knew plenty about our visitors, who sat squished and beaming in their fine dresses in the back seat. My mother had told me often that in Russia their father had been a millionaire, had owned three flour mills, each four storeys high, and had built the bank and the church in the large village where they lived. He had hired any teacher he wanted for the school. Here in Canada he had to peddle eggs in the streets of Winnipeg. Elizabeth and Martha worked in sewing factories; Mathilda was a maid for a wealthy English family. To me their changed circumstances meant very little against the overwhelming fact that they lived in Winnipeg, a city with street after street of fine houses, a park with a zoo and flower gardens, and Eaton's. A city I had entered two or three times in my life, accompanied by unbearable excitement and, of course, my parents.

Although we had not visited Elizabeth, Martha, Mathilda on our rare excursions to Winnipeg, I could easily picture them walking smartly along the sidewalk, their elegant heels clicking on the pavement. They stepped into Eaton's, their fine dresses swishing around their sleek legs as they ascended on escalators. They came home from work, home to a spacious house, sat down to dinner at an elegant table, and afterwards Mathilda would sit at the piano and passionate melodies would float up from her fingers and swirl around delicate china figurines: ethereal angels, rearing horses, long-necked swans placed here and there on ornate furniture.

My mother came rushing to the car, her cheeks flushed. "Hello, hello there," she called out, imperiously shooing away the skittish leghorns, all signs of nervousness gone, as if she'd flung it into the closet with her everyday dress. She had changed to her paisley cotton, her favourite, and a clean white apron over it. Ellie skipped furious circles around everyone, her pale braids flying, her small, bare feet kicking up the dust.

"Stop it," my mother said.

After my father's lengthy prayer there was an awkward, decent silence around the table and then, as if eating and drinking dissolved all barriers, the visitors spilled out a rhapsody of praise for my mother's chicken, tender under the crisp, brown skin, the thick farm cream, the garden-fresh peas, the gravy, richly golden and smooth as silk.

"Delicious, delicious, delicious," Elizabeth gushed, and Mathilda, "Gravy like satin, Frieda, how do you *do* it? Like satin!" Their delight was so unconstrained, so boundless that I found it embarrassing. My mother made me leave my full plate of chicken and sent me to the kitchen for more of everything for our guests.

She was transformed, her voice so animated it sparkled, and I was surprised at the way her laughter bubbled up and flowed out into the room. Her brown hands flitted and gestured, her tongue danced. "More chicken," she urged. "Elizabeth, your plate's empty. Pass it here, right now. Just plain farm food, but you must eat. Pickles, Mathilda? Coffee? Take cream, it's one thing we've got lots of. Come next week and you'll get ripe tomatoes and the corn's just about ready. The garden's got more than just plain old peas. Too bad everything's so late this year. I guess in the city you make sage dressing, all I can offer you is *bobbat*." Her comparisons left me cringing.

When everyone's plate was filled, and hers untouched, she went on, "What's Tina Poetker doing, have you heard? Susie Gerber—she still working for that Scotch woman? Susie Gerber, I can just hear her, how she could *sing*. Like a lark. Is it true Neufels' Lisa married that widower from Winkler? Haven't had a letter in months. Where *is* everyone?" Words flew across the table and multiplied to fill the afternoon.

"Think of it," my father said that evening, in a voice that could have been the prophet Jeremiah's, ready to deliver a pronouncement, an oracle. "Such a life. Such a misdirected life."

"What." My mother's voice was flat now, the word not quite a question. She had changed into her everyday dress and was sweeping up.

I stared at my sister, who was flitting like a drunk puppy between the blue tea set and the colouring book and crayons that had emerged from the lumpy packages Elizabeth, Martha, Mathilda had carried off the bus. "We forgot you're twelve already," Mathilda apologized when she gave me the colouring book. I had washed up the dinner dishes and the afternoon coffee cups, dried them and even put some of them away in the cupboard. I had been everyone's slave for a whole day, a whole, entire, wasted day, with no time even to run down the road to see Eleanor Tymchuk, and for all that sacrifice there would be no reward.

"Think of it. Working from eight to five in a factory.

And what do they get? Don't think they get good salaries, because they don't. The unhealthy air, people always smoking. Living by the clock. Always doing what the boss tells you, no chance to plan or make decisions. I'll bet they're still making payments on a house that always needs repairs and always will. Can you see yourself working for English ladies, like Mathilda? It's not what we were meant for. When we came to Canada we promised to be farmers. A city is godless, if you ask me. You can thank God you don't have to live like your friends."

"How late will you be tonight, mixing the feed? Do you need help with the eggs?" My mother's voice, I could tell, invited a "No."

But my father didn't seem to hear. *As it was in the days of Noah*, he said. "Always buying and selling, eating and drinking. It's a sign. A sign of the times," and I wondered if he meant what Elizabeth, Martha, Mathilda were used to eating in the city or the meal my mother had worked so hard to prepare and of which he had eaten a good portion. I wanted to step up to my father and tell him I would rather live in the city, I would rather breathe that terrible city air, walk on pavement instead of mud. And if he liked the farm better, he could stay and keep Ellie. I and my mother would leave them behind and escape to the city. She would work for an English lady and I would learn to play piano.

"Mathilda said my gravy was like satin." My mother paused in her sweeping, stood with both hands clasping the broom, her head raised, her eyes bright, as if something unexpected had happened to surprise her, someone had given her a prize. "Did you see she took a second helping? I said it was the cream, you need fresh cream for good gravy. I gave her a jar so she can try for herself. Hedwig, get Ellie to bed, quick. It's late."

As it was in the days of Noah. My father raised himself reluctantly from the chair. He had changed to his old overalls, stiff and dark with stains. "You stay inside," he told my mother. "I'll manage."

I imagined Mathilda in her summery print dress, sitting next to a closed window on the Grey Goose bus, carefully holding a jar of farm cream on her lap, as wheatfields and poplar bush and clusters of lonely farm buildings rushed by, mile after mile, until they gave way to tall, stately buildings, paved streets and clipped green lawns, smooth as velvet, and nobody there gave a single thought to the Days of Noah.

I WAS SIXTEEN, AND WE HAD MOVED TO ANOTHER FARM, not a better one, but closer to town so I could go to high school. Beside the dusty gravel road leading to the house, the poplars in summer were dust-choked, just like at the other farm, and the leghorns revelled in dust baths all over the yard and in the afternoon found shade behind the drab buildings or under bushes. Between my parents and my new friends' parents there existed an impossible abyss. That hadn't changed. I had resigned myself to the dismal reality that immigrant accents have the tenacity of sow thistles, that my mother wasn't about to cut her hair and get it permed like the English ladies. "Why should I?" she said, skilfully and quickly twisting the brown, waist-length cascade into a shining rope which she fashioned into a huge figure eight and secured with hairpins. I knew I had no answer that would satisfy her.

Gathie Thiessen was coming to the farm, a friend of my mother's who lived on Vancouver Island, in Victoria, a city none of us had ever seen, and therefore must surely be more wonderful, more out of reach even than Winnipeg.

"I want Gathie to see that my life is a good life too," my mother told me the week before her coming. I understood with a stab of amazement that her words were both a con-fession and an enlistment of my good will, a plea for congenial behaviour, something I didn't find it necessary to practise those days. My mother didn't usually take me into her confidence, and her words startled me, as if she'd walked naked into the kitchen.

When the occasional English ladies dropped in and my mother ordered me to lay out a teacloth and bring out her best cups, was she measuring her life against theirs, as I measured mine against my friend Carol Carson's? The idea that my mother too examined her life—was it good, was it bad—stopped me short that day.

"There has to be a green salad," I informed her, in the spare way of communicating I had perfected. "Tossed."

"Tossed, what's that?" she asked. "If it has to be, then you make it." Her voice was bordered with scorn for what she considered the needlessly frivolous and fancy English cooking I was learning in home ec class. At the same time, her words were a plea for help. She stirred and stirred the gravy and spread out the white damask tablecloth Elizabeth, Martha, Mathilda had brought her from Winnipeg four years ago. As if she considered chicken too common for someone from Victoria, she had coaxed my father into buying a roast of beef. Ellie was big enough now to help me with the dishes. "No use begging," my mother warned, and I knew she meant both of us.

I didn't bother reminding her that, for other people, "dinner" was not the noon meal. What would be the use? I regretted mentioning the tossed salad. I should have known my mother would use it against me. But having suggested it, I felt bound to check out the garden for lettuce, the last doubtful radishes, carrots that were still young and thin, but very sweet. "It's always the dressing makes the salad," our home ec teacher repeated *ad nauseam*. I knew with a sinking heart that our kitchen shelves held no olive oil, no Worcestershire sauce, no tarragon, no fresh lemon.

The amazing thing about Gathie was that, although she had come from Russia on the same boat as my mother, she had studied in Strasbourg at the university, and was teaching high school French in Victoria. No other Mennonite woman my mother's age, at least none I knew of, was a teacher.

My mother kept a pile of Gathie Thiessen's letters in a box in a dresser drawer that held other valuable treasures hoarded over the years: boxes of newspaper pictures and clippings about the royal family, a collection of faded pictures from Russia, tatted lace grown yellow. Gathie wrote on paper tinted pink or mauve and always bordered with exquisite flowers. The handwriting was delicate and spidery. Before she stored the latest letter in her dresser drawer, my mother read it out loud to us.

"It's hard to believe June is just a month away," Gathie would write in spring. "I have to take summer school, but then I'm driving to Los Angeles. I'm so looking forward to this change from routine and responsibility, you can't imagine how much." In December it was, "You'll be surprised to hear I'm flying to Bermuda for Christmas. These things have to be done before one is old. I wish you were going with me, Frieda. Can't your family spare you? Not at Christmas, of course, but maybe in summer."

The idea was preposterous, and naturally it was never even considered. "Gathie just has no idea what happens on a farm in summer," my mother said, in that defensively impatient tone she used when speaking of the ways of city people, when there were no city people present. I was disappointed she didn't at least put up a fight for Bermuda.

Once, at Easter, Gathie wrote in her card: "Last week I took my class to the art gallery. It was a long and difficult afternoon." That was all, and the spareness caught me unawares. I had never been to an art gallery. Why was it difficult? This year she had written, "I'll be driving to Winnipeg in July. Can you send me directions to your farm?"

Gathie was easily as tall as my mother, her stylishly short hair just beginning to grey around her forehead. Her lips were crimson. I could tell she wore eye makeup too, just a touch of blue-grey. She looked queenly, years younger than my mother. Her hands cradling the coffee cup were soft and white, her nails smooth and pink as wild rose petals. She took very small helpings of vegetables and of the tossed salad, but no meat. And no gravy. When she spoke to me in perfect English, I was impressed.

"Don't ever be a teacher, Hedwig," she said, shifting her attention to me. "Children can be so cruel. And teenagers—teenagers are monsters, plain and simple. You just have no idea." As if she'd forgotten I was a teenager. As if I didn't know exactly what she was talking about. Billy Stefanik and the other guys at the back of the room firing off a barrage of spitballs and Mrs. Crane always too slow to catch them at it. My best friend Carol would spend all of English class writing notes to everyone near by. Even when we were reading *Wuthering Heights*.

"They wear you out," Gathie said, her voice desperate, almost bitter. "They're always lashing out against authority. Never interested in anything you want to teach them, just endangering their lives tearing around in those noisy beat-up cars they always manage to get from God knows where. Or they hang out in the cafeteria and fill their stomachs with greasy French fries swimming in gravy."

"A sign of the godless times," my father said, but his voice lacked conviction, as if Gathie had taken the wind out of his sails. It was hard to tell if he had really heard, or if he was thinking it was time for water and mash, the eggs should be collected, he better get going. He always heaped his plate with potatoes and lots of gravy, enough so there was never need for a second helping. I was afraid he was going to speak about the Days of Noah, about eating and drinking, buying and selling, but Gathie wasn't finished.

"The phys ed teacher, now he knows how to discipline," she was saying, admiration and envy mixed in her voice. "When he wants to punish students, he just makes them run laps around the gym, or if it's summer, around the outdoor track. And just to be sure they get thoroughly worn out, he runs with them. He's really fit, you should see him. Now that's a fine idea. But it's not something I can do."

No, I could see that. I tried to picture Gathie running in her sleek navy pumps, her wool plaid skirt flapping around her thin legs, her hairdo losing its perfect shape, puffing to keep up with a guilty student who, out of spite, would tear like crazy around the track. I choked and sputtered, holding back the giggles that threatened to erupt.

There was no real conversation. It was more like our guest was lecturing, and I found myself putting her in Mrs. Crane's place, in front of the class. Would her face turn red with helpless anger like Mrs.Crane's? Would she give boring assignments? Would she ever laugh?

My mother sat silent and somewhat detached from Gathie's outpouring. Then a flicker of surprise crossed her face, as if she had caught a glimmer of something she hadn't seen before. The detachment gave way to attentiveness; she leaned forward to catch Gathie's every word. Then, as if she had been given a nudge, she rose briskly and, in the voice she kept for preventing juvenile protest, said, "Hedwig, Ellie, the dishes now."

As I roused myself unwillingly to help Ellie clear the table, I heard our mother say, as if to a small child, "Come, Gathie. Come, we'll go into the other room."

Ellie insisted on washing and that was fine with me. "You're way too slow," she said. "We'd be doing dumb dishes till supper." She was quiet, almost sullen. She wasn't usually like that; I was the sullen one. I figured it must be because Gathie hadn't noticed her, hadn't said, "What a fine girl," hadn't even asked her age. Had brought no presents.

Ellie's silence was fine with me too. I was determined to hear what my mother and Gathie were saying, seated side by side on the faded green living-room couch over coffee. I made sure the door was left open just a little, so that above the clatter of dishes I could hear their voices, intense but subdued, threatening to disappear. Straining, I made out snatches: "Vassilyevka" or "Gusarovka," something about orchards and watermelon fields and old Johannes Martens, who refused to leave the village with his family because the ocean was so terrifying, Canada so far away.

"Where in God's name do you think he is now?" Gathie asked.

"Taken," my mother said in hushed voice. "Sent north."

Sometimes they spoke Russian, a sign that my mother was aware of the open door. They're telling each other everything, I thought. Like Carol and me. My mother and Gathie, reliving a life I had never known, growing up again in a Russian village I would never see, speaking a language that shut me out. There they were, on the windswept deck of a fabulous ship, seaspray on their faces, the lucky ones, the saved, leaning confidently against the railing, staring across the huge ocean for the first glimpse of a new shore. A brand-new life.

Did my mother have any warning, any inkling that she'd land in this bleak, adventureless corner of the world? Could that be my destiny too? The idea was unbearable.

The sun was still far from sinking into the horizon, but the wind had begun to die, leaving an early calm, when the four of us stood together on the driveway, following the retreat of Gathie's car along the gravel driveway. We watched it make a left turn onto the highway, gain speed, gather a cloud of dust and vanish into another world.

My mother raised her hand to shield her eyes from the sun. She was the last to turn away. I wondered if she longed to be in that car with Gathie, the two of them hurtling away from the farm, away from the leghorns and the huge garden with its endless rows of carrots and beets, past wheatfields and bleak bush into a more splendid existence, one more chance for adventure. Or were they satisfied with the promised land that ocean voyage had brought them to?

"She's wearing herself out," my father said. "Teaching city kids is too much for her. You saw that, didn't you? Did you see how thin she is? She won't last."

"We'd better collect the eggs before it's dark," my mother said. "Come," as if putting an end to the afternoon, an end to Gathie.

I almost said then that I'd get the eggs for her, she could stay inside, she didn't have to change into her old clothes. She could read the "Home Loving Hearts" pages she cut each week from the *Free Press Weekly Prairie Farmer* and collected in stacks for the day when she'd have time to read them. Boring letters from farm women like her who sent in recipes for feather-light cakes, hints for keeping the outhouse odourless, awful poems they had written about the sunrise or about their cows or roosters. I wanted to tell my mother that her life was as good as Gathie's—no, much better, though I didn't for a minute believe that.

But I kept silent. Freedom from barn chores was a victory I'd won through a long and difficult battle, my chief strategy an unrelenting sullenness, complaint, exaggerated comparisons of my life with Carol's. I had strengthened my siege with just enough grudging cooperation where inside chores were concerned. I couldn't retreat now. My parents, careful to avoid leghorn droppings, walked wordlessly back to the house to change into chore clothes.

"Hedwig, there's nothing to do," Ellie's voice was restrained, deliberately reasonable. "Do you feel like walking down to see Mrs. Yaremchuk? Her cat has six new kittens, they're so cute and still blind."

I said nothing, knowing Ellie wouldn't nag or whine, she never did. But as I walked alone to the house, leaving Ellie forlorn in the yard, I felt as if I'd missed something important. An opportunity. I found the copy of *Wuthering Heights* Mrs. Crane had loaned me for the summer, and began reading where I'd left off, the part where Catherine is deliriously plucking feathers from the pillow and accusing Heathcliff of shooting lapwings on the heath. As I lost myself on that heath, the lapwings kept turning into leghorns. Rows of white eggs materialized on the page. The assured hand reaching for them was my mother's.

MY FATHER WAS TAKEN AND MY MOTHER LEFT. The hand of judgement reached for him some months after I had escaped, with Carol, to the dingy fourth-floor room in the bleak residence at the University of Manitoba. It came in the guise of sudden failure of the heart, one morning after hours of hoisting the heavy bags of feed from the back of the truck to his shoulders, then loading the truck with filled egg crates to haul to the city. This farm, like the previous one, had resisted productivity the way quack grass resists eradication.

Evenings he would spread the *Free Press Weekly Prairie Farmer* on the kitchen table and in a few minutes his shoulders would slump, his head drop to his denim chest, and from his altered breathing it was obvious he'd fallen asleep. "Don't sit there," my mother roused him, sometimes impatiently, sometimes gently. "You won't get rest that way. Come to bed."

I was surprised how much at rest he looked in the coffin. And how thin, despite a lifetime of large helpings of chicken and potatoes and gravy. Only his shoulders, under the dark blue fabric of his suit, were broad and substantial. His hair was thin too and had begun to grey. My mother, whose hair showed no signs of grey, was left to sell the farm and move to the city with Ellie.

One Saturday morning, and not to my delight, I found Mathilda drinking tea at the kitchen table in my mother's tiny apartment. The fresh cinnamon aroma of the apple cake my mother had baked filled the kitchen. I was surprised to see how heavy Mathilda had become. Glancing surreptitiously at her feet, I detected puffy ankles swelling over the edges of worn grey sneakers. My mother was still slender, her ankles firm.

"Good you came, Hedwig," my mother said. "Ellie's a lazybones today. Still sleeping. Have some cake."

"Mmmm," Mathilda crooned. "Wonderful. Frieda, your apple cake is so wo-o-onderful." As she reached for another slice, her face, her body, her plump hands spoke of repose, of being replete, of perfect contentment. My mother's hands were restless. They wanted to be thinning beets or slicing tomatoes. They wanted to grasp the carcass of a chicken and rip the entrails from it, tear out the hard stomach and the tiny heart.

"Isn't Saturday like heaven?" Mathilda gushed. "Just

sitting here like this. Tea, and your scrumptious baking, Frieda. Oh Frieda, weren't we lucky, you and me, getting out of Russia alive, thank God. So lucky to live here in peace. So happy."

Mathilda was working at the post office now, my mother had told me, handling bulky packages, always on her feet, her legs often in pain, the veins in them swelling darkly. What was so lucky about that? And I couldn't believe my mother taking her hand and telling her, no strings attached, "You and me, Mathilda, we have to be always grateful."

"This afternoon I'm making *Bodentorte* with strawberries and whipped cream," Mathilda said. "*Real* whipped cream. I always buy a pint at Safeway on weekends. If my sisters don't bring me some."

Elizabeth and Martha had married farmers, widowers with children who needed mothers. There were also gardens that needed tending, houses to be kept clean. "Of course they're happy," Mathilda said when my mother asked. "They have children. A home."

"The Kroegers are coming tomorrow," she went on, "and Susie Gerber. And you come too, Frieda, of course. And Hedwig, you too. Can you come, Hedwig?"

"Wish I could, Mathilda." I had no intention of reliving the Flight Out Of Russia with my mother's friends. Not that it didn't intrigue me, that familiar litany of narrow escapes that could easily fill a Sunday afternoon. The marauding hordes of bandits, the famine, typhus, the lice-infested Red Army. The villagers fearful of staying, fearful of leaving. Those who chose to leave crammed into trains that rattled them past the infamous gate with the red star. Those who stayed—silence. All my life I'd heard stories of the saved and speculation about those left behind.

"After the bandits ransacked the village, your grandfather read Psalm 37," my father used to tell Ellie and me. "*Trust in the Lord and do good,* that's what he read to us. *Dwell in the land and enjoy safe pasture. Delight yourself in the Lord and he will give you the desires of your heart.* And next day we fled. Left

115

everything behind." Then he would fall silent, a wry smile flickering around his mouth, as if he were meditating on the irony.

Carol and I had staked out Sunday afternoon for our own Great Escape—from term papers, from the dingy residence. Yesterday after class we had tried on last year's bathing suits, taking turns strutting for each other and for the mirror, judging and being judged. Stripped to skin and swim suits, prone on the white sand of Grand Beach, our innocent contours fitting themselves into its soft warmth, we would no longer be shy and awkward. No one would be able to tell we had grown up on a farm. We would become miraculously sleek and golden brown all over. We would be tempting as the newborn Venus. We would be irresistible.

I was saved from making excuses to Mathilda when Ellie appeared, still warm and pink from sleep, still in her pyjamas, her hair a blonde tousled halo. Mathilda reached out with both arms and my sister walked warmly into them. My mother cut her a slice of cake, poured a glass of milk.

"Hedwig, did I tell you I'm starting work Monday." It was an announcement rather than a question and my mother made it on the way from the stove to the table. Her face glowed with delight, as if she were the lucky contestant chosen for adventure, and the coffee pot she carried a winner's trophy.

"What? Where?" The idea of my mother working anywhere but in a garden or in a chicken barn or at the kitchen stove startled me. I wasn't sure whether I should congratulate her or show sympathy. What did I know about my mother? What did I know about her desires, about what would make her happy? I didn't even know if she has a favourite verse from the Bible. I stared at her patterned, cotton dress, her worn hands.

Ellie had told me she no longer subscribed to *The Free Press Weekly Prairie Farmer*. "You know all those clippings she kept from the 'Home Loving Hearts'? One day she burned them, every last one. I couldn't believe it. Said she wouldn't need them now."

After her friend Gathie had been killed some years ago in a car crash near Nanaimo, my mother had taken out her letters, read through them methodically, out loud, carried them over to the trash can, then at the last minute bundled them up with a scrap of ribbon and stowed them once more in her dresser drawer.

"I'll be cleaning the doctors' offices at that medical clinic. In that strip mall behind the Esso. And they asked did I want to take the gowns home to wash. They still use cotton gowns for the patients. I'm planning to buy new curtains, and it's time we got a new living-room couch, don't you think, we've had this old green one forever, and there's always bills waiting to be paid and groceries to buy. With you at university and Ellie just in grade eleven, well, the money will come in handy. Good thing Ellie saw the notice."

She spoke with a conviction that kept questions at bay, that forbade doubt and fear. Her voice was the same one that had announced one summer on the second farm that the clouds were gathering for rain and the long rows of beets were thick with weeds.

"Hedwig, you'll come with me, quick. And you too, Ellie." She had a hoe for each of us. My mother gripped hers firmly with both hands, raising it, bringing it quickly and imperiously blade-down on the roots of pigweed and sow thistles and the tenacious quack grass that grew everywhere. "Go deep. And don't leave the plants with their roots still in the ground," she instructed us. "They'll just grow again." From time to time she bent down swiftly, without losing her rhythm, to pick by hand a weed that grew right in the row. Ellie was quickly left behind. Urged on by a sort of pride, or stubbornness, I struggled to keep up.

We followed our silent course, the three of us, up and down the rows, our backs bent, our hoes whacking, uprooted weeds and earth flying. The sky grew ominous, the thunder that had rumbled in the distance moved closer, the afternoon turned dark. Past the barn I could see the first brilliant jag of lightning smash to earth behind the poplar trees. "If a rain's going to be a short one, the chickens will find shelter," my father always said. "If it's going to be long, they don't bother."

Beyond the garden the leghorns were scratching energetically in the dirt and weeds, their white backs eerily luminescent in the greyness. The first few pellets of rain broke, cold on my skin. "Ellie, you run to the house," my mother called from her position slightly ahead, to my left. "No use all three of us getting wet." Ellie flew to shelter.

I waited for my turn to be ordered to the house. I didn't want to ask. I had a desire to be as brave, as resolute as my mother. An orange flash lit up the next crack of thunder and I felt a quick, fierce tingling in my right leg and along my right upper arm. A crackling covered the top of my head like a swift burning. In my terror I kept on hoeing for several seconds before I stopped and yelled out, "Did you feel that?" I was ready to drop my hoe; surely now my mother would send me running to the house.

"What? Just keep going, or we'll never be done." She didn't look up. Her arms kept their rhythm, her shoulders remained in motion. When she finished her row, she turned to work mine. When we met, the whole world had grown opaque and filled with the rush of pounding rain. The tingling in my limbs and head was diminishing like the receding thunder.

"Run," she yelled and we raced, two drenched fugitives, to the dry safety of the house.

If I had been a little further right, I thought with a sort of wonder, or a little further forward, or behind, I might have been the one taken. And my mother left. I didn't even think that it could be the other way around, my mother taken. I was too shocked for anger, too frightened to tell anyone I had felt the lightning.

"Pay sounds good," Mathilda was saying, and I knew that everything about the new job had been confided to her. She lifted the cup to her mouth one last time and rose to go. I still couldn't think of anything to say to my mother, although I wanted to with all my heart.

"Mom, you'll like the job." Ellie was enthusiastic. "It'll be great. You'll see." My sister, still warm and glowing, still emerging from sleep, took dainty bites of apple cake. A smudge of milk glistened on her lip.

When we had arrived at the house that wet summer day, dripping, Ellie was there holding the door wide open for us, sobbing out her fear of the storm and her fear for us. "Stop bawling," my mother said. The race against the storm left her exhilarated. She shook off the wetness triumphantly. "Get some towels. Run." From the kitchen window we watched as the heavens opened, sending the deluge down like a judgement. Instant pools of water dotted the yard. The wind whipped the crowns of the poplar trees with growing force and fury.

"Where's Dad?" Ellie howled. I had forgotten him and so, apparently, had my mother in her elation over having finished the rows of beets. Was he unloading sacks of feed that shouldn't get wet? Was he waiting out the rain in the hen barn? Had he been struck by lightning?

"Shush, Ellie," my mother scolded. We watched silently at the window, the three of us, until he appeared, a nebulous, ghost-like figure running toward us through the rain, his raised arms holding a gunny sack over his head for protection. It was Ellie who ran to the door. My mother had turned to the stove to begin supper.

"Frieda, a job, that's something to be happy for," Mathilda was saying. "Congratulations. Look at your daughters. Of course you need work. Weddings cost." She stood to leave.

"You and me, Mathilda, we're the lucky ones," my mother said, her face flushed and glowing from the baking, but also because of Mathilda's visit and her job, and maybe even because of her daughters. "Good you reminded me."

I left soon after Mathilda. On the bus to the university

I shut out the shoppers settling in with their packages, the high school kids chattering and jostling at the back. I shut out the traffic in the street, but it was impossible to shut out my mother's glowing face, and maybe I didn't want to. I let my body anticipate the hot sand and sun at Grand Beach, to feel the wind on my face. I wanted to hear the cry of gulls as they soared and plummeted. I longed to be floating on the wide wetness of the lake, buoyed by the waves. There must be a way that I too could tear free from dread and bitterness and receive, finally, the desires of the heart.

AGENDA

IN THE MIDDLE OF THE STAFF MEETING Janice scrawls a message on the back of her agenda with her immaculately groomed hand, shoves the paper across to me and returns her full attention to Hunsberger, our principal.

"Lachinsky's gone bonkers," I read. "Tried to strangle McGrath in the lunchroom with his bare hands."

I'm struck with disbelief. I have to read it again. It hasn't ever occurred to me that Trevor Lachinsky, from English 200-7, third row from the windows, second desk from the back, is troubled with anything deeper than dullness of mind. Or boredom. Or that lethargy not uncommon in adolescent males who grow too tall too quickly. He's apathetic, indifferent. He fails to achieve. I have to force myself to picture him confronting a teacher. *Trevor Lachinsky raises his large awkward hands to Greg McGrath's swarthy neck, his fingers encircling the sinewy thickness with murderous intent, his pale visage moving inexorably toward McGrath's ruddiness.*

Should I imagine the expression on McGrath's face as one of disbelief or outrage? And how to picture Lachinsky's face? *A rush of fury replaces the usual absence of expression on*

121

Lachinsky's face. His eyes burn with hideous fury. No. I'm unable to reconstruct the assault scene. Is McGrath huddled now, somewhere at the back of the room with the other science teachers, nursing his hurts and creating a whispered fiction, reinventing Lachinsky, exaggerating his hands, fabricating scandalous words for him to say, while his colleagues fiddle with their calculators or mark tests during the discussion of school business?

Lachinsky regularly shuffles into class just before the second bell, carrying his books as if they are logs of wood in his clumsy hands. They land with a thud on his desk and he stares morosely into them or at the desktop until the bell. No one ever jostles him or calls out, "Hey, Trevor." Other students get up to sharpen pencils, pass illicit notes, initiate surreptitious conversations, stare out the window or at the posters of rock stars that glitter on the side wall and explode into iridescence when the light touches them. "Simmer down, class," I have to say. "We've got work to do." Lachinsky, though, can't be set in motion, although in my mind I try. *As the ascendant morning sun pours her rays like streams of gold into the classroom, Trevor Lachinsky's pallid face becomes transfigured, changes, imperceptibly at first, then surely, from circles of grief in the blank oval of his face to clear pools of light.* No, it's not true. His face is usually a blank above his worn, black sweatshirt. His thick dark hair is sometimes reasonably clean.

Once, though, on a stormy day in November, the wind flinging the first snow against the north windows of my classroom, I was startled by a glimpse of his face as he craned his neck to see around Lottie Bergen's plump shoulders. His eyes reminded me of a painting I'd seen in our art gallery of Christ on the road to Golgotha. As they peered past me at the chalkboard from behind Lottie's lank blonde hair, they reflected suffering, as if he bore in his heart the whole world's despair. But whose face, including a student's, doesn't from time to time hold more than a fair measure of agony?

Hunsberger, our principal, has steered us through point three on the agenda: attendance policy. Does he know about Lachinsky? Even if he does, he isn't likely to bring the matter to the staff meeting. He prefers to dwell on what's orderly, what's running smoothly. He unfolds policies and strategies he's convinced will work. In spite of all the framed degrees in his office, I judge him to be a slow learner, though there's not a scrap of consolation in that. He has finished speaking about the need to nip truancy in the bud and has delivered a barrage of statistics that prove Riverview has fewer absences than any other school in the division. Easy for him. He doesn't have to spend his lunch hours phoning parents, who are always at work, always preoccupied. "Yes, of course I'll make sure Jennifer doesn't skip any more of your classes. Thank you for calling." Click. Sometimes they are petty and complain: "I wish Adam found his courses more interesting. I have a feeling he's not really being challenged."

Hunsberger stares at the next agenda item: lunchroom supervision. It's clear he considers the attendance policy dealt with; further discussion of it would be unnecessary, a display of tolerance on his part if he allowed it. There is nothing more to say. The late sun illuminates his bent head, revealing the thinness of the hair on top and deepening the lines in his sallow features. He holds notes in his thick hands. His stocky shoulders are rock-firm. Hunsberger is not a man to shift position. I can see him clearly from the table where Janice and I sit. The pale light that touches Hunsberger's head hovers over the entire meeting, over each raised or lowered face, over fingers that tap tabletops or clutch pens and write notes or doodle on margins of the agenda. It falls on shelves of paperbacks lining the shadowed section of the library where all staff meetings are held. The titles dance in the wan light. *The Prime of Miss Jean Brodie. Breakfast of Champions. A Tender Torment. The Guinness Book of World Records.*

I am a doodler. Every letter of the agenda that offers enclosed space is inked in compulsively, the corners filled with fantastic curlicues, the margins cross-hatched. I clutch the pen so the skin of my knuckles is stretched and white. This compulsion is evidence, I like to think, of my desire to do more with my pen than doodle.

It's March and the long winter clings tenaciously to everything. The history teachers are struggling against it as they engage with the agenda. They have spared no effort to formulate arguments for and against the attendance policy, and now, with equal resolve, they vie with each other to formulate strategies for fool-proof lunchroom supervision. The phys ed teachers seem least affected by the seasons. They jog daily along the hallways in winter and around the outdoor track in summer. They perform push-ups to ward off middle-age weight gain and at lunch unwrap whole-wheat tuna sandwiches and gulp apple juice while they discuss the latest scandals or standings of sports leagues—baseball or hockey or football, depending on the season. Their eyes move restlessly to wristwatches or to the wall clock. As soon as it's 4:45 they will rise to their feet and, with important scraping aside of chairs, march out, a small, smart army, to coach basketball or track and field.

The rest of us will be left to grapple with what remains of the agenda.

Marion Browning, who arrived after Christmas to replace a burnt-out guidance counsellor, is speaking. *It is not winter on Marion's face, but spring. There are no discernible lines around her lovely brown eyes, nothing weary in her stance, nothing false in her speaking. Not one wrinkle in her sapphire blouse. Her translucent skin glows, her hair is a gold halo. Almost she lifts the battle-weary colleagues gathered around her out of the deadweight of their defeat.*

Actually, she's wearing a beige sweater, not a sapphire blouse, but I haven't exaggerated much. Marion gestures with her graceful hands and her words have the eloquence of a Haydn aria as she speaks of the need to phone parents promptly, to be gentle with students, quick to encourage, slow to punish. Words pearl from her mouth and we listen to what she says and are convinced. It won't surprise me if she concludes with a benediction, "May the everlasting peace..."

Gusdahl, late as usual, enters quietly as a cat while she speaks, and finds a chair facing the rest of us, slightly to the left and behind Hunsberger. Seated, he stares at Marion, rapt. His hands are stuffed into the pockets of the black overcoat he is wearing. I wonder if the overcoat is intended as a crude signal that this meeting had better be short. *All expression has been cancelled from his usually animated face, wiped out like a sin forgiven, replaced with a sombre innocence, as if in preparation for a fresh start.*

Not true. His face, as he watches Marion, is alert and animated. He's probably up to one of his wild tricks. At the last staff party he delivered an impromptu speech on flatulence, providing his own sound effects, and the next Monday there had been a session in Hunsberger's office. His attentiveness to Marion could be a ruse. Or he could be in his most earnest mood, which happens now and then, like the time I showed him Lachinsky's paper on *Macbeth,* my January assignment to grade eleven.

"Write about the darkness of the heart," I instructed my 200-7 class, with all the authority I could muster. "Write about Macbeth's struggle and Shakespeare's poetry, how they are still relevant in the decade of the '90s." Lachinsky responded as I expected, with no response. No questions. No small glimmer of interest. Such apathy no longer infuriates or amazes me. After twenty years I'm used to it. I'm able to adjust my expectations as well as any other teacher is. He handed in his completed essay two days after the deadline; this was speedy for Lachinsky and I acknowledged it. It took me a few minutes to read his short, more-or-less predictable attempt to link the bloody conflict in Scotland with the looming Middle-East crisis, the Oka stand-off, the violence in East Kildonan streets and shopping malls.

Only a few sentences drew me back for a second reading. They were embedded in the longest paragraph, midway through the essay, where Lachinsky, in a rare attempt at elaboration, was trying to comment on good and evil. I imagined his hand clumsily grasping the pen as he struggled with the words.

> It's like comparing someone like maybe our
> principal and Miss Browning whose beutiful-
> looking and her hair you'd like to touch and you
> know you can trust her. You can't trust
> Hunsberger, he's foul-hearted and doesn't know
> what the word fare means. Most teachers don't
> know what it means no more than Macbeth.

Gusdahl didn't smile when I pointed this passage out to him, or make smart remarks about a student having the hots for a pretty teacher. He didn't echo my hunch that this pathetic foray into analysis was just a fluke. He only said, in his most enigmatic voice, "Well. Hmm. Blessed are the pure in heart." He studied Lachinsky's lines with respectful, or mock, concentration for a few more minutes, handed back the paper and walked away. Gusdahl is like that. He either buttonholes you for an hour or he cuts you off without mercy.

His twelfth grade history students adore him. Every semester, registration for his course zooms off the charts even though history is optional. Janice is convinced his theatrical antics are his lure. "He doesn't teach. He entertains," she says, disdain coating her words. "Hunsberger just has no idea what goes on."

Gusdahl has moved his chair. From where I sit, he is mainly invisible, concealed by one of the pillars that make meetings in the library awkward. As I watch, an arm moves out from behind the pillar, blocking out *The Prime of Miss Jean Brodie*. At the end of the uplifted forearm, his short stubby fingers wiggle, as if sending out signals in code. At the same time his face, owlish behind framed spectacles, appears between arm and pillar, and his tongue emerges stiffly, a pink stub of a snake, and remains there for seconds. Small explosions of scattered chuckles give evidence that the gesture has been observed.

I have been thinking of asking my classes to do research on the language of small gestures. Gusdahl is given to gestures. I might say he is master of them.

"He's just plain nuts," Janice whispers, dismissively. For Janice—she teaches office management—everyone, staff and students, can be summed up, packaged neatly and, if necessary, dismissed. I'm quite positive that once or twice I've barely escaped dismissal. That even now my position remains precarious.

Gusdahl is writing a novel about the army, and, from what I can understand, it's to be a cross between *M*A*S*H* and a Le Carré spy story. His plots are exotic, or funny. Sometimes both. He lives alone downtown and every morning he sits at his computer for an hour or two before work, writing. *Heavy with sleep, driven with a compelling urge to create, and to record what he creates, the man splashes cold water on his face, puts on the kettle. His mind, his subconscious self, has been at work while he slept and new images have surfaced. A motley cast of characters that will people his inspired stories has sprung to life and is pushing newborn at the edges of his awareness. Ideas spill over, fully formed, complex, and so fiercely insistent his morning fingers can't keep up.*

Is it possible that writing could ever be that easy?

Every few weeks I'll find part of a chapter shoved into my mailbox, with the request, "please comment." And I always do, flattered by Gusdahl's perception of me as someone discriminating enough to pronounce judgement on his writing. Once when he sat beside me at lunch I admitted to him that I'd like to write. Short stories. "If only teaching wasn't so draining," I said and waited for affirmation, for a sign that, yes, educators are a burdened lot. I wanted sympathy. He turned to me, puzzled.

I envy his energy, the inspiration he is blessed with. The dedication. I can't imagine myself going to work after spending an hour at the computer. I always take pains to correct his syntax and spelling, make suggestions for vocabulary. Could I write as well as Gusdahl? Could I write better? Sometimes I'm haunted by the uneasy conviction that there's something elusive in his narrative, something he's trying to say but isn't saying. Or perhaps he is saying it and I am unable to comprehend it, just as I'm unable to comprehend Lachinsky's attacking McGrath.

I pick up my pen and write, "Why? What got into him?" on the back of Janice's agenda and hand it back to her, as sneaky as a student passing notes, and return to my cross-hatching. It bothers me that a boy in my class is deeply troubled and I've been unaware of it. I try to reconstruct the familiar image of Lachinsky in the lunchroom. *Trevor sits hunched over French fries and Coke, lost in contemplation that leans dangerously toward self-pity. He exists always on the periphery of things, the lonely circumference, never at the warm, safe centre. He doesn't know why there's a towering wall between him and the whole world, why the thundering solitude draws him in and holds him prisoner, his Walkman his only companion.*

In my intentional progress up and down between rows of tables, I occasionally stop where he's sitting and try to speak with him. There must be, I am certain, somewhere, the right words to speak, the words necessary to the moment, to each person. The words for Trevor Lachinsky have so far eluded me.

Lunch-hour supervision is one of those duties that hangs like a lead weight around our necks. *The students surge into the cavernous grey lunchroom at noon, a tidal wave of turbulence, of undetonated explosive energy, of undefined but palpable apprehension. The apprehension seems even darker this year because everyone is wearing black. The mood swings easily to ominous, threatening to overwhelm the few islands of adolescent eagerness that persist here and there in the turbulent, noontime ocean.* All right. This is overstating it. But if lunchroom duty falls on Friday, that's what it seems like.

Music pulses and blares from speakers placed on the back wall of this windowless room, high enough to be beyond the reach of destruction. The smell of fried onion rings, adolescent sweat and stale cooking oil mingles with the mad jangle of voices. It can unhinge the sanest teacher. During the dead of winter, food fights erupt, banana peels and squashed pop cans fly, students scramble onto tabletops, calling across the room at each other and hurling defiances at the two unfortunate supervisors who move quickly away from the centre and stand with their backs to a wall, in a desperate effort to avoid surprise.

This year the computer spit out my name and Gusdahl's for joint supervision on Mondays. "Nothing ever happens on a Monday," I'd remind Gusdahl each week in a rush of gratitude. Monday is a day for recovery, for regaining consciousness after the weekend, a day for feeling your way back into the week's agenda. Gusdahl doesn't seem grateful for this. It's taken me a while to realize that he doesn't share my aversion to the lunchroom, that he is equally charged with peculiar energy every day of the week. He welcomes a brawl, anything that tears through the stifling shroud of routine or boredom, anything that sparks with life. If no student is causing a ruckus in the lunchroom, he'll wait till no one's looking, then, with cool nonchalance, he'll retrieve an apple core or a crumpled brown lunch bag from the floor and fling it across the room. His target is always a student known to react explosively. He hauls the student off by the ear, ostensibly to Hunsberger's office, and then, as if he's lost interest, he abandons his victim, leaving him or her baffled, halfway down the hall.

I was his target only once. I pretended nothing had happened, that I hadn't felt the missile he hurled with accurate aim across a whole spread of tables lightly striking my left shoulder. I continued my patrol as if all was well. It was a reaction he found wanting.

"Do you ever feel persecuted?" he asked, placing his hand on my shoulder and peering at me through his dark-rimmed glasses in mock fatherliness.

"Why don't you fling something at Lachinsky?" I countered weakly. "He needs to get the lead out."

I can remember one occasion when Lachinsky's face

was anything but passive. It was a Monday, the day before report cards were to be handed out, and tension raced through the entire student body, as if on a network of fine wires. A noticeable increase in pitch and volume pervaded the hallways and spilled into my classroom, stretching each fifty-minute class to an eternity. All movements were erratic and nervous, every question charged with insubordination, each moment rife with imminent eruption. I became ill with headache and accepted Janice's offer to take my lunch-room supervision. I poured myself a coffee in the staff room and sat beside Marion Browning, who asked me if I'd heard that Trevor Lachinsky's father was refusing to go to Alcoholics Anonymous. No, I hadn't heard.

That Monday only Lottie Bergen, placid and bland as a *blancmange*, remained anchored and composed. Lottie approaches each day with good will and assumes that all her classmates do the same. That Lachinsky, for instance, is as willing as she is to discuss school problems and receive or offer help. "Did you get those questions on Mr. McGrath's science test?" she asked the minute Lachinsky lowered his long body, not quite late, into his desk after science class, period six, day three of the cycle. "The last one, I mean. What did you put down?"

From my desk I sensed an instant altering in the lines of Lachinsky's neck and shoulders. I saw his hands tighten. His cheeks flushed and his normally blank eyes burned. And then the outburst, "None of your goddamn business." Lottie spun around as if struck by a fist, her arms, shoulders, hair, her whole being appeared to shrink as she turned away from him, drawing snail-like into herself. Before she lowered her face I could see that her cheeks had lost all colour, that she was about to cry. As for Lachinsky, it wasn't till near the end of class that his hands became unclenched and the rage in his eyes subsided.

When she first joined our staff, Marion Browning sent me a memo about Lachinsky.

Re: Trevor Lachinsky. Confidential. Trevor's parents
have separated and he lives with his father. There
may be substance abuse involved. His mother has
attempted suicide twice. Please keep this in mind
in any dealings with him and please report to me
any unusual behaviour or absences. M.B.

I hadn't known. And knowing, I was helpless. What should
I do with knowledge that was so intimate, so exposing? It was
knowledge I didn't want. How should I know when a
student's behaviour is unusual? Isn't it always unusual?

That memo is probably still somewhere in my desk.
There's no need, of course, for me to feel guilty or respon-
sible for what happens to every single student. Split families
and drugs are common as two-car garages in this area. How
am I supposed to keep track of which student is saddled
with which problem? I'm at least as concerned as any other
teacher at Riverview. And a good deal more than Janice.

The list of unfinished agenda items is still unbearably
long. There is no hope of a short meeting. I feel a headache
coming.

"Apparently McGrath gave Lachinsky hell for. . . ,"
Janice has written in reply to my question, but before I can
finish reading her explanation, my head jerks up in
response to some signal, some change in the room, in the
quality of air or light. There's a converging of attention to
a point slightly behind and to the left of Hunsberger.
Flanked on one side by a pillar stands a white apparition, *a
presence large and luminous with a face that glows around dark-
rimmed, lake-blue eyes. The arms of the apparition lift and spread
like monstrous wings, their blackness forming a dark aura around
the body, whose almost translucent whiteness is flecked with shadows. The apparition wavers before us and begins to lift. It rises, an
awkward heron, flapping its ungainly wings and circling the room,
a crazy transcendence hovering with grim menace over us. Above*
The Guinness Book of World Records. *Above* The Tender
Torment.

"Oh my god," Janice squawks in disbelief. "He's completely berserk." The apparition, instead of rising, fades, or rather, folds into itself. Gusdahl lowers his arms, pulls his black coat over his nakedness, and sits down. Later, there is disagreement about details: the amount of hair on his chest, paunch or no, and so on down. Were his pants slumped around his ankles?

Hunsberger has become aware of the disturbance. The converging force lines of everyone's attention draw him to turn around and face Gusdahl, who by now sits upright in his chair, his spectacled, unengaged gaze aimed vaguely at a point past books and heads. Past the agenda. Behind me I hear the groan of suppressed laughter. It sputters and ripples, and finally dies. As Hunsberger turns, puzzled and uncertain, his expression is that of a man exposed, or found guilty of partial knowledge. He straightens his shoulders bravely and returns to the agenda. The phys ed teachers, already risen to their feet before the disruption, make their noisy exit now, smirking. Marion Browning looks tired.

When at last we have reached the end of the agenda, Janice and I leave the building together. She wants to stop at the pub, but I'm exhausted. I want only solitude. I want to go home, lay out the rough pieces of the day and fit them together, although I know my chances of succeeding are modest. I'll begin with Lachinsky. His misery will cling to me like a shadow. And Gusdahl's craziness. I'll wrestle a while with that. And with Hunsberger's blindness. I'll want to turn everything and everyone into stories, something Gusdahl never does. "I reach way out for my stories," he told me once. "Not that there isn't lots of drama right here. But I wouldn't touch it. Close to home is dangerous. It's best left alone."

What will stay with me longest, fastening itself barnacle-like to my memory, is *the weariness that crept on small feet, gentle as the evening's first faint shadow, across Marion Browning's perfect face.*

THE LITTLE MEXICAN

ADA MCPHAIL STARED at the single row of spindly carrots
as if accusing them of wilfulness. Of stubbornly refusing to
flourish. September and they were hardly worth harvesting.
Next door Nellie Krawchuk's garden had produced long,
fat carrots that were already stowed in a sack in the basement. Ada turned from the meagre row and began yanking
at the remaining bean and cucumber vines destined for this
week's garbage. She'd leave the carrots for later, along with
the cosmos that confronted her whenever she crossed the
church parking lot on her way home from Safeway. Their
pink and white faces were raised perpetually east to the
rising sun, as if in adoration. But also, Ada thought, in sup-
plication. Their importunate yellow eyes in fall pleaded for
more time, though she wasn't sure if they were as innocent
as they seemed at first glance, or conniving.

It wasn't just the carrots that irritated Ada. This morning over coffee at Nellie Krawchuk's, her neighbour had slid
into a mood of belligerence brought on by reading in the
paper that the 7-Eleven on Henderson Highway had been
burglarized last night. It was the third time since spring.

"Ada, you got no bars on your basement windows. That's where they break in, you know."

"Would have to be a very small thief," Ada said. "Have you seen my window wells?" She wasn't opposed to advice when she asked for it, but unasked and from Nellie Krawchuk, it didn't sit well.

"Aren't you at least having that alarm system put in?" Nellie's husband had looked up from the newspaper he was scanning for the bizarre stories he fancied. The Krawchuks' security system, recently installed, was the biggest and best. "Very sensitive," Kurt said with pride. And he was right. An inadvertent motion on his part triggered its ill will and a high-pitched *whee whee whee* issued forth like a banshee call into the quiet neighbourhood, putting an end to peace. Ada was always taken off-guard and jumped, perhaps not literally, perhaps only a slight leap of her nerves, in alarm or irritation or protest. Once or twice she suspected Kurt had triggered the alarm deliberately. Once the police came.

It wasn't that Ada thought slightingly of security. She agreed that a person needed to feel free of fear, and safe. Both her doors were old, the wood cracked and dry, but they had good locks and the back one had a deadbolt too. She had an aversion to going overboard on anything and believed she possessed common sense and anyway nothing much for thieves to steal. What was wrong with some old-fashioned trust in basic human goodness? And faith in providence. Surely life offered something besides the convenience store break-ins, the battering of innocent children, the devious schemes of con artists aimed at the elderly and reported to her by the Krawchuks. Not once in her entire life, and she was nearly sixty-nine, had she personally observed violence in the streets, and no one had ever entered her life, or her house, with force. Beyond the murder and rape detailed in the news, the predictable tax increases, the perpetual fighting in Bosnia, there must be another dimension to this world, or what would be the use of anything?

She had no particular quarrel with this world. She rather liked it, especially in autumn. She liked to work in her garden and looked forward to the time of falling leaves, even though she wondered how many more years her back could manage the bending. Her husband had never been one to worry about the world. Nor had he ever noticed anything that needed doing around the house or garden.

"You planning to move earth as well as heaven?" he used to call from his place on the deck, where he'd be having a beer or half dozing while she dug peat moss into the flower beds. If Ada hadn't taken it upon herself to become the partner in charge of maintenance, the place would be in a royal shambles by now.

Struggling with the last cucumber vines, Ada became aware of the pain in her back, the last thing she needed with winter coming. And of someone sitting on the concrete curb in the church parking lot on the other side of her wire garden fence. She pulled herself erect to examine the visitor. A schoolgirl, nothing odd in that, the children were always taking shortcuts across the parking lot. But Ada had a feeling there weren't too many girls like this one sitting in the classrooms of Ellerton Elementary School.

She was a rather chubby girl. Actually, a *very* chubby girl. Last night Ada had watched a documentary about obesity in children. The TV camera showed a fat-farm for kids where wealthy North Americans could send their offspring for slimming down. This girl could benefit from a fat-farm, Ada thought. Watching the documentary, she was aghast at the way parents overfed their children and then paid to have them made thin. She herself had always been thin. "You don't eat enough," Nellie had complained this morning, cutting herself another slice of strudel with her plump hand. "You keep on eating like a bird, one of these days you'll just disappear."

"I eat what I need." No way was Ada going to turn herself into an elephant.

The girl was dressed in purple sweatpants, a worn black t-shirt and new white running shoes. She carried several books in one hand, a pair of new rubber boots in the other, and on her back she had one of those pink and purple fluorescent knapsacks stuffed most likely with her school things. It seemed to Ada she was overburdened. Her face was round and dark-skinned; a tousle of black curly hair gave her head a moppish look. But it was the attentiveness of her extremely bright, dark brown eyes that convinced Ada she was not an ordinary schoolchild.

When the girl said nothing, Ada turned again to her garden. The tomato plants were tough to pull, the roots not deep but stubborn. She was determined to make a start on them at least. She braced for their resistance, mindful of her back as she worked, feeling all the while the eyes of the young, silent watcher. She became self-conscious, as if she were under scrutiny, and wondered if she was doing things right, if her movements were stiff and halting, her baggy brown slacks unfit to be worn even in the garden, her thin, greying hair untidy and unbecoming.

When she straightened up again, the brown eyes were still fixed on her, the dark-skinned face alert. No details were being missed. What was the girl waiting for?

"You planning to wade in some deep water?" Ada asked, nodding in the direction of the girl's rubber boots. The fall had been dry, no puddles.

The girl shook her head, set the rubber boots down on the pavement.

"I'm only seven," she said, "and I'm in grade three."

"You must be a very bright girl."

"No. My mom wants me to be in grade three." And after a pause, "If I knew how to get into the garden I'd come help you."

That's all I need, Ada thought, a child underfoot when I'm trying to get things done. Maybe she'd better just go back into the house and shut the door until the visitor went away. But the vitality in the dark eyes prevented her. She tried to place the slight accent she detected in the child's speech, something somewhat foreign.

"Where do you live?" Ada asked.

"On Edison. Across from the church."

It was also across the highway. What sorts of parents would let a child cross alone? Ada had always walked her boys to school until they were ten, no matter how they protested.

"I didn't want to cross at the patrols today," the girl said as if she could read Ada's mind.

"Well, then, what do you plan to do?"

The girl shrugged. "In Mexico I had a dog. You don't have a dog, do you?"

Ada shook her head. Dogs enough in the neighbour-hood without her adding another to the population. She didn't know whether to take that seriously, about Mexico. It might just be a child's fantasy. Her own boys got top marks in the fantasy department. But she asked, "Where, in Mexico?"

"Far, far away from Mexico City," the girl said, some-what vaguely. Ada had no idea if her accent sounded Mexican.

"I'm meeting my grandfather," the girl was saying. "He's taking me in his boat on the lake. As far as we can go."

"Which lake?" Ada asked quickly, as if she might trip up the girl.

But the girl didn't reply, just stared past Ada to the wheelbarrow, half-filled with the wilting remains of the gar-den. Besides the wheelbarrow, Ada had taken a spade and a hoe from the tool shed. All her tools were old. She didn't rush out to Wal-Mart to get the latest trowel or hoe or hose, or chemicals for growing plants or discouraging weeds and bugs. Bird baths and ceramic elves and twirling birds cut from wood and painted in brilliant colours were absent from her yard. She didn't want to accumulate too many things that needed attention and space. Her kitchen, to Nellie Krawchuk's perpetual disdain, was devoid of microwave and dishwasher, and there was only one TV in the entire house. She had always had a desire to travel light through life. In case of moving, she thought, though she hadn't moved in forty years. Even when her husband died three years ago, she had decided to stay in the house.

Ada surveyed the recalcitrant carrots and bent to one that looked more promising than the others. She pulled it, wiped it clean on its own greens. "Do you like carrots?" she asked.

"Yes." The chubby girl rose quickly to her feet and the brightness in her eyes increased as she took the skinny carrot from Ada with more eagerness than the poor thing warranted. "Yes, I do. Thanks."

Instead of eating it as Ada had expected her to do, the girl tucked it into the hand that also held several books. With the other one she picked up the rubber boots. "In Mexico we had red peppers in our garden and lots of beans," she said. "Your garden doesn't have red peppers." And after a while she added, "Those flowers, that's why I came. It's like they wanted me to come."

"Cosmos," Ada said. "They're cosmos."

She bent again to the tomato plants, moving slowly. When she turned her lowered head the girl was still standing there, as if waiting, not staring at Ada now but at the cosmos.

"You want some?"

The girl nodded vigorously. Ada straightened her back and broke off three of the best stems, counting a total of eight open flowers and some tight buds. She handed them over the fence, wondering how the girl could manage with her full hands, but the child uncurled an index finger from the boots and extended her arm so Ada could insert into the curved finger the three stems of cosmos. The finger tightened around them and the arm moved closer to the chubby body. She still didn't leave. Just stood there with all her possessions, perfectly serene, as if she was waiting for something more. But then, as though had received a nudge, she turned abruptly and ambled off in the direction of the church.

As Ada watched, the girl turned around and called back in a voice that took on the quality of music, "Thank you. Ever so much. I'll come again. Next time I'll help you." Ada wanted to call back that she didn't need help, but the girl was moving rapidly, her chubby figure growing small and vague, as if it were vanishing into air. A sudden feeling of loss came over Ada, as if something significant had slipped away. She should have given the child more than one thin carrot.

The roots of the tomato plants remained unwilling to be yanked from the soil, but Ada persisted until she heard the sound of footsteps on the parking lot and a breathless voice calling, "Hello, hello." It was the little girl again, her face more radiant, still holding carrots, cosmos, boots and school things, and running so hard she was panting. Ada was sure she was about to stumble.

"I forgot to tell you," the girl said, "when I grow up, I'm going to have a garden. I'll have tomatoes and peppers and carrots. Fruit trees too. Oranges and grapefruit. And flowers. Lots of flowers. Like these, I forget the name." She stopped for breath.

"Cosmos. They're called cosmos."

"Cosmos. You have a beautiful garden, Mrs. . . ."

Ada wasn't about to give her name to this child, no matter how intensely her brown eyes shone or how eagerly she praised the depleted garden. But she wanted to say something and all she could think of was, "Cosmos always turn their faces to the sun."

"Cosmos always turn their faces to the sun?" The girl repeated Ada's words, but as a question, and then added, "I have to go. My grandfather is taking me on his boat."

She hurried off the way she had come, turning around, like before, to call, "I'll come again. I'll help you," leaving Ada with the music of her young voice. What might this child be called? she wondered. This girl who had come a second time on this fall day to her garden.

Ada wasn't sure how she felt about winter coming. She

dreaded the icy streets that made walking to Safeway treacherous for weeks on end. But sometimes, standing in her barren garden, she longed for that covering of white snow, that purity spreading forgiveness like a blanket over the black earth. As a child she had loved winter. She had revelled in snow and ice. As soon as her own boys had become toddlers, she had dressed them in snowsuits and taken them out, year after year, to make snowmen and forts right here on the garden. Those snowmen with their carrot noses and stocking scarves had long subsided into memory that had flattened with the passing decades. Her boys were men now. They had moved on. But if Ada could, she would roll up the intervening years and return to those days when she would wrestle her two squabbling boys into boots and parkas after the first snowfall; or hover on the beach as they raced screaming into the lake at their summer cottage and threw themselves into the waves; or tuck their warm and squirming bodies into bed at night.

Before Ada returned to the house she found herself glancing back in the direction of the parking lot, as if she expected the little Mexican girl to reappear.

That evening the moppish dark head of the girl remained in her mind as she made her omelette-and-tea supper. She couldn't shut out those attentive eyes. She was certain she would dream of them. But when she went to bed she fell into a deep sleep that was, as usual, dreamless.

In the morning, before the kettle had boiled for coffee, the phone rang and Nellie Krawchuk's querulous voice came over the wires, half accusing, half triumphant: "Did you see, in the papers?"

"What?" Ada had just last weekend cancelled the paper. Too many inserts.

"A break-in at the Andersons', just three doors from you. Better look around your yard, Ada. If anyone's been there."

It was raining when Ada opened her back door, the deck was wet and the garden muddy, good thing she'd had the sense to go at it yesterday. The gate to the back lane stood wide open and a trail of muddy footprints the rain hadn't yet washed off led from it across the wet grass to the garden. For an instant, she imagined them to be tracks made by a child's rubber boots, but they were much too large for that. The garbage cans had been knocked over. Plastic bags trailing bedraggled bean plants and cucumber vines lay scattered on the grass. There were tracks on the sidewalk too. They came right up the steps to the deck. But no farther, as if they had been ordered back.

"How long do you think you'll be that lucky?" Nellie asked later, peering accusingly at her neighbour as if to draw from her a statement of confession, or at least commitment to prompt action. Ada didn't reply. She had already asked herself that question.

"You should at least get a dog maybe," Kurt offered, but Nellie disagreed. "A damn nuisance, dogs." She was quicker than Kurt and probably imagined dog turds on her lawn.

That evening, Ada noticed how everything had changed. How she caught herself after dark, when she had turned on all the lights of the house, listening for footsteps, for unfamiliar noises. Even the familiar ones seemed unfriendly and suspicious tonight, every one. Would she always live like this now, trapped under a shadow of uneasiness?

When the rain stopped three days later and the sun came out warm as in August, Ada returned late afternoon to her still-wet garden, her mind and body soaking up the warmth. Her mind and body were also, she noticed, alert to the parking lot, her eyes pulled by a persistent force in that direction. She kept looking up, and when no tousle-headed girl appeared, she was disappointed. She worked half-heartedly without noticing that it was long past suppertime and then, starting with guilty embarrassment, gathered her muddy garden tools. She wondered if Nellie had noticed how she had dawdled over her work today. None of her business, was it?

In due course the Krawchuks' maple shed its annual

offering of yellow leaves, most of them falling on Ada's lawn. Each day she waited until the sun had risen above the trees before she took her rake from the tool shed. A little each day, she thought. There was no hurry. The fall held such beauty this year, such peace. And yet she felt restless. Evenings continued to be the time for shadows and fear. Occasionally she dreamt. This pleased her, though in the morning she could never recall what she had dreamt.

She thought frequently of the little Mexican girl. That's how she thought of her, the little Mexican girl, though she was, of course, very chubby. And perhaps not Mexican at all, kids could invent such outrageous stories. But then, why couldn't she be Mexican? All kinds of people pouring into the country these days.

The girl had said, "I'll come again." Ada pictured the child sauntering across the parking lot and this time she would tell her to come around to the gate and the girl would run laughing into a pile of brown leaves. Ada would give her the rake for a bit. Let her have a go at the leaves. Let her help. "Pull as many carrots as you want," she'd tell her. They were still in the ground. She'd let the girl carry home all that her chubby hands could hold. Too bad the carrots were so thin.

But the girl never reappeared, though Ada often saw a child with dark curly hair coming around the corner of the church. It always turned out to be some other child, or a large dog, or sometimes simply a shadow. Had the family moved? Had there been an accident when the grandfather rowed the child out on the lake that evening in September? Once she was sure that was really her dark-eyed girl halfway across the parking lot, but at that moment a high-pitched *whee whee whee* coming from the direction of the Krawchuk house caused her body to jerk around in the direction of the alarm. It was a few minutes before she regained her presence of mind and glanced back to the parking lot. There was no one there.

An urge to learn more about Mexico took hold of Ada,

as insistently as a tune that can't be eradicated. She searched for the school atlas her boys had used years ago and located Mexico City. Where on the map should she look for a place that was far, far from the capital city? A place where the child might once have lived. One night in mid-November she dreamt about the girl, but the dream was very faint, and though she struggled when she woke to hang on to it long enough to make out the details, it slipped from her like sand. In the morning she looked out her kitchen window to see the deck and steps and garden inches deep in snow.

By the first week in December, Nellie Krawchuk had made ten dozen perogies and four kinds of cookies and stored them in her freezer for Christmas, and Kurt had exchanged his old snowblower for a better one, the biggest on the street. He demonstrated it for Ada with the enthusiasm of a child with a new toy and informed her, rather imperiously, that he would keep her sidewalks clear this winter. He's so patronizing, Ada thought, but she figured she couldn't afford to show resentment.

"Thanks," she said. "That's good of you." There had been no further break-ins anywhere in the neighbourhood.

One late afternoon Ada, resisting the strong temptation to stay in the warmth and comfort of her home, put on her down-filled winter coat and walked cautiously to the Wal-Mart to buy Christmas cards for her sons. She took a long time to decide, rejecting an amazing array of Rudolphs and Santas. Although she was intrigued by all the angels with their ethereal wings, in the end laid them aside. She liked the winter landscapes, but finally chose one card with the three wise men following the star and one with the holy family at the manger. When she returned home in the already diminishing light, the back door had been brutally kicked in, her TV and electric kettle stolen, and mud and snow slopped into every room of the house.

"Now you see why you need an alarm?" The triumph in Kurt's voice grated and Ada didn't reply. Inside her a wound had opened and she wanted to whimper like a hurt animal. The raw pulsing that spread fear to every corner of her body would still be there, she thought, when she went to bed and pulled the comforter around her. She was sure she would spend the night sleepless, appalled at this invasion of her innocent, eventless life. Who was the enemy who had done this to her? Now she'd have to look in the yellow pages for someone to fix the door. Should she consider a modest alarm system?

"This time of year, that's when they get aggressive," Nellie and Kurt both assured her with smug authority. Nellie had the presence of mind to call the police while Ada, still in her down-filled coat, stared out the kitchen window at the large footsteps that left the sidewalk and crossed the snowy lawn and the garden, and stopped at the fence. The intruder must have scrambled over the fence and crossed the church parking lot. Maybe she had passed him unawares on her way back from the shopping mall.

"Could be they'll come again," Kurt warned.

Ada did not buy an alarm system. Nor a new TV, though she replaced the electric kettle. But she was sufficiently unsettled to forget about the cards for her sons. A week later she came upon them, still in the Wal-Mart bag. She admired the cards once more—the brave light of the star, the radiance around the manger. In one of them she read *We have seen his star.* In the other *A child is born.* She added a short note to each and was about to lick the stamps and stick them on the envelopes when she was stopped short by a stab of remorse. Whatever had she been thinking of? A mother has to do more than this for her children. This isn't enough. She would go back to Wal-Mart tomorrow and look for something more substantial. A pair of gloves. No, not gloves, gloves would require exact size. Wool scarves would be safer. Navy for Dan and maroon for Robert.

But between intention and action there had appeared in the last weeks a gradually widening gap. She would have to get across that gap. She had noticed it soon after she had rallied to pull the last carrots and then locked her garden tools in the shed for the last time in October. A growing weight of inertia pulled her down, as if her limbs held lead. Everything became cumbersome. Even something as simple as gathering the ingredients for a coffee cake and inviting Nellie appeared as difficult as if she were faced with climbing a mountain. Putting on overcoat and boots and hat to go out became arduous. In school she had learned about the law of gravity, but now for the first time she thought she knew what it meant. She *felt* its meaning, felt it dragging her down. Kurt Krawchuk had shown her an article in *The Winnipeg Free Press* about how in the weeks before Christmas the short days and overcast skies spawned depression. "They say we can expect a rise in suicide rates," he said more than once, with satisfaction.

Ada had always believed that life held duties important enough to keep a person occupied, and that occupation with duty would ensure a healthy body and a sound mind. That night she ate her supper with deliberate intention, not allowing herself to dawdle over tea. Afterwards, she dealt with the dishes more briskly than usual and then dug through her old albums until she found one where the boys were small. There they were, carrying out the garbage, helping her fix the garden fence, raking leaves, washing the car, even doing dishes. Her husband, always the observer, the recorder, had taken the pictures. Hadn't there been one where she and the boys were making a snowman? She found it tucked into a series of birthday party pictures. Dan was dressed in the green parka she'd bought when he was nine. He was laughing and there was a snowball in his raised hand. After the camera had clicked he'd flung it at Robert, who stood half-hidden behind the grinning snowman.

"Your boys coming home this year?" Nellie or Kurt would be sure to ask. "Seems like they haven't for a while."

"Did we give them too much or too little?" she used to ask her husband when the boys stopped visiting, Dan from Vancouver, Robert from San Francisco. They had wives too. Ada had met them once or twice, but that was long ago.

There were no children. When the boys stopped writing, she had stopped too. Her husband hadn't stopped because he had never begun. She looked a long time at the picture, then resolutely stacked the albums in a neat pile on the shelf. She had no reason to blame herself for anything, as far as her boys were concerned. She was sure she had done what she could, had given them the love she had to give. Anyway, children weren't property of parents, for them to control. They changed and became something quite separate. Something unexpected, baffling. And it wouldn't be any different with girls. Rose, the Krawchuks' daughter, came home three, four times a week after work and stayed for supper and the evening, and all they did was quarrel, according to Nellie. This didn't surprise Ada. Afterwards Kurt would be morose and go on about the way children sponged off parents. "They'll suck you dry," he'd say.

When Ada walked to Wal-Mart the next day it was snowing again. She shook the white flakes from her featherdown before she entered the store. "Deck the Halls" was playing loudly over the PA system, not her favourite carol, she didn't care for all those silly fa la la la la's. She wished they'd play "Joy to the World" instead. Every aisle was so crowded with Christmas shoppers, she had to hold her ground firmly on the way to men's wear. The scarves had been picked over but she found two, not the colours she wanted, but of good quality. A green plaid for Dan and a solid brown for Robert.

In the long lineup at the checkout she had time to catch her breath and look around at her fellow shoppers. They look tired, she thought. A blur of faces without much joy. Then, out of the blur, her eyes picked out a specific face in the lineup two checkouts over. A child's face, partly hidden in a fur-trimmed hood. Ada didn't immediately recognize the bright eyes and tawny complexion of the little Mexican girl. The too-large parka the child was wearing made it impossible to tell if she was still chubby. Ada was jarred into full alert. She wanted to shout across the lineups, "Where have you been? I've been waiting for you." She wanted to give up her place in the queue and rush over to where the girl was talking to a short, stout, dark-haired woman. Her mother, probably. Ada remembered how once she too had been accompanied by children, two small boys, their warm hands in hers, when she attended to the various errands life required. The little girl seemed to have grown.

Ada had heard that intense concentration on someone who isn't noticing you can get you that person's attention. When the girl responded to Ada's stare, the dark eyes, uncomprehending at first, lit up with glad recognition, and two small, red-mittened hands rose above the curly head, exuberant and joyful and waving. But by then the mother had paid for her shopping. She pulled her child past the checkout and toward the door, where the child turned and waved once more. Her lips were moving, or at least it looked that way to Ada, who was convinced they were saying, "I'll come again."

Then she hasn't moved away, Ada thought with a surge of excitement. And there was no accident on the lake. What a relief! And maybe she really is Mexican, that wasn't just a summer tan. Ada was infused with energy. The child had not let her down. She paid for the scarves and hurried out into the snowy day. Soon as she got home she would do the wrapping and mail the packages the next day. With luck they'd arrive before the new year. And she decided to stop at Safeway for candied fruit and nuts so she could make that jewel fruitcake her husband always liked, even though there wasn't enough time left for it to ripen properly. After Christmas she would invite the Krawchuks. Nellie would be impressed. Not that she needed cake of any kind, with her bulk.

Walking home across the pure white snow with her packages, Ada was grateful that Kurt Krawchuk was taking care of her driveway. And all the fuss and bother about Christmas would soon be over, and she could begin waiting for spring when she would once again plant carrots, two

rows this year, and dahlias and cosmos. The bright eyes of
the cosmos would turn to the sky, the little girl would
return, sit on the concrete curb, and they would talk about
Mexico. The sun would warm them both.

By the time Ada arrived home her back ached, and her
fingers were chilled and stiff from clutching the packages.
Some of the confidence triggered by seeing the child at the
checkout had subsided. She was no longer as sure as she had
been at Wal-Mart. She set her things down on the deck and
felt a moment of panic when she couldn't find her key. But
it was there, in the zippered section of her purse. I'm not the
only one coming home to an empty house, she thought
defiantly, as she unlocked the door. Lots of people do. I'm
not alone. As she entered her kitchen she pushed aside the
possibility that, come spring, she would wait in vain for the
little Mexican girl. Of course she will come, Ada told
herself. Even before removing her coat, she reached for the
kettle, filled it with water, plugged it in. While she waited
for it to boil, she found scissors and tape and wrapping
paper enough for both presents. She pulled cookbooks from
the shelf and paged through them until she found the recipe
for the jewel cake. She read it through three times while
waiting for the tea to steep:

one cup dried apricots, whole
one cup maraschino cherries, red and green
one-half cup candied pineapple cut in chunks
one quarter cup whole almonds ...

MURDER

THE SPRING JESS GALLAGHER WAS MURDERED and her battered body shoved into the dumpster beside the low-rental housing, I had developed the habit of visiting my mother every day right after school. I'd lock my classroom door, shooing any lingering students ahead of me. If there was a staff meeting I couldn't be excused from, I'd sit near the door and slip out early. After the close, chalkdust-laden classroom, the street always took me by surprise. There's a whole world out here, I'd think, amazed how every leaf on the Chinese elms was a miracle of precision, every dishevelled sparrow flitting from shrub to shrub an unexpected delight. Bunches of students rushed to the 7-Eleven or clustered at the bus stop or headed for their cars parked at Safeway, as if in pursuit of some urgent enterprise the schoolday had interrupted.

On the way to Donwood Manor I had to walk past the low-rental housing with all those identical wooden steps, identical doors, some flanked by a blazing manifesto of red geraniums. After Jess's death I always walked on the far edge of the sidewalk, as far as possible from the dumpster.

My mother had read somewhere that if arthritic hands and feet are coated with wax as warm as your skin can bear and then wrapped tightly, the inflammation and the aching will be relieved. When I let myself into her small apartment at the Manor, she'd be sitting at the kitchen table, erect with stoicism and hope. And with the stiff corset she always wore, though it was becoming impossible, she admitted, for her aching fingers to pull the laces tight. Both legs and her left arm ended in lumpy, towel-wrapped appendages; the pale right hand was taking its turn in the pan of liquid wax. It lay there, submissive, lifeless. When she lifted it out and the wax hardened around it like a grey carapace, it looked dead and so ghastly I was repelled by it. My mother would be waiting for me to help her wrap the hand, first in plastic, then in a thick towel which I pinned tight. The idea was that the warmth would be held prisoner by the layers— wax, plastic, towel—and the pain and stiffness would dissolve, the way a bad dream dissolves in the morning.

"I can feel it," my mother assured me. "It's now not so bad, the pain. My fingers aren't quite so bent. You can see that, Emma, can't you?"

Her knuckles were red and swollen, her wrists mis-shapen, but I didn't say anything to disillusion her. She knew I wouldn't stay long and sometimes, to delay my leaving, she had a list of requests for me.

"Emma, sweetheart, scrape for me, please, a few carrots," she'd say. "Bottom bin in the fridge. And while you're at it, could you slice them maybe."

It might be opening a can or jar, getting a vase down from a high shelf, a pot from a lower one. I didn't mind. It was a relief to be doing something, anything, completely unconnected with *Hamlet* or the poetry of Robert Frost.

On days when I had to rush away and leave her ban-daged and trapped, unable to get up to answer the door, unable to pick up the telephone, I'd turn up her radio and make sure the timer was set for forty minutes. Or forty-five or even an hour, whatever time she named, depending, I suspected, on the degree of pain and immobility she had wrestled with getting up that morning.

"Don't forget, Emma, the telephone," she'd say. "It has to be where I can reach it."

"What do you do when it rings?" I asked.

"Oh, I just let it."

I suspected that it didn't ring often, and when it did, her right hand instantly broke free of its multilayered prison, regardless of the timer.

Once in a while I'd sit with her the whole time, until a sharp buzz signalled freedom. She liked that. "How's school?" she'd ask and I'd say, "Oh fine. Just the usual." I didn't want to talk about school with classes just barely over for the day. I didn't want to tell her how my north windows were sometimes smashed after a warm spring weekend, the splintered glass creating bizarre patterns on the classroom floor, the guilty rock come to rest under one of the desks where a student would find it. I didn't want to say how trapped and tired I felt after all teachers were assigned an extra class because of budget cuts.

I never told her about Jess Gallagher, who had been in my literature class. My mother's world was already beginning to shrink, her frail memory so overloaded with more than eighty years of living, there wasn't room for more. She couldn't keep up with the rush of events beyond the walls of her building: the wave of purse snatchings in East Kildonan, the Elmwood man dead of flesh-eating bacteria, the number of women murdered this year in Winnipeg risen with Jess's death to six. She listened to gospel programs on CFAM instead of the news. I encouraged that.

Best to get her talking about Mrs. Jensen, two doors down, who kept a pair of cockatoos and sometimes brought them with her when she came to borrow an egg for an omelette. Or about the Tuesday morning craft hour in the activity room. My mother's gnarled fingers could no longer fasten wire to plastic, or twist crepe paper, or even handle the scissors very well, but she went anyway for the coffee.

If conversation lagged, I'd ask her about Naumovka, a farming village in the Ukraine where she had grown up. She described the pear trees, how they blossomed in April, her father's horses. Or the beggars straggling into the village during the hungry years, in their rags and rotten shoes, the despair of beaten animals stamped on their features. Her stories carried me along to village weddings or funerals. I helped with the harvest in the brilliant light of late summer, heard the nightingale sing at night. Other times I watched the morning collection of the stiff, gaunt bodies of those who had succumbed the previous night to typhus. I could easily have changed roles with her, becoming the storyteller.

One day she told me a new story. She had asked, "*Na, mein Kind*, what did you do today? You and all your pupils?" And I said, "Sometimes, Mother, teenagers would rather not do very much. Were you like that?"

"Me? Sure I was like that. We didn't have so many books, but if I found one I'd sneak it away somewhere, like a squirrel with acorns, and you wouldn't find me."

"Some of my students don't even want to read," I said.

"Well, I liked to read. And Anna too. Didn't I ever tell you about Anna?" And as the timer ticked away the minutes, she told me the story.

NAUMOVKA HAD REALLY JUST ONE STREET, EMMA. *I know,* I've told you that a hundred times, and across the street from us behind a row of chestnut trees huge as giants lived the Wielers. I'd say the richest or among the richest in the village. His riding horse was black as ink and grand enough for the Czar, and even the workhorses had always such shiny coats. Katya Wieler kept the garden like a picture book, not one weed allowed in the rows of cabbage and beets. Like a park, her flower beds, she had lilies no one ever saw before. All the rooms in the brick house, spotless. Well, there were no children to make a mess, you know. No children, and that bothered Katya terribly, and Johann Wieler too. Everybody said how it was like a worm gnawing at his heart that he had no sons. The best farmer, think of it, but not one son. And not so young any more, the Wielers.

So they decided to adopt, but a girl. Everybody said that was playing it safe. If the girl doesn't turn out so good, well, she marries some day and doesn't carry the Wieler name forever, you see. They got Anna from a village near Kharkov. How they heard about her I can't tell you, only that her parents didn't want her, that was the story. So terrible, Emma, to give a child away like a kitten because the litter is too big, only this is a person. She was five only when she came and I was seven, but we lived so close we were friends even though we were so opposite. Me always kind of shy, scared really, and skinny, my mother kept telling me to eat, eat. Anna round and pretty, Johann Wieler called her *mein goldenes Voegelchen*, such blue eyes, and not scared of everything like I was. So even if I was older, we usually did what she thought up. And Emma, she could think up lots to do, believe me. She was like a bird, flitting here and there, everybody fussing over her. "We are princesses," she would say, pretending. "We live in Petersburg. And in summer we will travel to the Black Sea."

Katya Wieler of course kept Anna dressed like a princess, better than the rest of us girls in the village. Stylish, her dresses. Made by a seamstress, not handed down like mine from older sisters. I'm not saying she never showed off, but mostly I liked her. When she started school she was so quick and learned easily.

But not everything was easy for Anna, especially when she got older. Katya Wieler's tongue was sharp like a paring knife, you might say, and her eyes even sharper, if that's possible. She was very strict. As if she was looking for fault, especially when Anna started being a woman. She had lots of rules, Katya did, but Anna was …what should I say? Free, I'd call it. She had trouble with rules. So there were tears and she sulked.

We grew up happy mostly. I never thought, oh, she's adopted, though of course she was and everybody knew it, but it was somewhere back there. In the past. When she was fourteen, what a beauty. Already the boys my age looked at her, and I got a little jealous, because I wasn't getting that kind of looks. From boys, I mean, even if I was older.

And then the war came and the revolution. Naumovka wasn't so bad off, we were spared the worst of it, but our men had to leave. Naturally they didn't go to the army, Mennonites didn't do that. In the first war they could serve in the forest, sometimes far up north—I know, I know, I've told you that a hundred times too—but some of the younger ones wanted to be in the *Sanitaetsdienst*, and that was allowed too, by the church. Anyway, pretty soon there were no young men left in Naumovka. But life went on somehow in our small village, the war was not so close to us, or the revolution. The bandits left us mostly alone.

And then, what a surprise, I should say rather shock, Emma, when I found out Anna was going to have a baby. A sparrow's feather could have knocked me over, so surprised I was. She told me before she told anyone, before her parents, and I couldn't say anything, my tongue was like wood. I mean, she was just fifteen, so young, and if that happened to me, I just couldn't imagine even living after that. Anna didn't seem even terribly upset about it, but a bit nervous, all the same.

"Who?" I asked her that, of course. She wouldn't say.

Katya Wieler couldn't get it out of her, either, not for a long time. People were starting to say maybe it was Johann Wieler himself, but my father said it wasn't fair to think like that. "Not Johann." My mother agreed with him. Katya Wieler got so angry that her daughter was pregnant. Such a disgrace. She wouldn't go anywhere except once in a while across the street to see my mother, she had to talk somewhere. But Anna kept her secret. She could be like that.

"I have to go away," she told me one day. We were sitting on a bench in the garden. It was spring and near the house the tulips were opening red and yellow, and butterflies in and out of the shade, or settled so pretty on the grass. Everything so pretty there and Anna so deep in trouble.

"Where will you go?" I felt cold inside. I couldn't imagine, Emma, if I was sent away from home.

"Mama wrote my relatives in Kharkov. Not my real mother. An aunt. I have to go there."

I almost forgot she came from Kharkov. Anna told me once she thought the reason they gave her away was because her father died and the man who wanted to marry her mother said she could keep only the oldest boy, not the others, so places had to be found for them.

"Are you scared?" I asked. Well, I sure would be. Having a baby would be bad enough and no husband even. And to go to a strange place, where you know already they aren't glad to see you.

"No," she said. "Why should I be?" But she was, Emma. I could feel it.

Just before she left, Anna told Katya Wieler it was old Alyosh, the cowherd the village hired when the young one went in the army. I couldn't believe it, Emma, I didn't want to. Alyosh was old enough to be her grandfather almost, and not clean, not clean at all. Right away I imagined them in the barn, in the hay or some place, and it made my stomach sick to think of it. It was a relief, I have to say, when Mama told me, "Anna's getting the train this morning, to Kharkov." I don't know what I would have said to her. But I was ashamed for feeling like that, and sad too. I missed her.

A few weeks later Katya Wieler crossed the street with a letter, crying. I stood in the front room very quiet so I could hear everything she said to my mother in the kitchen.

"Now she wants to come back," Katya said. "This is her only home, she says. She's lonely. Well, she should have thought about everything beforehand." And she read from the letter. Such a heartbreaking letter, Emma. "Mama, please let me come home," it said, something like that. "Don't say no, dear Mama, I can't stay here with these strangers. Please let my baby be born there in Naumovka with you and Papa. I will not be any trouble, I will help in the kitchen and in the garden, all I can. Here I feel with every glance and word they are throwing me out, every minute of the day. I can't sleep at night. Please write and say I can come. You don't know how afraid I've been. And lonely." She went on like that, Emma, it just broke my heart.

"You have to let her come," my mother said right away. "The child is scared to death. Send for her, Katya."

Katya Wieler didn't say no. "But just till it's born," she said. "The girl can stay that long. But not afterwards. It wouldn't be right."

Right away I wanted to ask, "Then what will happen to her, afterwards?" I couldn't imagine living like that. No one who wants you. I wanted to ask Katya Wieler, how can you do this to your own daughter and to a baby, innocent and not even born yet, how can you, but I kept quiet when she walked past me. Young people didn't speak like that to their elders and, like I told you, Emma, I was a rabbit. But I felt afraid, as if I was somehow guilty. As if we were all guilty.

Anna showed just a little when she left Naumovka, but when she came back, she was big already, not much longer to wait. I went to see her, wondering what should I say, what was there to talk about? I thought, a baby to be born, that's something you should get excited about. And very glad. It shouldn't be, so to say, a weight on my tongue. It shouldn't hang there like a black thing in our village.

Anna seemed happy to see me, but not like herself. As if her mind was far away, not anywhere close to her body. This sounds maybe funny, but I thought her soul was floating just above her head, like a summer cloud. I asked her about her train ride. Imagine, talking just about the train ride, as if that's important. I asked should I come next morning on my way to church. I thought she would say no, she wouldn't come, but she said yes, we would go together. Katya Wieler said this is shameful. A girl so far along and without a husband yet should stay home. But Johann Wieler said let her.

Everybody stared when we walked in, even those who turned away were sort of staring. I felt that. Anna did like she wasn't noticing. Her eyes looked straight ahead. And I thought I was being very brave, sitting with Anna. Stupid, to think that. So stupid.

It wasn't one of our preachers that morning, but a different one, Adam Elias, he came sometimes from Petrovka to preach, and I remember the text he read. *You will go out in joy and be led forth in peace.* And something about all the trees clapping their hands. Mostly our preachers read verses that were a threat almost. They would read *Be sure your sins will find you out,* or some other warning. I think Adam Elias knew how everybody was sick and tired of chaos, first the war, then the revolution, and always scared those terrible bandits would come, and the typhus, so much fear still there in the village. He wanted us to think of joy. He wanted to comfort us.

And something else. He said if he could have one wish it would be that he and his wife could die together. On the same day. They were just two, no children to leave behind. It seemed like a strange thing for a preacher to say in a sermon, so personal. My father said it didn't belong, from the pulpit, but I thought it was sort of lovely, as if he loved his wife really so much. By then Kasdorfs' Gerd was visiting me and I wondered if he would ever love me that much.

The baby was a little girl. Very cute with black eyes and lots of dark hair. Anna called her Esther. A fancy name. In Naumovka girls were just Katherine or Lena or Elizabeth. The first time I saw Anna after the birth she was breast-feeding her baby and looked so satisfied, so calm, I thought there was something almost holy about her. That sounds not right, so Catholic almost, but I thought that. For the next few weeks Anna looked happy, holding her baby close, letting her suck, changing the diaper, rocking her to sleep, and I thought maybe Anna can stay after all, for the sake of the baby, you see. Maybe Katya Wieler changed her mind.

But no, Katya said Anna would have to leave now, and the baby too, but just then Adam and Lena Elias sent word from Petrovka that Anna and Esther should come, they would be glad to give them a home. I was so relieved, so happy for Anna. To me this was like a big load lifted from my

heart. I thought God did a miracle. Anna didn't show any
sign, was she relieved or not. Just very quiet. Her last days in
Naumovka she helped Katya Wieler in the kitchen, but
mostly I think they didn't say anything much to each other.
As if now Anna was not a daughter, just a maid, just like one
of the Ukrainian maids. Anna spent all the time she could
with Esther. I was tongue-tied whenever I went to see her.
Couldn't think of anything to say. My head was so full of
Gerd, only Gerd. That plagued me very much, afterwards.

At Wielers' when I said good-bye, was the last I ever saw
of Anna. It was a fall day, the leaves not yet fallen down but
coloured already, shimmering all gold, I remember that.
There she was sitting in the *Droschke* with Esther already. She
leaned out and the sun made her hair so bright. Golden, you
could say. I thought yes, she looks like a princess riding in
that fine black *Droschke*, she doesn't belong in the village.
Johann Wieler lifted her suitcase on. Katya Wieler stood in
the door. I was glad Anna had somewhere to go where she
was welcome and not back to Kharkov. But I felt as if a terrible crime had been done, to Anna, you know. Why
couldn't she stay here just as good as in Petrovka? I didn't
look at the Wielers, that's how I hated them.

I think, Emma, there was darkness over Naumovka and
no one to hold a light for us. Someone should have shown
us. We heard our ears full about sin, but where was the love
that would make room for a person who didn't keep all the
rules exactly? Katya Wieler, she just couldn't see a single
rule broken. But where is her pity? If there's no love, can't
she at least have pity? I think sometimes the war and revolution brought the darkness that hung all around us. Or
maybe the other way around, the war was a punishment for
our darkness. I don't know.

One letter I got from Anna and I wish I kept it, but
coming to Canada, crossing the ocean, so much had to be
left behind. She wrote how she was helping Lena with the
canning and cooking and how Esther was smiling and
growing fast. Adam and Lena Elias were kind to her, she

wrote, and Lena was teaching her how to sew things for
Esther. She had made friends with someone called Agatha.
They went together to *Jugendverein*. I thought the letter
should make me happy, but it didn't. I read it over and over,
and always the tears wanted to come. And I felt as if for
some reason, happiness was not possible any more.

And the rest we heard afterwards, in spring.

Agatha came to visit Anna one morning. Knocked, but
no answer. Strange, someone should be home. She came
back later, still no one answered. The house quiet as the dead.
She told her father and when he came, the cow was bawling
to be milked. The door opened easily. Agatha could have
walked right in when she was there alone, but thank God she
didn't. Everything so lifeless, quiet, only the sound of a child
crying, very faint. And on the floor, the bodies. All dead.
Murdered and cut up very bad and lying in blood. Adam and
Lena Elias. Anna. And a Russian official who was billeted
there, dead too. Only Esther alive and crawling like a little
worm among the dead, her hands and face streaked with
blood and dirt and crying for her mother. Crying for food.

Anna was brought back to Naumovka for the funeral,
but the coffin was kept shut. Too terrible, they said, how she
was cut up so bad. And Katya Wieler, Emma, she nearly went
crazy, I can't tell you, sobbing from so deep inside, it got in
the way of the preaching at the funeral. I was too shocked for
crying. I couldn't. When they let Anna down into the ground
in the far corner of the graveyard, it felt like there was a stone
inside me, and in the centre of the stone a large aching. To
think of Anna dead. Mind you, even then I thought maybe
she wasn't so bad off dead, but hacked to pieces like that?
No, who can even think of that? The hurt inside, that stayed.
That kind heals very slow. You can't do nothing about it, but
wait and hope some day it will let you alone.

THE TIMER HAD SOUNDED before my mother finished her
story and I had shut it off. She sat in silence, her lumpy

159

hands motionless in her lap. I unwrapped the towels, slipped the plastic bags from her hands and feet, broke away the wax, collecting the bits in the pan for next time. After sitting still so long, my mother could hardly get up. I could see how every joint and muscle raged with pain, how difficult the smallest movement must be.

"I don't want to think what Katya Wieler suffered," my mother said. "She was the worst off of anyone, in the long run. She and Johann. I can see that now, how it made them old. But then I hated Katya, like she was the murderer, the one who butchered Anna. But that is no use, thinking like that. A family in Petrovka took Esther, and I hope she found a good mother because she lost a very good one."

My mother walked slowly, painfully toward the stove. "I'll make tea."

"Who was it?" I finally asked. "Who murdered them?"

"We never found out. Those days, after the Revolution, well, things weren't always orderly, you didn't expect even a real investigation. But they said maybe who did it wasn't after the Eliases at all, but after that Russian official, a quiet fellow, sort of mysterious. They never found out. But the worst thing, Emma, was to think how Anna suffered. The fear. You have to be terribly afraid when someone lifts against you a knife, even Anna, although she was a brave one, like I told you."

When I left Donwood Manor that evening I felt disoriented, as if I were a stranger on the street where every crack in the sidewalk, every greening shrub, every fence, wood or wire, should be familiar. I walked there every day. That evening the traffic rushed by menacingly and the normal shapes and voices of the people who passed me were infused with hostility. Everything seemed cold and indifferent and none of the elm trees looked as though they might begin clapping their newly green branches.

My briefcase was crammed with my students' final *Hamlet* essays on the nature of tragedy. I knew I couldn't face them, not tonight.

Two months ago, I had prepared my classes for the matinee performance of *Hamlet* at the Warehouse Theatre. Jess was still alive then. I told my students that to see or read a tragic drama is to participate in the suffering. It's an experience that purges you of all emotions. I taught them words like *catharsis, vicarious, hubris, hamartia.* I told them tragedy was invoked by an interplay of character, circumstances and powers beyond the natural world.

"Can those powers beyond, or whatever you called them, keep it from happening?" Jess asked. It was an urgent question. Jess wasn't talking about Shakespearean tragedy, not entirely, I realized afterwards, and wondered what it was she feared. What she knew and didn't speak.

She used to stop by my classroom after school, though never to ask, "Why did I get such a low mark?" Her marks could have been the highest in the class if she had desired that. She had an uncanny understanding of literature, an insight rare among my students. She could enter a story or poem and arrive directly at its heart. And the way she took it so seriously often startled me.

Once she told me there was a reason for believing in God: "There has to be one, I think," she told me, as if she was working things out in her mind. "So many people want God to exist, that it makes sense that something inside them must know, subconsciously maybe, that there is a God. But then there's this: why does God just sit back and let people kill and hurt each other? Like in Africa. Maybe no one's ever tried hard enough to figure that out. We're given this brain and no one knows yet what we can get done with it.

Shortly before she was murdered, she asked me, "Do you think I will ever be free, really free?" She spoke with a great wistfulness and looked so anxiously into my eyes as if to pull an answer out of them.

Jess was the president of the Literary Club and a member of the student council and there had been meetings every lunch hour that week. She'd mentioned two overdue assignments she'd have to finish that night and on weekends she worked long shifts at the library, so I naturally thought she was exhausted, as overwhelmed as I was with work and deadlines. I had no trouble sympathizing with her. Someone like Jess, I thought, will always have more to do than she can handle. But I wanted to say something reassuring.

"Maybe the freedom can be there, inside, no matter how crazy things get," I said and added lamely, "In the heart." What did I know about the lives of my students, of their fears, of what excites or shackles them? What did I know of tragedy?

I really wanted to help Jess. I should have let her talk, but my mother's arthritis had flared into a full-blown inflammation and although I knew I could do nothing for the pain, I also knew she would be waiting for me.

Our principal phoned to tell me about Jess. "It was brutal," he said. "The police were shocked at what they saw." Jess had been raped and clubbed to death on her way home from a shift at the library. I didn't ask for the details.

At the memorial service, the family friend who read the eulogy used the word "tragedy" about a dozen times. I sat there numb, listening for words that might console the mother and sisters. Words to console me and the students who had come. But there was no hope offered, nothing to make bearable the grief moving inexorably into our memories. No one said we would one day be able to go out with joy, clapping our hands like the trees.

So far the police have been unable to come up with either motive or suspect in the Jess Gallagher case.

My mother usually repeats her stories, over and over, but she's never mentioned Anna to me again and I haven't asked. Why would I ask for a story so devoid of solace? It's as if my well-meaning mother reached into a chest for something to give me, a treasure, an inheritance, and found this clutched in her bent fingers. I wonder what else she retrieves from her crammed memory those long hours with her aching feet and hands in warm wax, waiting for the minutes to tick down to zero?

MAFIA

I HAVE NO SUSPICION OF TROUBLE, no idea at all, until after Inga flicks her agile fingers for the last time through my hair, holds up the mirror so I can see the back and insists on sweeping up the curled, mouse-brown bits from the floor. "It's my job," she says stubbornly, even though we are in my kitchen and she has to ask where I keep the broom. She's said nothing about it the whole time, cutting and trimming. Later I recall a slight nervousness as Inga moved around me lightly, quickly, combing and clipping. A barely perceptible tension.

Last Sunday, walking along the beach, we felt winter in the air and when the wind grabbed my limp hair and blew it straight up, I said to Inga, "I need a haircut." She said, "I do it for you." Inga has a temporary position in a German-Lithuanian enterprise that imports used washing machines from Hamburg, and no longer works in a salon. But she still cuts and styles hair for a few clients in their homes. We huddled in the shelter of dunes and arranged a time for the haircut while the autumn sun warmed us and the gulls hung like phantoms in the chill air or plunged and rode the

163

cold waves of the Baltic Sea. Inga's body glowed; she had been swimming.

"Tuesday," she said after a long pause during which she studied my hair. "Tuesday the moon is right."

I first met Inga in the park last winter, when the Canadian Travel Association sent me to assist the airlines in Klaipeda. At twenty, she was young enough to be my daughter, and as we became friends I thought of myself as her mentor, but in truth it was usually Inga advising me. In January she took a cure at a sanitorium in Palanga and urged me to do the same, describing how at midday they would run hot from the sauna across the frozen sand into the sea. Before leaving the water they would turn their faces toward the sun and bow their thanks to it.

"It feels wonderful," she tells me often, her eyes luminous, voice reverent. "Now every Sunday I go early to the sea. You come with me. You try it."

But my schedule has no space for a three-day cure and anyway the prospect of plunging into icy water doesn't tempt me. I don't have Inga's unhindered courage. "I'll watch," I always tell her.

Inga is quieter than usual tonight, though not silent, and nothing she has said so far suggests anything is wrong. Her long blonde hair is too fine and frizzy to fall to her shoulders. It seems to swirl and float around her head, giving her the appearance of an angel. As she sweeps she tells me the city treasury is low and her mother, a teacher, will not be paid this month. I put the kettle on. It's when she finally sits down that I first notice how pale she is, and how her shoulders droop. Her hands are unsteady when she takes the cup of tea and there's a smudge of fear in her brown eyes, though she lowers them to hide it.

"Are you okay, Inga?" I ask.

"Okay, okay," she says, with a dismissive shift of her slumped shoulders.

"How was work? Are you tired?" I feel guilty for allowing her to come by bus after a long day at work. She'd been delayed and came late. I should have offered the tea first and maybe warmed up yesterday's beet soup.

"No, no, not tired." But there's a slight giving in as she speaks and I press her.

"What's the problem, Inga?"

"No big problem. Only at work, something. I can't say you." And then she adds, "Something criminal."

I've heard enough about the challenges to private enterprise in Lithuania's changing economy to suspect immediately there's been a threat, a demand made of her company. After more insisting on my part, she tells me. Two men— "they did not have kind faces"—arrived at her desk and demanded she call the director. He led them into his office and when they emerged some time later, his face was ashen. After they left, he locked the door and explained the simple threat—the demand for money. Within a week, or "something will happen."

"We know plenty such thing," Inga says, her English crumbling under the burden of her anxiety. "Plenty fires. Cars breaking. Crashing, bang into air."

"Are you afraid?" I ask, though I know the answer. What else can she be but afraid?

"Yes."

It's nearly eleven and I have a seminar on flight scheduling to review for the next morning. Inga has to get home by bus, and very likely half the street lights will be out, the city given over to darkness. We stare at each other, helpless, wordless. Our tea grows cold. I feel as if all sensation has been suspended while Inga explains that in such cases most enterprises simply comply, but her director called the German owner in his country home outside Klaipeda and he directly notified the police.

"Two hours they question me. I had not a good feeling."

"What will you do? What does your director say?"

"He very afraid. I afraid for him."

The other thing she's afraid of, she says, is a summons to court, if the men are arrested, to identify them. She has seen their implacable faces clearly for a few brief seconds and they've seen hers. This mutual knowing is not safe for either side. As I listen, a nervous emptiness forms inside me.

"Do you wish the police hadn't been told?" I'm uncertain which questions are wise to ask, which stupid. How do I move beyond mere comprehension to genuine concern?

Inga shrugs. "We not trust the police." Her empty hand is clenched on her knee. Her eyes, vivid and scared against her pale skin and hair, begin scanning the room as if searching its corners for danger. And I remember irrelevantly that I haven't yet looked into the mirror to see the result of Inga's work.

"Are you afraid?" I ask her this again when we leave the building and walk along the dark street, careful not to trip on the broken pavement. Inga doesn't reply. The huge lime trees, shadowy and threatening, reach for the sky. Their grotesque shapes alter and shift in the stiff night wind. They are still leafy enough to obscure the few street lights not burnt out. And where's the moon? The moon that Inga promised would be auspicious today. Clouds have moved in from the sea, unexpected and swift as the wings of monstrous birds. They cover the moon and leave the city of Klaipeda in darkness. The wind that brings them is unpredictable; it blows as it pleases. It could as easily blow fog and snow over the city. Or dispel the clouds. Right now it breathes cold on my exposed neck.

We turn onto *Zuvis Gatve*, where a renovated white building looms, an authoritative, elegant presence with bars protecting the stained-glass windows of the first floor. Behind the building there's a matching car shed housing a row of waxed and gleaming vehicles. Day and night, stern guards and ominous guard dogs are on duty. There's no sign to identify the building, and whenever I pass it with any of the expatriates I've met in Klaipeda, we speak the word "mafia" jokingly and speculate about the activity behind those closed doors and barred, stained windows. The impeccable lawn stands out in a city where neat lawns are not important.

As we near the pillared entrance the sensor lights come on, and we move from darkness into blinding light, and then, as we pass beyond their range, back into darkness. None of the buildings on the street offers a friendly light. Inga doesn't want me to walk all the way to the bus stop with her and I don't want to let her walk alone. We compromise. Halfway we stop to say our goodbyes. A car speeding down the street swerves toward us, its headlights hostile and glaring. It slows down as if coming to a stop, then regains speed and veers away, roaring toward the city centre. We remain rooted, unwilling to let go the small comfort of each other's presence. Inga assures me she's perfectly safe on the street, and when she asks if I'm afraid walking alone at night, I naturally say no, I'm not. We leave, in opposite directions.

Alone, I walk as quickly as I dare on the rough sidewalk, terrified. The sound of my footsteps, the moaning of the wind in the trees: everything announces danger. When I come once more to the sensor lights I will their automatic radiance to last and see me safely through the darkness. It's a relief to see the lighted windows of the hulking Soviet apartment block where I live. It's like coming home.

The next day, Wednesday, I think constantly of Inga. Walking along the frosty street to work, I pray with every step: please, please let her be safe. I pass the familiar kiosk where I stop regularly for bananas and candy bars. The woman imprisoned in it is sliding her window open for a customer. In the next block a dozen shabby men of all ages are already queuing at the beer-store window, sepia figures in the subdued autumn light. They huddle against the dilapidated building. The one-legged beggar is in his place just outside the food store, his brown coat pulled like a loose sack about him, his eyes fixed on the pavement. For the first time I throw a couple of *litas* into his hat. He doesn't look up, though his lips move. Has poverty pulled him beyond the reach of fear or more deeply into it?

Nothing will happen until the week is up, Inga has assured me, but the waiting and the fear loom like a punishment over every hour. "Please not call me," Inga insisted before we parted on the dark street. "My mother, she should not know." The thought of a terrified Inga constantly looking over her shoulder as she goes to work this morning is unbearable.

It's raining when I leave work, and the wind has increased. Rimantas, one of the Lithuanian travel agents, offers me a ride home. His car—a sporty thing, fiery red—is parked ostentatiously on the sidewalk. His slender, deft hands release the security device from his steering wheel.

"Your car ever been stolen?" I ask as he drives off with unabashed pride and at a speed too exaggerated for the cobbled streets of Klaipeda.

"No," he says. "Never. But in summer I am driving with this car very fast through Poland. The mafia is after me." And he tells me about the high-speed chase, a hundred kilometres along Polish highways, through countryside, through towns and villages, his foot hard on the gas pedal, hands gripping the steering wheel, the pursuing car a dark, terrifying speck advancing and receding but mostly advancing in the rear-view mirror, his two friends in the grip of panic, shouting instructions. One of them demands hysterically that he stop so they can run into the forest where they might hide in the trees, the other urges him to drive faster, faster, faster until finally they reach the safety of the Lithuanian border.

"My friends and me, we very afraid."

At the border, he tells me, the mafia car stopped and the leather-jacketed men who got out ignored him and his friends. They shared jokes and cigarettes with the border guards before they got back into their car, turned around and disappeared into Poland.

"What did they want?" I ask, breathless from his telling.

Rimantas shrugs. "They want maybe money. 'Tax' they say it. Or they want car."

"Did they have guns?"

"Maybe. I hear sometimes about Lithuanians disappear in Poland."

"Why didn't you stop for help?" I ask. "At one of the towns."

Rimantas flashes a glance my way, a touch of pity for my ignorance about life. My naiveté.

"Will you drive again through Poland?" I ask.

"Maybe."

By Thursday I can't stand the waiting. I phone Inga. "Okay, okay," she says when I ask. "Nothing happen. One week nothing happen," she insists impatiently and changes the subject. "How you like your hair?"

When I tell her about the compliments from my colleagues at work, she laughs with pleasure, no tinge of anxiety in her voice. She says she has a surprise for me and suggests we meet after work next day at a cafe where, we both agree, the best espresso in Klaipeda is served.

Inga is waiting at a window table when I arrive at the Flamingo, but I don't recognize her, even when she waves. She stands up and comes toward me. Her hair has been cut short and dyed black. In contrast, her skin appears chalk-white and in the dimly lit cafe her face glows eerily. She attempts a laugh at my surprise, but it's unnatural and loud. When she asks, "Do you like?" I am too stunned to speak.

"I think it is good," she says as we wait to be served, her voice lowered to a confiding tone. "We must do something," and she gropes for words. "We should not, we must not just wait. We must, can do something..." She falters. The bravado she's trying to muster slips from her.

"Is this a disguise, Inga?" I ask, and when she doesn't understand, "A mask. Are you trying to hide?"

"Not mask. No." She shakes her shorn, dark head, irritated, but doesn't offer anything more. Instead, she launches into a description of the brown and black uniform she had to wear as a schoolgirl. Because she was the treasurer for the Young Pioneers, it was her duty to collect the small fee from each classmate. Only one or two paid. By that time communism had become an outgrown coat, ready to be cast off, and she can't remember anyone who wanted to join the Comsomol.

"We not scared of them like before," she brags. "We make jokes about important people. About the party. About Gorbachev." As she speaks, colour returns to her face and it becomes vibrant with that capacity for joy I've come to associate with Inga; her brown eyes burn with it.

"Now you say from Canada," she orders, mustering her new assertiveness, and I'm at a loss what to tell her about this large subject for which she has an endless appetite. "About your life," she adds. Well, this narrows the field considerably. But what is there to say about the ordinariness of life in a country that seems distant, and because of that distance, vague as a huge landscape painting seen at some earlier point in life and more than half forgotten? I've already told Inga I've been married once, not unhappily, but that was long ago. My only children have been the young travel agents I've trained over the years. I'm embarrassed at having nothing to offer her, nothing to compare with the stories of exile and fear and loss I've heard since coming to this country.

Inga's grandfather spent ten years of his youth labouring in the mines of Kamchatka, where his hopes became as bleak as the geography he woke up to every morning. He returned eventually, his spirit and body diminished, though not destroyed, to the forests and rye fields of Lithuania, where he married and had children and worked, when his health allowed, in a collective, making parts for television sets.

"They not say me, about the mines," Inga has told me more than once. "They not say me about Grandfather until I am sixteen. About that terrible years."

"What did you think when you found out? How did you feel?" I always ask.

"Of course frightened."

She's told me how her grandfather, stooped and frail, used to take her hand and lead her into the forest when she was small and there he taught her which mushrooms were safe to

170

pick. While they searched for wild herbs and mushrooms, the sound of the sea came to them through the trees. I try to imagine them together, the bent old man and the little girl, but with Inga's short, black hair directly in front of me, I have to close my eyes before I can picture a blonde fairytale child walking hand in hand with her fairytale grandfather through a fairytale forest that in earlier years was the gathering place for freedom fighters and a haven for fugitives.

"With my grandfather in the forest I am not scared," she always says. "He tell me stories, only happy stories. Not Siberia."

What fascinates me about the forests in Lithuania is the way light enters them, leaving the trunks and forest floor flecked with patterns of moving light. On weekend excursions to Vilnius I stare, mile after mile, through grimed bus or train windows into that mottled brilliance. The forest is so unlike the bush of stunted oak and modest poplars that grew in the Manitoba interlake where my brother and I played as children, encouraged by our mother, who didn't like us to stray onto the highway that passed our farm. Light could not pierce that bush because of the dense undergrowth, but the clearings were filled with light.

A maze of shaded paths laced the dense bush, paths where Indian warriors, springing full-blown from our young fantasies, moved like mysterious shadows on moccasin-padded feet, always beyond our vision. My brother and I expected them, longed for them to stride toward us through the trees, carrying bows and lethal arrows. Impatient, we slung our own crude poplar bows across our shoulders and ventured out with brave and quaking hearts to meet the enemy we had invoked. And sure enough, one day as evening deepened the shade of the path, a dark shape, indistinct, unrecognizable, came toward us. My heart froze, my knees turned to water and a scream gouged the silence.

"Shut up." My brother turned and clamped his hand over my mouth. His rasping whisper conveyed warning and a fear so real it intensified mine. I dared not look at the appalling apparition coming toward us. What punishment had we called down upon ourselves?

And then another voice spoke in the dusk, a voice both terrible and familiar. "What are you kids up to? Isn't it a bit late to be chasing around in the bush? Your mother wants you home." From the alien shape came the stern voice of our father. In the failing light his tall, broad-shouldered form, clad in his oldest, grungiest work clothes, towered over us and filled the narrow path. In his hand he held a length of poplar sapling, lithe and leafy, to swish away mosquitoes.

"See any of our cows?"

His face, I noticed later in the light of the warm kitchen, was grimed where he must have brought his hand to it to brush away twigs or mosquitoes. The lines in his forehead, accentuated in the shadowy dusk, seemed carved to unusual depths, perhaps by disapproval of his children, perhaps by worry over the cows that had broken once again out of the farmyard fence. The stern face and stern voice of my father pervade all my memories of childhood. At night, moans would come from my parents' room and I imagined him struggling with an assailant I couldn't see, the way he struggled, alone, against the relentless bush that surrounded our small farmstead, taunting anyone who tried to subdue it. Our mother, transplanted from the warmth of a large family and a circle of friends into this desolation, completed the solitude by retreating into her mind and her kitchen. She was no help in any struggle.

"Get on home. Quick."

We never argued with our father. Abandoning our bows in the undergrowth, we flew weaponless down the path ahead of him. Underneath my giddy relief at being safe I felt a faint tug of regret: we hadn't met the adventure we longed for. Adventure that would complete our dreams and prove our courage.

"You okay?" Inga's curt question brings me back to the coffee. My hands have curled themselves around the cup and cling to it, the taut knuckles white.

I release the cup and push it away from me, embarrassed. How long have I been sitting here, caught in the capricious grip of memory? When I look up, Inga's eyes, brown and wary, are fixed on me.

"I'm okay," I say, sheepishly.

Inga insists on walking me back to my apartment. "I must tell you I have plans," she says, her words brisk.

"Plans? What plans?" Inga strides so quickly I can scarcely keep up.

"I will leave my country now. I will find new country."

"How, Inga? Where will you g?"

"I will become nanny. Maybe Denmark, maybe America. My English is now fine. I can help with children." This barrage of information is delivered with a swagger as grating as Inga's black hair. I have no idea what my invest-ment should be in this venture that terror has driven her to. It's not uncommon for young Lithuanian women to find positions abroad with foreign families. Should I encourage her? Or caution her against hasty expectations? Does she expect my help?

The following days I'm busy untangling schedules and putting words to airline policies so pressing they drive every-thing else from my mind. On Wednesday, in the middle of the morning, a surge of guilt jolts me when I remember Inga. My concentration on arrivals and departures snaps instantly. How can I find out if Inga's all right? Frantic, I con-sider asking Rimantas what he's read this morning in the local paper. Has there been anything unusual on the news? Has he heard of a recent explosion of a car or a building?

Inga calls that evening. She's been in bed with a sore throat since the weekend, but now she's fine, though she sounds tired. "I believe we go on Sunday to the sea," she says. It's an announcement; she doesn't ask if I want to go. Nor does she mention work, and there's no discernible fear in her voice, only that new brusqueness. I don't know how to ask her what happened, if everything's all right. I agree to accompany her on Sunday.

Once again Inga surprises me. A short, tight skirt reveals her long legs, her blouse is low-cut, and sandals with narrow straps and fantastically high heels make her appear taller than she is. I have never seen her dressed like this. Her lips are painted a blood colour, her heavily made-up eyes challenge me from under the black lashes. She looks like the prostitutes I've seen near the downtown hotel and I can barely refrain from shuddering. Is she finding ways to finance her future?

"Those shoes, Inga...," I begin, thinking of the sandy beach.

"Let's go," she interrupts, her voice brittle. As we set off down the cobbled street, heading out of town, she walks quickly, as if to prove the ridiculous shoes are no hindrance. Her brazenness annoys me. I decide that I won't ask her about her plans for leaving the country. In the last few days the trees have begun shedding their red and gold, leaving more space for the brilliant autumn sun to pour through to the damp forest floor. As we follow the shaded path to the sea, a quiet beauty surrounds us. Our steps slow to a stroll. The air is cool, the breezes icy in spite of the sunshine.

Inga relaxes a little and tells me her mother is happy now because she's been informed all teachers' salaries will soon be paid. At work Inga's director has decided to renovate the office and she has to help him pick the wallpaper and carpet and draperies. "Because I have good ideas," she boasts. "I know what looks fine."

I find shelter from the wind in the dunes and spread my jacket to sit on. Inga pulls a magazine of the latest hair fashions out of her bag and hands it to me. "You choose for winter a new style," she orders as she kicks off her sandals and jogs toward the small wooden building that houses the sauna.

"It's a pity you not come with me," she calls back. Is she challenging me?

"I'll watch."

174

I flip through the pages of the magazine, looking up from time to time, watching for Inga's dark head to emerge from the sauna. She steps from the building in her blue and white striped bathing suit, strides with grace and confidence across the sand, and stops at the water's edge, a traveller pausing for a moment to contemplate what lies ahead. Then, raising a hand to shield her eyes from the sun, she enters the water. Waist-deep, she turns and waves to me. Then she slips into the sea and her arms stroke steadily, propelling her pale body and dark head into the grey distance. I shiver as she heads further and further out into the cold water. She is disappearing from my sight and I want to shout a warning: "Inga, not so far." I am suddenly and terrifyingly convinced she has another surprise in mind: She has chosen this day to vanish, to let the Baltic Sea swallow her, and I am to be the witness. I can scarcely hold back the outcry that forms inside me.

When she finally turns and begins her way back, I'm elated. I want to shout encouragement for her quick progress back to the beach. Before she leaves the water she stops and turns toward the sun, lifting her face to it. Is it a general gratitude she offers, or is she thinking of the disaster that hasn't happened?

Inga lets herself down on an arm of my outspread jacket. Her dyed hair streams water. Makeup streaks her face. The wind is increasing and her body shivers. As she gazes out over the sea, she looks oddly forlorn.

IN JANUARY INGA LEAVES THE IMPORT COMPANY for a new job at the local telecommunications company. "I use every day my English," she tells me proudly. The plan for becoming a nanny is not mentioned, nor is the mafia incident, and the mundane things that prevail each season fill the weeks. Winter forges ahead uneventfully, except for one afternoon when Rimantas offers me a ride home after work. The days are short and darkness should be shrouding everything, but we see the vivid glow of flames when we arrive at my street to find it blocked by police cars. Rimantas parks one street over and walks with me to where the police have cordoned off the area across from my apartment block. We can't tell which building is on fire.

"Lucky the wind it is down," Rimantas says. "Fire like this, it could go anywhere," and I think, yes, the wind governs everything.

Smoke billows from the place where the small kiosk should be, the kiosk where I stop regularly for bananas and pop. Police uniforms are everywhere, trying to muster authority over the confusion of onlookers crowding as close as they can to the dark cloud of smoke and ash from which leaping flames throw light across the neighbourhood. An ancient firetruck arrives; a ragged clutch of firefighters climbs out and gets to work.

Rimantas approaches a policeman for an explanation. He is brushed aside. The kiosk has become a charred, broken husk and someone says the woman has been taken away in an ambulance. She won't live, that's the verdict. She will no longer slide the window open and shut, dispensing candy bars and beer to her customers, receiving their *litas* and making change. She will never speak again through that small opening. No one will see her muffled in a scarf and wool hat next winter, her breath escaping in a thin vapour, or sentenced to the moist warmth of her cramped workplace in summer. Her husband has refused to pay protection money— that's the rumour spreading through the curious crowd. It's dangerous to ignore mafia threats, Rimantas says. No witnesses will come forward. The police will not do anything.

IN SPRING, INGA AND I WALK along *Zuvis Gatve*, where the lime trees are greening and the first anemones and violets are poking through the earth in front of the apartment buildings. Inga has lately returned to wearing decent walking shoes and modest skirts. Her hair has grown, its pale roots exposed at her forehead. Hardly a trace is left of the brashness she practised sporadically throughout the winter. I'm curious to know if she was rejected as a nanny, but I don't ask. Maybe she never applied. Never intended to. We pass the white renovated building with the barred windows. The lawn is an emerald carpet. The guard dogs lie in the shade of the building.

"Is this a foreign company?" Why haven't I thought to ask Inga before?

She laughs. "Of course not foreign. Lithuanian company. But rich. You can see. Very rich."

I hesitate before I ask, "Do they pay money to the mafia?"

"Of course, to the mafia." Her voice is impatient. How else could life go on except through compromise and adjustment?

And then I ask her about the threat to the import company, surprised how easy it is to shape the question I've avoided for months. "What happened? Were they caught?"

"The police not catch anybody," she says sornfully. "But the owner, he not pay."

"And nothing's happened?"

"Not yet."

"Is your director still there?"

"Yes. He like very much the new decoration."

I have never seen this man, but now I imagine him going about his work in the ambience of new draperies and wallpaper, doomed to wait fearfully for the calamity that will always be imminent. The disaster that may or may not come.

"What about your plans? About leaving the country." I might as well ask this too.

There is a lengthy pause before she speaks. "I will stay," she says, and there's no artifice. "You see, it is sometimes wise to wait. In Klaipeda we know the sea. It is there always. It does not change so much."

The sea is *always* changing, I think. It is restless and

unpredictable. The wind too. But I don't have the right to instruct Inga who has struggled all winter, alone.

IN JUNE, WHEN MY ASSIGNMENT IN KLAIPEDA is completed, Inga comes to the train station to see me off to Vilnius where I'll begin the flight back to Canada. She brings a jar of dried mushrooms—"my mother give it for you"—and a yellow rose. She's given my hair a trimming the day before, "so you look on the airplane very fine." Inga's hair too has been cut. It's mostly blonde now, fringed with what's left of the black. I won't be here to see the transformation completed.

Inga's eyes are sombre at the finality of our parting and I am tired from winding up at work, the fuss of farewell parties, packing. The words of friendship and encouragement I find for her are awkward, but I blurt them out before the moment for speaking them is gone. We hold each other close, briefly, little more than strangers, the fleeting intersection of our lives, the shared pleasure and fear less than a blink in time. In that blink I have seen terror and joy in Inga's eyes. I have watched her, a small speck on the sea.

On the way to Vilnius the train's noisy rhythm sings to me: let her be safe, let her be safe. I stare through the grimed windows into the forest I'm seeing for the last time, the forest that for generations has been a place of refuge and a place of terror. Today the sun-flecked spaces between the trees shimmer. As the wind sends clouds scudding across the sky and bends the branches, it sets in motion an endlessly shifting pattern of radiance and shadow, a restless sea that sweeps past my vision and is left behind.

A Time to Gather Stones

INGRID DID NOT EXPECT to be conveyed from Sudak to Simferopol in an ambulance. The vehicle is an old rattling one, banged up and rusted. She wonders if it will actually get her there. She watched nervously as the driver kicked each tire several times before departure and poked around under the hood like a doctor examining a patient. He is swarthy, probably one of the Tatars that have been trickling into Sudak ever since the failed coup in 1991.

The road is pitted and gouged, the driver determined on speed rather than safety. The countryside they are being hurtled through is green. The lush almond trees and apricot orchards have exploded into such extravagant blossoming Ingrid would ache with pleasure, if she were able to give it her full attention, and in the distance the Crimean hills shimmer in the morning light. Wind roars through the windows, kept slightly open so they won't all suffocate. Although it is not yet ten, the June sun pours unforgiving heat down on them, draining their energy.

The road leads north, away from the Black Sea, where yesterday Ingrid and Natalija kicked off their sandals and waded one last time into the water, not stopping until it lapped their shorts. Surrounded by the dark ripples, Ingrid thought of Tim: she wanted him there beside her, steadying her against the current.

Afterwards they walked along the beach, carefree as children, stopping from time to time to collect stones. And later, leaning from the balcony of Natalija's flat, she rejoiced at the unobstructed view of the hills, the way they curl around Sudak, cradling it in their craggy, earthen arms. To the right, the remnants of an ancient, crenellated fortress snake along the crest of the hills, a stone stronghold built by the Portuguese in the Middle Ages.

"Can we climb up to it?" she asked the day she arrived in Sudak. "Is there a path?"

"Of course. But we go first to the sea."

Naturally, the sea came first. When they met three years ago in Kiev, Natalija gave her a stone with a small hole through which she had threaded a thin string. It was one of many such stones decorating the wall in Natalija's tiny room.

"From the Black Sea," she said gravely, her grey-green eyes intense with memory.

Ingrid was spending that summer on a cultural tour that included Kiev, where Natalija had lived before the coup. They had met by chance at a performance of *Carmina Burana* and after that often spent an evening walking on the grounds of Saint Sophia, or wandering through the market. One hot afternoon they bought candles at the Lavra and entered the cool catacombs, making their way with the tourists past crypts where the preserved bodies of monks, shrouded in embroidered satin cloth, lay on their stone slabs. Sometimes they took a picnic to the park. Natalija spoke rapturously about the Black Sea, where people came to be healed and where she hoped to live one day; Ingrid told her friend that her grandparents had lived in Ukraine before coming to Canada.

One day they came upon the foundation of the

destroyed Church of the Tenth Part. In the thirteenth century the dreaded Tatars had invaded, demolishing the church and slaughtering the women and children and cripples who had fled for refuge into the sanctuary their own small tithes had built. The restored foundation stones gave witness to their sacrifice. Natalija had been reluctant to leave the site.

At the summer's end, when Ingrid was preparing to return to Winnipeg, Natalija announced that she was moving to the Black Sea, where her future husband lived.

"He builds for me a house." Her voice was tranquil, her words infused with faith. And when she told Ingrid, "You and me, we meet again, at the Black Sea. Keep, please, the little stone," her voice was firm and her eyes, usually the dreamy eyes of a mystic, grew clear and unwavering as planets.

In Winnipeg, Ingrid hung the stone over her desk. She showed it one day to Tim, an architect, recently graduated, for whom nothing ever seemed difficult and nothing unclear. His dream was to leave Winnipeg and go east. She tried to tell him about Ukraine, about Natalija, but he only wanted to move his hand along her hip, his mouth along her mouth and throat and shoulders. "Ingrid," he entreated. "Ingrid, don't ever leave me."

It would have been easy to rest in the warm, hungry strength of his arms as they tightened around her. It would have been like coming home, but Ingrid wasn't sure that she was ready for home. Whenever Tim spoke of leaving the limitations of Winnipeg to go east, urging her, "Come with me," Ingrid told him, "Not now. Not yet."

Occasionally she heard from Natalija, who had married and lived with her husband in a small flat in Sudak. Their dream of building a house was abandoned after the collapse of the Soviet Union, but her letters contained no hint of disappointment, not a breath of complaint. Ingrid wondered if her friend still believed they would meet one day at the Black Sea.

There was no time for the fortress until last night, her final night in Sudak, when they returned from the sea and

Natalija said, "Tonight the moon is shining. We go this evening to the fortress." She was ladling out *pelemenje* and pouring tea. Ingrid scrambled to dig out the hiking boots she'd already packed.

"Everybody like our fortress," Natalija said.

"It's mysterious. A piece of fabulous antiquity. Just think how long it's been there, how much it's witnessed."

"The broken walls, they can tell much stories," Natalija agreed. "Such sad things."

"It's history, isn't it? History we can see and touch. Don't you think we can learn from it?"

"Sometimes we learn not much. An empire grows big. An empire dies. And now a pile of stones. Only for tourists."

"Makes a good picture." But Ingrid had used up all her film.

In Sudak, the legacy of a recent empire's rising and falling was a pervasive state of decay. Jungles of graceless apartment buildings, thrown up hastily in Kruschev's time, occupied their designated spaces, grey and ponderous. Only around the tourist hotels near the beach was an attempt made to keep the stone buildings in repair, the grounds groomed, the flourishing oleander bushes trimmed. Along the road to the beach an astonishing row of palm trees strutted exotic fronds, always catching Ingrid by surprise.

When they had finished their tea, Misha, Natalija's husband, came from work with the news that the Lada had developed a transmission ailment and couldn't take them in the morning to Simferopol, from where Ingrid would fly to Kiev, then home. Natalija said nothing for several minutes, long enough for fluttering wings of worry to make themselves felt in Ingrid's stomach.

"We have much variants," Natalija insisted after the pause. She listed them and they included, as a last extremity, taking Ingrid's knapsack to the highway and "any car," would take them to Simferopol. "Yes, any car. Very easy. But not necessary, don't worry. I find a better way."

As if to convince her friend she harboured no doubts

about that "better way," Ingrid took the opportunity to explain "hitchhiking." Natalija possessed an insatiable hunger for English idioms. "Hitchhiking," she repeated, letting her mouth savour the word. "Yes. But hitchhiking I believe not necessary." No flicker of shadow disturbed those calm eyes that at this moment are focussed on the fields rushing by, fields where the wind-whipped poppies dance like crazy crimson puppets. Ingrid did not sleep last night. The hike to the fortress, weighed against the necessity of negotiating a ride to Simferopol, was abandoned. Ingrid, her stomach more queasy by the minute, did not repack her hiking boots.

Ingrid, Natalija and a third, older, woman occupy the space in the ambulance where the stretcher would be placed if the vehicle were used for its intended purpose. In the last few days Ingrid has observed how frequently things are not so used. A decent gas stove in Natalija's flat is display space for ferns and books and a cluster of pictures. There has been no gas in Sudak for five years.

"The bathtub, it has lost function of bathtub," Natalija announced airily, ushering Ingrid through the flat on the first day. "It has become a reservoir." At seven in the morning every tap in the city is turned on to release the cold water that rushes through the pipes for one hour while everyone scrambles to catch it in all available containers.

Ingrid has twice seen Misha's battered Lada stuffed window to window with hay for a friend's goat, and one day the goat itself shared a ride with him and the friend.

Ingrid is relieved that Natalija found out about the ambulance and its unscheduled business trip for the medical clinic. Their places on it were confirmed only this morning when the possibility of hitchhiking had already become, in Ingrid's uneasy mind, the only way out of Sudak.

"Does she work for the medical clinic?" Ingrid asks, motioning toward the third passenger.

"Maybe. I ask her now." Natalija turns to their fellow traveller, a matronly blonde wearing a white sweater over a flowered dress. Her shoes are worn but, like Natalija's, they are dressy, with pointed heels. Her solid body hardly sways with the motion of the ambulance. Her hands look older than her face, a strong face with blue eyes, a solid chin, and precise cheekbones. It is a face held resolutely in check until Natalija speaks, and then it becomes animated. As the two speak, their Ukrainian words struggle against the wind's shrill piping.

"Jelena say about herself," Natalija says, turning to her friend. "I translate you."

Ingrid leans forward, inclining into the story.

IN THE VILLAGE MOLOCHANSK, in Ukraine, Jelena plays with Vladimir, the neighbours' boy, on the crumbling stone staircase of a ruined building that according to the villagers belonged once to a rich German family who owned much land around the village. The children's play, carefree and innocent, magically translates the ruins into a castle where prince and princess are surrounded by adoring courtiers. Servants, summoned by the children's desire, materialize instantly like so many willing genies.

In addition to the stone steps, sections of an ornate fence and the remnants of a gate have also escaped decay. Daily the children's imagination replaces the missing parts so that everything is beautiful and whole, a grand enclosure for the fabulous domain where they spend the idyllic hours safe from all invaders. When their mothers call them home to supper they run, shouting to each other that tomorrow they will marry, will become King and Queen and rule their empire with pomp and great happiness, forever.

Jelena's family lives in a village house distinguished from the others by two arched windows in the gable. She admires the graceful curves of those arches, but except for these and certain details in the red brickwork, her home is as humble as the others, the wooden fence in need of repair, the family's existence empty of luxury.

Because of the famine in Ukraine, they are forced to leave the village for a new home in the unfamiliar, distant Ural mountains and Jelena leaves behind forever young Prince Vladimir, whom she has married countless times on the broken stone steps. Their joyfully shared splendour becomes a pleasant memory. Her father, by this time a member of the Communist party, is retrained and given a teaching position in a technical school. Jelena grows up, joins the Comsomol, and studies cartology.

One day the Rulers of the Soviet Empire issue a stirring proclamation:

> Young People of the Soviet Union! Prepare to show your loyalty and gratitude to Father Lenin. There are new regions to be surveyed and made productive. There are splendid cities to be built, new factories to be planned. This undertaking requires advanced skill and enormous exertion. It demands devoted effort and great sacrifice. The task of building a glorious country is a task for the young and courageous. Therefore, young people, do not hesitate to dedicate yourselves to this great patriotic venture.

And so, Jelena leaves father and mother and her home in the Urals to follow an undeniable calling. She arrives in the mining region of Kazakhstan. Here, in the bleak city of Karaganda, she is given a room in a shabby hostel, from where she trudges daily to work in a grungy building. She is serving her country; she is part of something grand and hopeful. The whole area will blossom, boundaries will disappear and opportunities for all will burst like spring flowers from the barren ground.

The air in Karaganda is thick with coal dust; nothing is ever clean. She discovers that there is little glory in the service she performs, even for a sincere and dedicated servant, but she continues nevertheless. Occasionally, in the course of her work as cartologist, she is swooped up in an aircraft, away from the routine drudgery, lifted beyond the endless grey mining country. Flying weightless above Lake Baikal in the east, or over the southern mountains that border on Tibet, she stares amazed at the muted colours, the magnificent shapes and graceful contours. Hovering over such grandeur, she dimly remembers another kingdom, lost or imagined.

She marries in Karaganda, where almost everyone she knows is displaced, having come from somewhere else. Her husband, a Crimean Tatar, was a child when his people were driven out like cattle from their homes near the Black Sea. They left everything behind, he tells Jelena, except for their children and the clothes on their backs. As the little band of exiles moved away from their abandoned homes, their wailing rose, spiralling like smoke on a windless evening, and wound back into the shadowed curves of the Crimean hills and up to the remnants of an old fortress set high on one of its summits.

Her husband speaks with longing of the sea and the hills, although he hardly remembers them. When the great union of socialist republics finally sags and falls apart like an outworn shoe, he insists on returning to the Black Sea. To Sudak. Jelena, the former cartologist, finds works in the office of the medical clinic. Her husband is still looking for work. Their children have stayed in Kazakhstan. Life is not wonderful, but it's possible, though she's not sure Sudak can ever be home.

INGRID LEANS BACK, EXHAUSTED BY THE STORY, by the vying of Natalija's imperfect English with the perverse wind. While the other two continue the conversation in Ukrainian, she closes her eyes and gives her body up to the rude jostling of the old ambulance. That scene with two small children playing on the stone steps is imprinted with diamond clarity in her consciousness, and she holds it cupped in her mind the way one might guard a fragile shell found on a beach.

She reaches for her bag and pulls out her journal. She wants to write down Jelena's story and last night's disappointment about the fortress, but it's impossbile to write in the rattling ambulance. She'll do that when she is safely settled on the aircraft to Kiev. Maybe she can read.

Before arriving in Sudak to visit Natalija, she travelled in Ukraine, near the Dnieper River where long ago her grandparents lived, "in prosperity and God's blessing." That's how her grandfather still puts it. Throughout Ingrid's childhood, her grandmother extolled the beauty and peace of a destroyed world that would always be home. "I wish you could have seen the orchards in spring, Ingrid," she would say. "I can't tell you how lovely they were. Like pink and white clouds floating in the sunshine behind our house." Her eyes would shine or grow misty whenever she remembered the beloved country from which God delivered them after the revolution in 1917. Brands plucked from a blazing fire. From the time of that great escape, they have lived in exile, giving thanks for the miraculous deliverance and mourning the lost and ruined homeland so far away and at the same time lodged, unchanged and desirable, in their souls.

"You're young, Ingrid," her grandfather said. "Why don't you go on one of those tours to Ukraine? You should see where we come from. I'm too old, but you, you're young."

"Go," Grandma said. "Take pictures. Then come home and tell us. Tim can wait."

The last remark amused and surprised Ingrid, who assumed that Tim's presence in her life went unnoticed by her grandparents. Tim, whose desires and ambitions were directed toward the future. Toward the east and prosperity. "Come with me," he begged, and then, exasperated at her resistance, "Marry me, Ingrid." Instead, she took a leave of absence from her job at the advertising agency and joined a tour of Mennonite villages in Ukraine.

"Want to come with me?" she teased Tim. But Tim, lured by exciting designs, new materials and the latest techniques, dreamed fantastic buildings of glass and steel. The ancestral, disintegrated world that drew Ingrid held no fascination for him.

Ingrid pages through the journal she had kept in Ukraine.

ZAPOROZHE, MAY 24

A small stray bird flitted from table to table in the hotel dining room this morning at breakfast. I took it for a good omen and gave it a slice of sausage. The sausage is mainly fat; I can't eat it.

The hotel is huge. And ugly. The architect must have failed Design 101. Tim would despise it.

I feel out of place here, like that grey bird, even though the people in the group are Mennonites. *My* people. Mostly older. Some, like Old Gerhard Lepp, were born here. He's determined to see the village, maybe even the house, where he was born.

Today we visited Chortiza, the village Grandma Peters comes from. A foolish part of me expected things to be the way she tells it, so it was disappointing that everything's drained of colour, except for the blooming chestnut trees. The girls' school Grandma went to, though, is still a fine building. Its ornamented architecture struck me as surrealistic against the drabness and neglect you see all around. It's still used as a high school. A gaggle of curious students crowded around us, the girls giggling, posing for our cameras, the guys acting tough. Like kids anywhere in spring, they're antsy for summer vacation. They seemed carefree, and I envied them.

I recognized the ancient oak tree immediately, from Grandma's old photos. Massive trunk and a forest of mainly dead branches. Our guide, Olga, pointed out one brave branch that's still leafy, too high up for us to reach. Grandma told me the oak is 400 years old, but Olga says, 700. She says it was sacred to the Cossacks of the region. I wanted to say, "It's sacred to me too. My grandmother played under this tree." But I didn't. It seemed suddenly impossible to believe. Or too significant to just blurt out.

How much will I tell Tim? Will he be interested if I tell him about the school children, the old men with their goats, the kerchiefed women selling limp vegetables, the employees in our ugly hotel? If I tell him there is life in the midst of desolation, will he listen?

And how much will I tell Natalija when I see her? *If* I see her. Last night I woke in a sweaty panic because I dreamed I got to Simferopol and she wasn't there to meet me.

ZAPOROZHE, MAY 25

Today Olga taught us to how to recognize Mennonite buildings and fences. If a house has two arched windows under the gable, it's pretty certain the Mennonites built it, she says. (Would Tim be interested?) We all played the game of identifying Mennonite architecture. Not much of it left, just here and there the ruins of a vanished golden age. Takes a busier imagination than mine to picture this as the wonderful settlement Grandma gets so terribly nostalgic about.

Gerhard Lepp insisted we drive to Eichenfeld, the village where he was born and where his father and uncles were murdered in the chaos after the revolution. The Ukrainian bandits with their horses and sabres arrived just after dark and forced their way into the first house in the village. The father was hacked to pieces in front of his family and his young son was forced to accompany the bandits on their grim business of death. At each door the boy had to knock and call out his name. The villagers opened to his familiar voice, giving the bandits easy entrance. No guns were used, only sabres. A silent massacre that left behind a river of blood. Olga told us the whole story, her voice hushed with the grisly horror of it. We were all without words. Gerhard Lepp struggled a while to keep his composure, and then gave up and sobbed.

After the massacre, the women and children who survived left the village, Olga said. Most of them came to Canada.

"And now we're back," one woman muttered. "Visitors in our own homeland. My parents had to leave everything." She was rude to Olga, as if Olga had anything to do with it. I was embarrassed. The woman's family once owned two flour mills near the Dnieper River. All gone.

ZAPOROZHE, MAY 26

This morning we drove through the villages that formed the Molotchnaya Colony, where Grandpa comes from. Olga read their Mennonite names from her map: Liebenau, Fischau, Petershagen, Kleefeld, Alexanderwohl, Halbstadt. These names are forgotten now, replaced by Ukrainian names I can't pronounce or spell. Instead of prosperous farms there's poverty everywhere. None of the stately horses Grandpa speaks of, only a few mangy ones, here and there decrepit tractors. Lots of goats mean a well-off village.

The most marvellous ruins of all are located in Halbstadt, where Grandpa comes from. It's called Molochansk now. One particular building must have been a grand mansion. Olga said "palace." Even now that it's fallen to pieces the grandeur isn't completely gone. The broken steps and the stone fence are proof that this must have been an elegant estate at one time, the whole place prosperous. I let myself imagine it was Grandpa's home, though of course that's unlikely. I sat down on the steps to rest and Gerhard Lepp snapped a picture of me.

I wanted Tim to be here, to walk with me along the streets of Halbstadt. To sit beside me on those broken steps. To help me reconstruct the former glory.

ZAPOROZHE, MAY 27

My last breakfast in the ugly Zaporozhe Hotel. Today we take the night train to Simferopol. I'm leaving behind a geography that holds tantalizing bits and pieces of my heritage, of the proud empire my people built with industry and faith. And also cruelty? I wonder. Only ruins left. I'm taking bits and pieces of it with me. If I should come again, say in ten years, maybe I'd find a new and better empire.

My few days here are just a blip in history, you might say. In the morning I'll be in Simferopol, then Sudak. Five days of still another geography. Who knows what I'll find there. And then home.

Tim wants to marry me. But can a traveller who comes home carrying invisible treasure live with someone whose idea of treasure is quite different?

I pray to God Natalija will be there, in Simferopol, when the train arrives in the morning.

INGRID CLOSES HER JOURNAL. The other two women are still engrossed in conversation, Jelena listening, Natalija speaking and sometimes bending to read from a small Bible she has pulled from her bag. What is she reading in that strange Cyrillic text? Maybe that part about being strangers and exiles. Or about the search for an abiding place, a city that doesn't crumble.

The driver reduces speed sharply, steers the ambulance down a short side road and brings it to an uneceremonious stop beside a small, shabby building. He gets out, walks toward the building. The three women get out too.

"Something wrong?" Ingrid asks.

"Nothing wrong." The wind lifts Natalija's hair and it swirls in a pale nimbus around her head. "The driver wants maybe a coffee."

The driver enters the building, a dingy roadside store or cafe. It seems to Ingrid that they couldn't have stopped in a more desolate place. The hills have long since vanished behind them and the orchards and green fields have given way to a stretch of colourless countryside with only a few trees for the wind to bend. No poppies anywhere. Here and there a pool of stagnant water rests in a depression in the cracked earth. Two children float paper boats in one such opaque pool. The women walk slowly toward the building, but don't go inside. Ingrid wonders nervously how much time the driver needs for his coffee. Her mouth feels dry. Natalija motions her to the shaded side of the building. Above them the blue bowl of the sky has become a haze of heat dotted with a few twists of cloud. The air is oppressive.

"Well, here we are," Ingrid says to Natalija. "At least we've got this far." She regrets immediately the thin edge of doubt she has allowed to slip into her voice, the implied lack of faith in a good outcome for the journey.

"No problem," Natalija says, her voice unruffled, her eyes resting on the surrounding bleakness. "We get there. On time. Please not worry."

Both Natalija and Jelena have entered that state of intentional resignation Ingrid has observed in women of this country. They are wrapped in patience, as if they are accustomed to standing and waiting, have accepted both stasis and change and learned to discern when struggle is futile. When it is best to conserve strength.

"It was easier before," Natalija said one morning in Sudak while she waited for the water to come gushing from the tap. "Before, we have in the shops food. We have hot water." And then, as if even this small complaint was too much and must be atoned for, she announced with an air of gaiety, "Today I make you breakfast for queen. The Queen of England have for breakfast oatmeal and one egg. I read it in the book. Today you and me, we eat like the queen."

And while they enjoyed the breakfast fit for royalty, Natalija said tentatively, as if testing the words for validity, "It is easier before. But now is better for the spirit."

The three women stand together, perspiring in the heat—Ingrid in hiking boots, the others in shoes whose inexpensive elegance has long worn off—near the rough road to Simferopol, in the shade of this unlikely building. It seems incredible to Ingrid that she, a copy-writer for an advertising agency, twenty-seven years old, with a permanent Winnipeg address, finds herself in this forlorn place with two women who at this moment seem strange to her. And she unknown to them. Her life in Winnipeg has become as remote as the farthest planet, her apartment impossible to visualize. She tries to conjure the faces of her aging grandparents, but they come up blurred. When she thinks of Tim, she is desolate.

She turns to her friend. "What were you reading from the Bible?"

"I read for Jelena a blessing. From the Psalm."

Ingrid looks away. She wants to tell Jelena about the ruins she has seen in Halbstadt. She wants to say there is a link between them, a significant link, that their paths have crossed long ago, but explanations will call for more translation and Natalija must surely be tired. Maybe later, in the ambulance.

The driver emerges from the small building, his step energetic. Revived. His swarthy face is only slightly ingrained with the passing of years. Ingrid looks for humour in that face, for kindness she may have overlooked. He motions, unsmiling, for them to get into the ambulance where Ingrid dozes relieved that the journey has resumed.

They have reached the outskirts of Simferopol when she is jolted awake. The driver has once more pulled the vehicle off to the side and stopped. He turns around and speaks to Natalija, a conversation of increasing gravity during which a stubborn firmness appears on his face and Natalija's calm eyes become more agitated than Ingrid has ever seen them. When the conversation has reached its conclusion, or inconclusion, Natalija reaches for the knapsack and motions her friend to follow her out of the vehicle. Ingrid turns to Jelena, takes her hand and holds it.

"Good-bye. Thank you for the story." She wants to add, "I have a story too," but what would be the use, now that

their allotted time together has run out, and their translator
has already stepped out of the ambulance. Reluctantly, she
releases Jelena's hand and gets out. As the ambulance rattles
off into the heart of Simferopol, a feeling of abandonment
and loss engulfs her.

"The driver not go to airport," Natalija is saying, her
manner no longer unruffled. "We take here the bus." She
grasps Ingrid's arm with brusque purpose, and steers her
toward the nearest bus stop. Ingrid follows mechanically, her
heavy hiking boots clumping on the broken pavement.

Some distance from the bus stop, a car is parked at the
side of the street, the driver half-hidden behind an open
newspaper. Natalija slows her steps, hesitates, then
approaches the driver. She pulls bills from her handbag and
speaks to the man. He folds the newspaper and opens the
door for them.

"Don't worry," Natalija says as they settle into the
strange car. "Soon you are with Tim. Plenty of time."

"No, there isn't. I've still got lots to tell you. About Tim.
About everything."

The cruel ticking away of time is eroding much more
than her chances of catching the plane. How little she has
spoken to Natalija of what needs to be said. Of the way life
carries you too quickly on its unexpected byways. You move
along, unaware of the intersections, or indifferent to them.
She has slept instead of telling the others that she, Ingrid,
rested a while on stone steps leading to a vanished house.

"I still have things to tell you."

"We meet again," Natalija soothes. "Then you tell me."
She looks at her friend intently and with curiosity. Calm has
returned to her eyes. When she opens her bag, Ingrid
expects her to pull from it another stone on a string, or
maybe the small Ukrainian Bible from which she read to
Jelena, but it is a postcard her hand holds out, a picture of
the crenellated fortress near Sudak. The crumbling structure, dark and ghostly against the rose glow of a perfect
sunset, proclaims a stunning authority.

"Next time we climb to it."

"Next time?"

"Yes. We meet again."

"Next time, will Tim be with me?" Ingrid asks quickly, and only half joking.

Natalija gives her full attention to the question. But no answer.

"Which Psalm did you read for Jelena?"

"About the waters of Babylon. Where the people cry for the country."

And then they are at the airport, on time, as Natalija promised.

ON THE PLANE TO KIEV, INGRID IS TOO SATURATED with relief and exhaustion to write in her journal. Instead, she settles into the aircraft's shabby upholstery, closes her eyes, and rehearses her homecoming. What souvenirs is she bringing? There wasn't much to buy in Ukraine, except for those lacquered nesting dolls and endless embroidered blouses. She decided against them. The undeveloped film in her bag will produce an abundant crop of pictures of the former Mennonite villages; her grandparents should be pleased. She will give the prettiest of the stones she and Natalija gathered at the Black Sea to her friends. And Tim? She has nothing, really, for Tim, except the stories she can tell him, if he's willing, and Natalija's postcard of the ruined Portuguese fortress on the Crimean hills.

THE BARVENKOVO FACTORY

EDITH HAD READ that travel is an art, and that perfecting this art is not dependent on experience so much as on the traveller's state of mind. Inner tranquility, transparence, a humble spirit are as necessary as good maps, addresses of decent, affordable lodging, acquaintance with the language of the country you're travelling in, congenial companions, a trustworthy guide. Edith reflected on this travel wisdom in compartment #8, car #12, on the train heading east from Kiev, a cup of tea in one hand, the other spreading out a map of Barvenkovo across her jeans. It was a good map. She'd found it in the Mennonite archives in Winnipeg and made copies, one for herself, one for Irwin. The third copy, folded and already becoming dog-eared, was stored in the shirt pocket of the young man who lay in the bunk above Irwin's, face to the wall, asleep. Pants and pullover lay folded beside his pillow. It was too early to tell whether Vassilyj was a good guide, though he spoke English passably well. Among the three of them they had no information about lodging in Barvenkovo, but Irwin kept saying as long as they had enough cash he couldn't imagine that there'd be a problem.

As for a tranquil mind, Edith would have been the first to admit she didn't yet possess it. She was trying to still the ill-natured, pesky voice that threatened to undermine her confidence. *Is this some kind of mission you're on?* the nagging voice said. *Where do you think it's taking you, really? What are you looking for? Evidence that your roots are tapped into the Dnieper River your grandfather swam in? Shouldn't you just let those roots rest?*

"First thing when I get home, I'll start on the fence." Irwin, on the bunk opposite, was eating potato chips he'd bought from a vendor when they boarded the train in Kiev. "I figure if I get right at it, a couple of hours every day after work, I'll get done by September." He would much rather not be on the train to Barvenkovo, but he wasn't actually disgruntled. Nor did he get lost in the landscape rushing past the train window.

Edith had so completely located herself in the Ukrainian countryside they were travelling through that she could hardly picture their Winnipeg bungalow with its white, peeling fence. At Kiev the train had crossed the Dnieper River, followed its north bank for a while, then left it behind. The fields were fresh and green, the crops much farther along than crops in Manitoba. The farmyards and small villages they swept past looked desolate, the people forlorn. And now, darkness was settling over everything: villages, fields, the train.

Edith had with her two photos taken in Barvenkovo long before she was born. One showed the brick house her father had grown up in. The second was a blurred picture of a factory complex, the buildings ornate and impressive. A group of labourers posed near pieces of farm machinery. On the edge of the picture, part of a fence could be seen, a patterned stone fence. The factory had belonged to her grandfather and this visit to Barvenkovo, which by now would have grown into a sizeable town, was entirely her idea, she accepted full responsibility for it. Irwin did not share her passion for this journey; she didn't expect it of him. In an extremity she would have come alone, but extremities were what Irwin liked to prevent. He had shopped for a new camera and booked a vacation from the computer firm where he worked. He was here with her, like a conscientious schoolboy who would do his best to see a project through to a successful conclusion, then put it resolutely behind him and give his full attention to the next one. In this case, the weathered white fence.

By the time the portly woman in charge of car #12 came by, dusk was giving way to night. As she gathered teacups and money in her large hands, the burden of authority rested importantly on her stocky body, solidifying the slack, impassive features of her face. Edith couldn't imagine her saying "Have a good day" to anyone in any language. As soon as she left, Irwin unfolded a blanket and spread it on his bunk, took off his shoes, and rolled himself, clothes and all, into the blanket, leaving Edith wide awake in the steadily rocking darkness of the train that would deliver them to Barvenkovo early in the morning. She took out her notebook. All day she had been recording her impressions of the countryside and now she wrote: *We are nearing our destination.*

"Chances of the factory still being there are pretty slim," Irwin had kept telling her. "It could have been bombed in the war. Or demolished afterwards to make way for some grand Soviet scheme."

He was right, of course, but that didn't stop Edith from feeling the journey was meant to be, though she couldn't have said how she knew. Through the winter her anticipation had intensified. Anticipation was, she believed, another essential element of successful travel. Irwin had overleapt this part, as far as she could tell. For him the factory did not really exist. He assumed that after Barvenkovo they would return home and resume their normal routines of work, he at his computer job, Edith as employment counsellor for the government, a job she'd worked at for longer than she cared to remember. Unlike her husband, Edith didn't believe that visiting Barvenkovo would leave them unchanged. Sometimes she was uneasy concerning the outcome.

Occasional snoring, sometimes a moan, came from one of the two men, she wasn't always sure which one. She wanted to get up from her bunk and go to the restless dreamer, tuck the blanket firmly around him and say, "Sh, shh." Both men seemed equally helpless, and equally strangers in the darkness of the compartment, for which they had bought all four tickets, on the insistence of the travel agent in Kiev. "So it will be for you very private, very pleasant," the woman had said. She had recommended Vassilyj, a university student, to be their interpreter. "He does not drink so much." Travel tips from someone in the business were not to be taken lightly.

It was getting chilly. Edith pulled a sweater from her bag. It might have been an evening such as this one, chilly and a bit damp, when her grandfather, coming home early from the factory, had made the astonishing announcement that this night he and his wife and their six children would not sleep in their beds. They would eat a quick supper, then pack food and warm coats and blankets, and after the sun had set, they would all leave the house. Everyone would have to be very quiet. Horses and a wagon stood ready. But where would they sleep? the youngest children asked, and why must they leave their home where it was warm, where they all had beds? The oldest one, Edith's father, did not need to ask. He was old enough to help in the factory and he knew the workers were envious of his father, Ivan Ivanovitch, the hard-working, prosperous factory owner. Their own shiftless poverty made them restless, his father kept saying, and in 1917 that restlessness found its place in the larger turbulence of revolution and war. It was because of these disgruntled workers and their stubborn desires that the family was driven from home, a small band of fearful fugitives. Driven eventually from the country.

The wagon had brought them to an abandoned house a good distance from the factory. As they entered the strange rooms, the parents and their six children looked about them fearfully, and then climbed down into the clammy cellar, where they cowered for four days and nights in the dark, surrounded by forgotten potatoes whose pale shoots reached vainly for the sun. The occasional scuttle of rats startled them. Outside, the days and nights were filled with the constant tramp of feet, shouting, horses' hoofbeats. In the distance gunfire rose and fell. When it finally subsided, they climbed up, cold and exhausted, to the sunlight, and returned to the brick house. In place of the warmth and order they had left, they found chaos: chests and drawers ransacked, windows and chairs and china smashed, clothing and pillows slashed by sabres and flung helter skelter, the oak table gouged right down the centre. The vandals—the outraged grandfather was sure they were his own shiftless factory workers—had been thorough.

That was the story. But was there more? Edith could remember very little of her grandfather, only that he had been almost completely blind, somewhat stooped and tired, as though he carried around with him a heavy burden. A man who said little and never smiled.

Edith believed she would recognize the contours and colours of Barvenkovo. She hoped that some ingredient in the air, a certain quality of light, would welcome her. After living forty-six years with her father's detailed descriptions of the factory, she expected to find it. He had sketched for her the whole village as he remembered it: the wooden orthodox church; the muddy square in front of the market place; the medical clinic an altruistic aunt of the Czar had ordered built as a treatment centre for trachoma, a disease rampant in the village. Before his death, her father had given her his pictures of the factory and the family's red brick house. Of all the places he had described, Edith counted on the factory. It seemed a substantial goal, worthy of the journey.

"It was well run," her father had always insisted. "Your grandfather was an orderly man. He didn't put up with

shoddy work. He didn't permit laziness. The workers knew
their place."

The grandfather's near-blindness was the result of a
doctor's over-zealous treatment for trachoma. As a child,
Edith had believed it was poor eyesight that caused him to
walk bent and so slowly. She supposed that he couldn't really see her and that was why he paid little attention to her.
His sorrow was what she most remembered.

At the first grey streaks of dawn, the train stopped at the
station from where, two months after emerging from that
damp cellar, Edith's grandparents and their large family had
departed one morning, leaving everything behind. The
three travellers in compartment #8, groggy and disoriented
by the incessant motion of the train, braced themselves,
each in turn, against the train's swaying while they brushed
their teeth in the small washroom that by morning had
acquired an acrid stench and a slimy wet floor. Such travel
trials should not unsettle a tranquil mind, Edith mused.
Vassilyj had already folded all three allotments of bedding,
efficiently and energetically. Halfway through last night,
Edith too had spread her blanket out and slept lightly for an
hour or two.

The street in front of the station was coming to life
against a grey overcast of fog and dust and smoke. Men and
women carrying gaudy plastic shopping bags strode to work
or to market. A row of ghostly chestnut trees in full bloom
towered over the street, giving way further down to lime
trees. Near the entrance to the station, a grandmother held
two small children by the hand and waited for someone. A
drunk lay sprawled beside a smashed bottle. A lean, stooped
man lounged against an aging blue car parked in front of
the station, smoking. Vassilyj approached him. They talked
and gestured. The man's clothes were shabby and not
exactly dirty but not clean, either. Edith couldn't tell how
old he was, maybe seventy. Younger than her father when he
died two years ago.

Her father had drawn into himself and shrivelled, as if

his leaving them was a painstakingly choreographed act of disappearance. In his last days he ceased speaking, and his eyes focussed on a point past everyone, as if he had taken his leave of the familiar room with the people he knew in it. Then his eyes had opened wide and the muscles of his face moved underneath the dry skin, Edith had believed her father was trying to tell her one more story, an important story he had saved for the last. It was too late.

Edith wondered if the man beside the blue car had lived all his life in Barvenkovo and what kind of life it had been. Was he glad Ukraine was independent now, or was he a believer who regretted the demise of communism?

"He say he can to show us factory." There was excitement in Vassilyj's movements and in his voice, the adrenalin flow of a small success. "He drive us to factory. You come, please, inside car." Edith wondered what factory that might be. It couldn't be her grandfather's, for which she was prepared to search all day. And the next. Then they would board the train once more, for Kiev, and from there to Moscow.

The old man stood watching them. His gaze left Edith uneasy. Of course they wouldn't step into the car of this stranger. It would be like entering alien territory where they would be at a disadvantage. How was she to know if this man could be trusted? Vassiljyj was young, his judgement untested. She looked around for Irwin, but he had wandered into the street with his camera.

"Stand over there, Edith," he called. "Right beside the station. No, there beside the sign. Vassilyj, you get in too. No, no, I'll be in the next one." He was happy as a child with a new toy, innocent and unaware of foreignness except as a subject for a photo. And no, he didn't think they should get into this stranger's car.

"He might rob us," he muttered to Edith, who was looking around for a real taxi. "Might even murder us." He had listened with care to the travel agent's warnings about crime in Ukraine. Crime that fed on poverty.

The old man held the door open while Vassilyj beckoned with both arms, and the two foreigners, uncertain what else they could do, walked reluctantly to the car. Got in. Just before the driver closed the door, his eyes met Edith's. They were a deep brown, almost black, and veiled, as if they guarded secrets. Vassilyj seated himself beside the driver. Edith listened as they spoke. Tense. Were she and Irwin cooperating in a malicious conspiracy against themselves? All she could figure out was that Vassilyj seemed to be asking questions, the older man giving information, though at times it seemed the reverse, the driver asking for information, probably about the two foreigners in the back. She turned to Irwin, but he had his camera ready to snap one of the fruits stands outside the window.

"This factory, it was used for, how you say it, cranes, yes?" Vassilyj turned around to offer this new information. "They make large cranes, many cranes they need for construction of the apartment buildings, yes?" He looked directly at Edith. He understood that she was the one to whom these facts mattered. The one who wrote things down.

"Yuri say it is today empty," he continued. "Nobody work now."

And then Yuri spoke, as if repeating after Vassilyj: "No money. Factory—no work." Edith took it as an announcement that he too knew a few words of English. His eyes, in the mirror, were wary. Almost hostile.

The streets that rushed by—Yuri drove madly, flicking cigarette ashes out the open window—had about them a grey sameness. Edith felt disoriented and wondered if they were being taken on a wild goose chase, or in circles, covering the same ground again and again. She looked for buildings they had already passed and tried to decipher the Cyrillic signs in case they reappeared. And then they were there. The factory, blurred by the grimy windows of Yuri's car, was a shabby and unremarkable collection of buildings with enough resemblance to Edith's photograph to convince her that here, before them, stood the enterprise they had made such a long journey to see. The factory that, in a different era, had flourished and made her grandfather rich. Gazing at last upon this lost empire, the subject of her father's repeated stories, Edith felt nothing, as if her emotions had been put on hold, though she became aware of a startling concentration of thought and a clarity of her senses. They were acute, ready to register every line, every detail of the place. The buildings, some of them two-storey, appeared distinct, the weeds that reached the bricked-in windows incredibly vivid, the outline of the corrugated roof against the muddy sky precise, the decay obvious. Logs and boards had replaced the brick in many places. The patterned stone fence was gone, but that was to be expected.

Stepping from the stranger's car, Edith felt a small surge of excitement. She reached for Irwin's hand. She was glad he was with her, a fellow traveller, a second witness. They tried various doors, but none would budge, and after an initial flurry of pounding and kicking, mostly by Vassilyj, though Irwin joined in, they gave up and fell silent. A few of Barvenkovo's inhabitants stopped to stare with detached curiosity at the foreigners in their midst. Edith and Irwin, once more hand in hand, began making their way through weeds and around scattered fragments of stone and metal as they circled the buildings solemnly. Vassilyj trailed after them and the driver followed. When they arrived back where they had started, Edith and Irwin made another circle, alone. The two men were waiting for them when they returned, watching for their reaction. Edith was relieved when they resumed their conversation; the attention of the local onlookers embarrassed her She stared at the overgrown, junk-strewn yard where, according to her father's stories, the children had played. She imagined her father raising his small arms for balance and running along the narrow rims of huge fly wheels that lay on the ground, new from the foundry, awaiting shipment to some German estate. He was a prince, his father the king who ruled over the workers in the factory. No one would have believed that the king could die in exile, not quite poor and almost blind, leaving the prince to keep alive the legend of his lost empire.

Irwin shifted restlessly from one foot to the other until he remembered his camera and began assiduously shooting the buildings from all angles. Edith took out her notebook, unsure what to write. She stared at the empty factory, as if by doing so she could persuade it to yield up more. She really wanted more than these crumbling structures, these bricked-in windows, the rough wood of the door frames. She wanted the doors to open so she could walk in, hear the clang and whirr of machinery, watch the workers as they toiled over parts and assembled them. She wanted to turn back the clock, to see how her grandfather, his oldest son in tow, moved and worked within his domain.

Vassilyj came close and said, "Yuri asks, you come now to take your grandfather's factory?"

Edith shook her head. The idea amused her.

"All we take is pictures," Irwin said.

The driver and Vassilyj moved toward the blue car and stood beside it like valets, holding the doors open. Edith and Irwin walked once more to the vehicle and got in. No one spoke as the driver started the car and they drove away. Edith did not look back.

"We look now for the brick house," Vassilyj said, and Edith took the picture from her bag and handed it to him. All three maps of Barvenkovo remained folded, unused. Yuri had no need for a map.

There were numerous brick houses in the streets near the factory, many of them painted over, white or blue or grey. Edith glanced at each, unimpressed.

"Like looking for a needle in a haystack," Irwin said.

"Yuri say his father work in your factory."

This simple statement brought Edith to full alert. She looked quickly to the mirror and once again met the driver's gaze. It seemed more wary than hostile.

"What kind of work did his father do?" she asked, leaning toward Vassilyj, notebook and pen ready. "Ask him what his father said about the factory. About working there." The driver was transformed in her eyes, given a new role.

Yuri's father had been hired, two years before the revolution, to work in the foundry. He'd been eighteen then, on the verge of marriage. In the nearby village where he came from, there had been talk of the new German factory in Barvenkovo. Because he was tall and husky, the foreman had given him the heaviest work in the foundry. Yuri had been born in Barvenkovo. He remembered walking with his father up to a gate in a stone fence. He wasn't allowed to go in, but through the pattern of the fence he could see parts of tractors and harvesting machines lined up on the other side. German children played on the tractors. When the revolution came, the German owner had vanished and the state took over the factory. Yuri's father had continued to work there, though not in the foundry.

"Ask him how long they kept making tractors. Was the factory used during the second war? Did they make war equipment?" These were the questions her father had often speculated on and they came automatically to mind.

In the end Yuri could not give much information. Yes, the factory had been active during the Great Patriotic War, but whether for agriculture or war production, he couldn't say. His father had joined the Red Army and lost his life in the war. In recent years, before the collapse of the Soviet Union, cranes had been the chief product.

Yuri drove up and down the narrow streets of Barvenkovo and Irwin snapped pictures of every brick house that had a vague resemblance to Edith's photo until she told him to stop wasting film. "They've been rebuilt," she said. But he kept on, as if he had suddenly been awakened to the importance of capturing as much of Barvenkovo as he could.

Yuri brought the car to a sudden stop. "Church," he announced. "You like?" He seemed to have decided that the search for the brick house was over, and now he would direct the further tour of Barvenkovo.

The wooden orthodox church was not huge, but the blue and white brilliance of its fresh paint shone against the drab background of the indifferent neighbourhood. Startled and dazzled, Edith looked up to where the sun's rays glinted from the gold trim on two modest cupolas silhouetted against a dusty blue sky. When she ascended the steps to enter the sanctuary, the others followed. The inside was bright with renovation too. Four huge chandeliers glittered above them and wide mauve ribbons swooped down from the balcony to drape around white pillars that marched in two grand columns toward the altar. In front, flickering candles lit up pictures of saints on the icon wall. Several kerchiefed women knelt a decent distance from the altar. An old woman unrolled a red carpet between the columns of pillars. When she came close to the altar, she genuflected and crossed herself.

"I think today it is feast day," Vassilyj said.

As the four made their way along the pillars, Yuri kept glancing at Edith, as if to gauge her reaction, his eyes less hostile, though still enigmatic. A choir sang from the balcony. The mournful strains of minor harmonies carried by human voices filled the church with music. *Gospodi pomilui, Gospodi pomilui*, they sang. God have mercy. Edith closed her eyes. Beside her, Yuri knelt and folded his hands. Edith would have liked to kneel too. She wondered if she might be standing on the same spot her own father had stood as a school boy.

"Our teacher took all of us Mennonite kids to see the orthodox church," he had told her often. "I knelt and made the sign of the cross, just like the Ukrainians. I didn't tell my father that."

"Why not?" Edith had asked.

"He would have beaten me."

LATER THEY STOPPED AT A SMALL DINGY CAFE where Vassilyj ordered for them before joining Yuri, who sat and smoked several tables away.

"Disappointed?" Irwin asked, when they were alone with their cabbage borscht and boiled beef. There was a gentle concern in his voice that surprised and annoyed Edith. She avoided his eyes, shook her head.

"No," she said. "It was magnificent. I felt like we were on holy ground."

"At the factory?"

Edith laughed. "I meant the church," she said. "It's where the people go after work for a bit of beauty. And the factory—well, it was there. We found it. I knew we would. I could tell how fine it must have been in its time, couldn't you? I'm satisfied."

"Maybe you should reclaim it," Irwin teased.

She took out the old picture of the factory, scrutinizing it for clues she had so far missed. Clues to her grandfather's dark sadness.

"Pretty rundown if you ask me," Irwin said. "Coincidence, that Yuri's old man worked there. Or do you think he's pulling our leg?"

"No. I believe him."

"Uncanny, how Yuri met us at the station."

"He didn't go there to meet us. He didn't plan to."

"No, but he did meet us. Or we met him. Yuri, not someone else. It's like that movie, *Six Degrees of Separation*. Remember? It's uncanny."

"Not uncanny, Irwin. Not at all. Barvenkovo's not exactly a huge place and the factory was the only one. It would have been impressive, a place everyone knew about. My grandfather would have looked after it." She wanted to go on, amazed that Irwin was actually becoming interested, but she stopped, aware of the defensiveness creeping into her words.

"No offense, Edie, but I'm wondering what kind of boss your grandfather was. I mean, usually the industrialists weren't all that concerned about their workers. Not then. I wonder what kind of employer he was."

Good, Edith wanted to say. My grandfather was a good employer. A good man. Instead she found herself saying: "He had sad eyes. I told you how he was nearly blind because the doctor who treated him for trachoma used too much bluestone, here, in the clinic outside Barvenkovo. When I was little, I always thought he was sad about being poor. About losing the factory. But really, I guess I never knew much about him." Right now she wasn't sure she wanted to know more.

A SIDE TRIP TO BARVENKOVO'S MEDICAL CLINIC came about quite simply, as if it were meant to be. Late in the day, when they were all once more getting into or out of Yuri's blue car, Vassilyj managed to get the thumb of his right hand jammed in the door. He let out a gasp and put his thumb instinctively into his mouth. Edith cringed and turned away, Irwin offered his handkerchief to absorb the blood, and Yuri drove them all to the clinic that from her father's stories Edith had pictured on a hill outside Barvenkovo. They found it located within the slow sprawl of the town. The street rose slightly to a building as neglected as the rest of Barvenkovo. The name of the clinic and the red cross on the door were barely distinguishable. A grey cat watched them from a bed of petunias.

While Vassilyj's thumb was being stitched up, the other three waited in the reception room. Yuri spoke to the young woman at the desk and Edith felt sure he was explaining who the two tourists were, their connection with the old factory. The possibility that this woman too might have a grandfather or some other relative who had worked in the factory left Edith nervous. She wanted to tell the recep-tionist that her grandfather had been treated here for trachoma before he left for Canada, but the woman spoke no English and probably wouldn't care. Instead, Edith tried to ask her with words and gestures whether trachoma was still being treated here. Yuri came to her assistance.

"No," he said. "No trachoma. No."

A small boy with his right hand in a sling sat crying beside his father, who seemed to be turned to stone. There were two pregnant women, a schoolgirl, a young man talking to an older woman, probably his mother. The weight of resignation rested on them all. They waited as those who have no expectations, no assurance that the world owes them something. Edith thought of the unemployed who waited with similar apathy for their interviews in her Winnipeg office.

When Vassilyj emerged with his bandaged thumb cradled in the opposite hand and held high like a fragile treasure, Irwin ushered them out and lined them up for a picture. Flanked by petunias and a cat on one side, the clinic door with the unreadable name on the other, they blinked into the afternoon sun.

"That almost finishes my film," Irwin announced. "I'll save a few, in case."

THERE WAS NO HOTEL IN BARVENKOVO, in spite of Irwin's insistence that they had to have one for two nights. Yuri shrugged. No. No hotel. He discussed this lack of lodging with Vassilyj, who wasn't much help because of his thumb.

"Yuri find for you a house," he told them, finally. "Everything will be good. A house will be good." And while Edith and Irwin assured themselves he couldn't possibly be planning to lodge them with total strangers, Yuri drove on.

"Are you believers?" Vassilyj asked, interrupting his conversation with Yuri. He rested his injured hand tenderly against the soiled upholstery.

"Believers?" Irwin sounded puzzled.

"Do you believe in God?"

It was a bizarre thing to ask of two foreigners travelling

in a stranger's car. Yuri's eyes were indistinct in the rearview mirror.

"Yes," Edith said.

"Yuri take us now to a house where live believers." He spoke as if this information should set them at ease.

Past the older streets they came to a district of apartment buildings clinging to the edge of Barvenkovo, a joyless residential complex, the balconies decorated with lines of laundry, a few potted petunias, and everywhere the outcroppings of satellite dishes. Mostly they were five-storey blocks, but occasionally a highrise thrust its stark, concrete presence up against the sky.

"That's what the cranes were used for." Unappalled by the ugliness, Irwin turned the dusty window down so he could see better. "Your grandfather's factory helped Kruschev build homes for the expanding population," he said, as if that confirmed its existence.

Edith smiled, amused at his belated interest in the factory. As for Krushchev's drab housing, it depressed her. She didn't want to look at it.

Yuri stopped the car at the third in a series of identical doors in one of the apartment clusters, and when he got out, Vassilyj followed him. The two passengers watched the men disappear into the building.

"What do you think?' Edith said.

"What choice do we have?"

"If I had to come home every day after work to one of these shabby blocks, I'd need therapy." Edith shuddered. She was surprised that she felt no particular fear, though her mind and body had shifted once again into a state of sharp alert that left no room for the normal weariness a traveller has a right to feel at the end of a full day. She kept hearing Vassilyj's unexpected question, "Do you believe in God?"

"Too bad your dad never went back to see that factory," Irwin said, turning to Edith. "Why didn't he? Ten years ago the factory would've still been in operation."

The white Winnipeg fence had been pushed far into

the day's periphery. Irwin was satisfied with the pictures he'd taken. It had been a good day for him, and this helped tip the balance for Edith also, toward the good. They had, after all, found the factory. As for why her father had never travelled to Barvenkovo? Edith had wondered about that too, ever since his death. He had certainly had the means, unlike his father.

"I often wondered," Edith said, "why Dad never encouraged me to travel to Barvenkovo."

A bearded man emerged from the third door with Yuri and Vassiljy. He was shorter and older than Yuri and walked with a limp. His face, though not smiling, held a kind of assurance.

"Grigor has room," Vassiljy explained. "You stay here. I go with Yuri."

"If we stay, you stay." Irwin spoke before Edith could. "Who would translate?"

Vassilyj shrugged. "This man speak maybe one, two words English," he said. "You stay here? Or maybe we look for bigger place?"

"So Grigor is a believer?" Edith asked. She saw how strained Vassilyj looked. He needed a reprieve from the two tourists, a respite from speaking English. She knew he would rather go with Yuri.

Vassiljy nodded.

"We'll stay. You too."

Yuri helped them carry their bags up four unlit flights, accepted Irwin's *grivni* without comment, and left.

A woman in a dark skirt and brown shawl, shorter even than the bearded man, and as old, led them through a small hallway to a poorly lit room, obviously the main one. She smiled and made a sweeping gesture of welcome with both hands. "*Chai?*" she asked. "*Chai?*" Her voice was loud, as if by increasing volume she could make herself understood by these foreigners. Three of the four walls were hung with woollen floral rugs, and frayed sectional furniture was pushed against the rugs. A crocheted doily decorated the small table. In one rug-lined corner hung an icon, a gilded picture of Jesus.

When the woman, Olga, brought tea, Edith turned to Vassiljy. "Ask them if they remember the factory."

The conversation of the three Ukrainians became animated. It shut out Edith and Irwin, leaving them to their tea. Occasionally the host and his wife, and Vassilyj too, turned to look at Edith, as if appraising her.

"Yes, they remember," Vassilyj said.

"What? What do they remember? Do they remember the original owner?" And then she added, "Was it good to work for him?" It wasn't a question she had jotted down on one of the many lists she'd made in preparation for the journey. She hadn't expected to ask it.

Vassilyj hesitated, and conferred once more with the old man and woman, and once more their conversation meandered, leaving the foreigners forgotten.

"I want to know," Edith interrupted, her voice controlled and calm. "What was it like to work at the factory?"

"Many people work there." Vassilyj shrugged, clearly unwilling to go farther.

"And what about the pay?" Irwin spoke slowly, deliberately. "Were the people satisfied with their pay? Were they treated well by the owner?"

Vassilyj turned to the old couple as if for rescue, but they had turned toward their tea and said nothing. He shook his head.

"No?" Irwin asked. "No, what? The pay wasn't good or they weren't treated well? What does the old man say?"

Apparently the "no" meant both. Labourers in the factory had been of one mind about the wages: they were not enough for a working man to feed his family. The Mennonite owner and his foremen had a reputation for demanding long hours of work and handing out harsh punishment. There had been brutal beatings.

Even with the hesitation of the old couple and Vassilyj's translation slowing it down, the information was coming at

Edith too fast. She wanted to turn it off before it stunned her. Why had she and Irwin insisted on it? Now she would have to prove that it was all wrong, that these believers were misinformed, that they had given credence to false rumours, or were telling outright lies. Maybe age had distorted their memories, rendering their evidence unreliable. She could barely restrain herself from raising her hands to cover her ears.

"What else?" Incredible, that Irwin was asking for more, but Vassilyj questioned their host again and then he was silent, listening to Grigor. And then more silence as the old man sat with his head bowed, as if burdened by some grief that had returned to him. Irwin had to prod Vassilyj before he released the information that Grigor's neighbour had been beaten bloody and senseless by the factory's foreman, on orders from the owner, while the owner's son watched. A week later the man had died.

There was no need to ask or tell more. The import of the knowledge they now shared filled the room. Edith tried to conjure the sad face of her grandfather, the old man with damaged eyes, arms that once gestured imperiously, a mouth that had spoken orders. But the only image to appear in her mind was that of his grave marker in the cemetery north of Winnipeg, with his name, *Johann J. Lange*, carved in the stone, and below it the words: *Rest in Peace and Mercy*. Her father had taught her to read the words when she was too young to notice that on other stones there was no "Mercy," only "Rest in Peace." When she was old enough to ask, her father had said only, "Your grandfather wanted those words."

Olga carried the tea things to the kitchen. Her husband rearranged the sectional furniture and brought faded blankets and pillows to make a bed for the guests. When he was making up a bed for Vassilyj, on the floor in the narrow passage at the entrance, the doorbell rang. It was late, and the faces of the old couple showed consternation. When Olga opened the door, a man holding a camera stepped across the threshold. It was Yuri, and the camera was Irwin's.

"You forget, yes?" Yuri said, handing it over. In the poor light of the room his face seemed to have lost its disquieting aspect.

"My God," Irwin said. "I hadn't even noticed it was gone." He took it and shook hands with Yuri. "Thanks, man, I don't know what to say."

He reached into his pocket but Yuri waved the *grivni* away with a firm gesture. Vassilyj and Grigor and Olga crowded round, smiling, as delighted as if the returned camera were theirs. Yuri repeated with a kind of pleasure and with more animation than he had shown all day, "You forget. You forget in my car."

The old woman turned to face the icon. She crossed herself and mumbled a prayer. Her face creased into a smile and her eyes shone.

THE MAKESHIFT BED WAS NARROW FOR TWO PEOPLE, the covers and pillows musty. Edith didn't count on sleeping. Under the blankets Irwin's comforting hand moved over her body.

"It was long ago, Edie," he whispered in the absolute darkness of the room. "Long ago." He drew her securely to him.

Edith, knowing now why she had come, could not speak for grief.

"Good man, that Yuri," Irwin whispered.

"Yes."

"I thought he'd rob us all he could."

"Shh. Vassiljy's trying to sleep."

Irwin sighed and Edith moved in closer to him. As the events of the day and the knowledge gained pushed into her brain and her body, she felt Irwin's arms relax. He was asleep.

So this is where the journey had brought them, this narrow bed in the house of strangers. Believers. Irwin would

215

pay them, of course, but Edith was overwhelmed by the burden of debt so enormous nothing could ever be enough. And not just Grigor and Olga, but Yuri too, who had not robbed them, the old women in the church, the receptionist at the clinic, all the labourers who had worked long hours in her grandfather's factory and for their efforts received a low wage. And, in at least one case, death. And Vassilyj, sleeping on the floor with his injured thumb. In Kiev he had told them he wanted no money, only his ticket paid for, and the travel agent had assured them he was glad for the chance to practise English with "native speakers."

Edith couldn't shake off the conviction that she ought to have come bringing gifts of gratitude and atonement, not empty-handed. Desolate, she felt the beginning of a throbbing, not only in her head but in her whole body, as if the unrelenting rhythm of last night's train was melding with the pain she imagined pounding in Vassilyj's thumb. To counteract her misery she let the mournful choir music from the orthodox church flow into the surrounding darkness, willing it to wash the day's events from every corner of her mind and body. The stooped, sad figure of her once-rich grandfather appeared, unsummoned, and in its presence she repeated, over and over like a prayer, the five-word inscription on his lonely grave-marker. *Rest in Peace and Mercy.* Toward morning, she slept.

THE LEGEND

WHEN JONAS WAS ONLY FIVE, his father was flown home in
a sealed metal coffin. He insists he remembers the burial: his
mother silent and motionless beside the unopened coffin,
the rough chunks of frozen earth thudding on the lid, the
dead trees in the small winter cemetery in Minsk where
they buried him on a snowy day. He remembers how his
cheeks burned in the sharp wind.

After listening to him tell of it, Roger can't help wondering what other stories of loss and of tragedy lie untold
behind the apparently serene and unsceptical faces of his
students. The first day of classes he asked them to write
about themselves, introductions that are now piled untidily
on a shelf, hand-written fragments composed courageously
and written badly in a language they have yet to master. He
rereads one or two every day in a sincere effort to know his
students. They offer a richness of place names: Kaunas,
Vilnius, Kretinga, Joniskis. The older students name a
university, an occupation. The younger ones, with more
sentiment than Roger can digest, refer to grandmothers
who raised them. The words "beautiful" and "wonderful"

appear often. The evidence is innocent, for the most part, and he is sure the most significant things have been left out. He tries sometimes to imagine the unexpected return of a father no longer alive, his body concealed in a cold metal box.

Roger lives in a medium-sized room on the fifth floor of the building for foreign teachers, higher than he's ever lived before. There is no elevator.

I can run up the five flights without excessive puffing, he writes to Gail. *Prepare to see your dad fit and trim at the end of the summer.* He wants to add something about being "a different person," but the words lack a convincing ring. The change he feels within himself, if it's there at all, is too slight or too recent to define. And maybe he's just assuming that in a new place with a foreign language constantly humming around him, different air and architecture, the enchanting nearness of the sea, something should be altered.

The door to his room stands ajar as if to admit someone, but he's not expecting a visitor, and when Gita appears in the doorway, a book in her hand, he is unprepared. She is younger than Gail by a few years, he reckons. He has a habit of measuring his female students against his daughter—taller, more slight, prettier or less so. Gita is not pretty, but her eyes are set with enormous gravity in her pale, angular face and, from the first, their gaze has stirred him in a way that's always unexpected, just as the first glimpse of the grey-green sea when he has climbed to the top of the dunes always takes him by surprise.

"Can I come now?" Gita asks. She waits, not quite at ease, although her eyes are unwavering. There's a hot stirring inside him, and also a rush of pity. He's sure he made no appointment with Gita. He'd remember if he had.

"Come in, Gita. Sure, I've got a minute." There is no unsteadiness in his voice, nothing about him betrays either unwillingness or undue heartiness.

Gita steps across the threshold and looks around as if to discover where she is, what this place contains. As if she hasn't been here before, many times. Roger's room is also his office where he keeps appointments with students— Jonas finds some pretext or other for a visit several times a week—and he tries to keep his tabletop looking like a desk, the kitchen counter clear of dirty dishes, his bed made like the beds of his neatest colleagues. He's not particularly good at it. Not like Carol, who managed without apparent effort to keep their house in Winnipeg orderly, even beautiful in a plain sort of way. On the mantel she placed three roughly carved wooden angels with stubby wings, long peasant skirts painted blue, and the round, innocent faces of children. One held a candle in her carved fingers, another a book. The third raised her hands so they perpetually covered her face. He used to refer to them facetiously as the guardian seraphs of their house. Other times he gave them ordinary women's names—Catherine, Elizabeth, Grace— but Carol never appreciated his efforts to endow them with any kind of mortal identity. When she left she must have taken the angels with her.

Once a week Gita comes with mop and pail and rags to clean Roger's room while he goes to the market or takes a book to read in the park. She is thorough in her cleaning and enjoys arranging and rearranging books and dishes and furniture. In a short time she has given everything a place: the pattern of his room is a gift she has given him. And her presence that stirs him so powerfully has also a tranquility he wants to cling to.

"I bring you now the stories." Gita falters because she has noticed his distraction, his agitation.

"Stories?"

"About Lithuania.'

She holds the book out to Roger. He takes it and remembers then that on Monday he asked his students about the folklore of their country and Gita offered to bring a book of legends, translated into English. A painting of a mermaid with long pale hair decorates the brown cover.

"Here is Jurate," Gita points.

Not knowing quite how to proceed, Roger hands the book back to her. "Why don't you read, Gita?"

"I read? Now?'

"Why not?"

"What you like I read?"

"About this one—what did you say her name was?"

Gita hesitates, as if waiting for an invitation to sit down. He waves her to a chair and she sits on the edge of it, her long skirt falling almost to the floor, covering her shoes. She bends her head over the book and when she has found the page, begins to read: *A young fisherman fell in love with the beautiful goddess of the sea.*

As Gita's hair falls forward over her plain face, Roger sees its warm sheen, the flecks of amber in the brown. His hands want to touch it, and his body longs, suddenly and violently, for every warm crevice of hers, every softness. It's as if he remembers her entirely. Every limb and even, he thinks, every bone and muscle, though of course that isn't true. Isn't possible. His hands clench and unclench.

"Some of the students have a hard time with fees," Peter, the director of the Summer English Institute, said at the first staff meeting. "I've got a list of those who'd like to earn money cleaning your rooms or shopping for you. Or translating or even baking. It's okay, so long as we all pay the same hourly rate." That's how it started.

Right now the room is reasonably tidy. Very deliberately Roger orders his eyes to review the details: the floor is clean except at the entrance, the windows not smudged, the stove decent, the tea towels laundered and neatly folded on the counter. The top of the door frame is probably thick with dust. Why has he never thought of telling Gita to dust the top of the door frame? The fridge won't need defrosting for at least a few weeks. He has only been here for three.

After classes, walking along unfamiliar streets shaded by leafy lime trees, he invariably ends up at the small cobbled theatre square in the heart of the city. In the centre of the square there's a fountain, and in the fountain, the bronze statue of a young girl with braids and an apron. She holds a bronze flower in her hand. Her back is turned to the balcony of the theatre from where Hitler proclaimed in 1939 that this city would always be German. The girl, her name was Aennchen, married three times, always older men, widowers with children who needed a mother. At least that was the tale the guide told. Looking up at that statue silhouetted against a blue sky—day after day this summer, the sky is a peerless blue—it always seems to Roger he is alone in the middle of a vast desert where the sun beats down and the wind blows sand around his ankles. Nothing but the statue in sight, not in any of the wind's four directions.

Mother and I went to the Forks this afternoon and walked along the river. It's still high. For my sociology course I've got to write a paper on child abuse in Winnipeg. Gail will write regularly, he's sure, but is the one word, *Mother,* all he will get about Carol? Her name dropped naked into a letter is more than he can bear. You live with someone for more than two decades and then one day find yourself an ocean away from everyone and everything that has become familiar in all the precious years of living. An ocean away—and that's counting only physical distance. That distance was absolutely necessary for him to obtain, or so he believed, when the notice about teaching in Lithuania appeared on the staff-room bulletin board. He wonders if Carol too is overcome sometimes by this merciless longing that fills his days. He wonders where she has placed the three angels. Does the angel with the candle stand as he remembers her, left of the angel with the covered face? His favourite was the angel with the book.

Gita was the first student he met. She came early the first day and claimed a place in the second row. Among the more stylishly dressed students, her plain skirt and blouse always give her an air of modesty and containment. As for her mastery of English, she's somewhere in the lower middle of the class. Roger thinks the difference between her and other students is that while most of them come from towns and cities in Lithuania, she comes from a village, the village Kintai.

The god of thunder punished them. The beautiful palace under the sea lay in ruins. Gita's been reading steadily, though she sometimes stumbles over the English phrases. Her voice is pleasant; her accent lends freshness and fragility to the words. But Roger has missed the events leading up to the ruin of the beautiful palace under the sea. What roused the god of thunder to such anger that he inflicted this violent punishment?

Light from the west window falls on the pages of the book and on Gita's hands, turning them bright as angel wings. Roger can barely restrain his own hands from reaching for those hands, grabbing them more greedily than any living thing should be held. The longing slides damply down along his brow, his face, his neck. His body is sticky with it. He is impatient for the story to end, for Gita to close the book.

WHEN JONAS SAYS, "CAN YOU COME, FRIDAY? We like you eat with us," Roger assumes he will meet the mother who has taken to drinking after her husband was shipped home in a sealed coffin. "They say us he die from pneumonia," Jonas says. "We do not believe he die from pneumonia." But it's an older woman who opens the door after they've walked up the four unlit flights, groping like blind intruders for the broken metal railing. "Be careful," Jonas cautions at every step. "Please, very careful." From the tiny entrance hall a door straight ahead leads to a small kitchen that spills out savoury cooking aromas. An observant, long-haired cat occupies the doorway.

They follow the old woman into a larger room filled with odd pieces of furniture, shabby and uncomfortable; and wall units crammed with Lithuanian and Russian books; dainty china cups chipped and unmatched; various carved knick-knacks; a green tangle of plants. If Carol were here she would pick off the yellow leaves and dead bits. Roger looks for a picture of the dead father, but there isn't one. An old, dark red rug, the pattern worn bare, covers the floor. Everything in the flat seems ancient and weary. Dust-laden. Carol would find it impossible to breathe in this room. She would tackle the dust and clutter with energy, creating order and even beauty. Carol, and Gita too, would be at ease with the old grandmother.

"My grandmother say she make wine from apples," Jonas says and Roger understands he is being asked if he'll try it.

The grandmother hurries back and forth between the kitchen and this room and in her movements there's the lightness of a much younger woman. She speaks to her grandson as she brings cottage cheese *blyni* with a rich cream sauce and raspberry preserves and the pale wine she's made from apples in her garden. Roger has never seen such astonishing grace in one who looks so ancient, her wispy hair pure white. The wine is sweet and fruity.

"My grandmother say, you please take. Eat," Jonas says.

Roger heaps raspberry preserves on steaming *blyni*. "Your grandmother lived through the war," he says, and Jonas understands that his teacher would like to hear stories. He speaks to the old woman and then tanslates as she begins to tell about the years of Soviet occupation.

Her husband, a teacher in a village school, was sent east into exile where he vanished like smoke into the cold white vastness, while she began to hoe endless rows of beets on the farming collective to which she was assigned. Her daughter grew up and fulfilled her mother's fears by marry-ing a Russian, an officer in the Red Army. The officer quickly rose to a top position that required him to fly reg-ularly to Leningrad and Moscow and Odessa. His business was never talked about. It was connected with the military and consequently secret. Some time after his last departure he came home in a coffin to his wife and infant son, Jonas, who lived then in Minsk.

"Grandmother say, 'My son-in-law die not good. Some bad thing happen,'" Jonas translates.

Roger is about to ask about that "bad thing" that happened, what it might be, but he feels suddenly wary of the story. He is afraid that, unlike his students' stories, this one will tell everything, and the force of it will sap his strength. The grandmother's eyes are bright. She sits poised, waiting to be asked, ready to spill out more unrelenting details of the life she holds inside. But this would be unbearable, Roger believes. He is unprepared to receive so much memory, so much suffering, and all the surmise and speculation that by now must surely surround it like musty lace. He wonders how often she has told and retold it, and to whom. How does she decide which fragments to offer to which listener? What edges have been smoothed in the telling, which particulars abandoned? Or added? And he wonders how Jonas's translation alters or shapes the events that will always be at the core of his life and of his grandmother's.

Roger doesn't know what to say to the grandmother. What do you say when a person, not quite a stranger, tells you the story that is always present, invisible but palpable, as she eats and works and thinks, the story that is still there when she lies in her bed at night, that will follow her to the conclusion of her days? Does the grandmother recite her life, the way one recites an ancient tale, evenings when she stares out the window? Does the chronicle become a refuge, a haven against the demands of the day?

"My mother, she not eat with us. She, how you say, not able." Jonas indicates, with a slight movement of his hand, a closed door. If Roger were to open it, he would find her, this woman driven to drink by the story. He pictures her as colourless and transparent with grief, like an insect that has dwelt too long under a stone in the damp darkness.

As if she has spent her supply of energy, the grandmother leans back now, her face toward the window that overlooks the harbour where metal cranes loom dark as vultures against a rose-coloured evening sky. Her features settle and her mouth becomes slack in repose, though without losing its confidence. The cat has leapt into her lap.

"My mother and I, we come here, to Klaipeda," Jonas is explaining. "To grandmother."

And then all of them are absorbed into a silence soft and soothing as shade on a scorching July day. Roger feels that his mind is ready for reflection. But reflection is still new to him. His life as a teacher has left little room for it. He forces himself to speak.

"Ask your grandmother, what kept her going? Did she ever lose hope when all these things happened? Did she despair?"

"What means 'despair'?" Jonas asks and a discussion follows as they fumble and grope for definition. This, in turn, requires a lengthy exchange of words between grandmother and grandson before Roger gets the answer. He is watching one of the metal cranes swing slowly as it loads a freighter.

"She say she is not lose hope. She say hope is there, is beside her like a friend, when she work in the fields or in the garden or cooking."

She means God, Roger thinks, or some sort of presence, and because he doesn't know what else to say he asks, "Doesn't she ever think it's punishment?" He's not sure why he said that and regrets it at once, but Jonas is already translating. The grandmother becomes agitated and Roger is embarrassed. It was a stupid thing to say, here in a country where the past is crowded with suffering and the present uncertain and where he is a novice at life. "Be careful," Jonas is always cautioning him. "Our streets, for you they are not safe. Everybody know you are foreigner."

Gradually the old woman's voice grows calm and settles into a rich, liturgical lilt, as if she is recounting her blessings. When she is finished, it is too much for Jonas to translate and he says simply, "My grandmother say, no punishment. She say every year the garden get green. Every year is, how you say, harvest."

The grandmother tells more, a story for which Jonas supplies the translation: Lithuania is like a roof supported at its four corners by three women and a man. The man has long abandoned his place. The roof is still standing.

The grandmothers breaks into laughter at this anecdote, her wrinkles reshaping themselves into concentric circles in her face. Roger wonders if the woman behind the closed door can hear the laughter. Then, as if remembering forgotten duties, the grandmother rises to remove dishes and offer more wine, familiar tasks her hands and feet have practised a lifetime. She has known emptiness and loss, but her life is full. She chatters, and in her eyes Roger detects once more that youthful brightness. There is safety in this cluttered room, and he would like to stay here in the quiet presence of this woman who has not been defeated, not by tragedy, not by the Soviet system. She moves off into the kitchen and returns with coffee and a plate of gooseberry cakes for Roger to try. The coffee is strong and bitter. The gooseberry cakes are tart to his tongue, but also sweet, and he eats three pieces.

SATURDAY MORNING THE SKY IS A JEWEL. Azure. Every leaf on every lime tree is distinct and brilliant as if rain-washed, but there's been no rain. Roger catches the first ferry across the lagoon. Several old men with fishing gear sit together on a bench. A group of young men just out of their teens have taken their beer to the covered part of the ferry, out of the sun. They are drinking, laughing, jostling each other, half playfully, half in earnest. At any moment the playfulness could explode into belligerence, Roger thinks, remembering his teenaged students in Winnipeg. Three kerchiefed women with baskets find seats near the front. They remind Roger of the three wooden angels.

The rest of the passengers stand. Roger has never taken the ferry so early, and it's never been so empty. I'm the only one travelling alone, he thinks. Alone, with strange people whose language I don't even understand. But he doesn't mind. He watches the ducks swimming near the boat, alert for scraps. Gulls float overhead and clouds roll in from the sea, casting a thin haze over everything.

Leaving the ferry, he heads for the cool, spruce-lined path to the beach. He walks slowly, letting the others overtake him. He relishes the solitude. At a wayside bench he sits down and rummages in his knapsack for Gita's book of legends. He opens it and turns to the one about Jurate, the sea princess in the enchanted palace, punished for falling in love with a mortal. Or maybe the mortal was punished for falling in love with the sea goddess. *Her hair was yellow as the sun,* he reads, *and her eyes the colour of the sea.* Gita, of course, is the sea princess, and the Lithuanian grandmother is the the old woman who does not lose hope, waiting for her fisherman son to return. Carol is outside that story. And so is he. A foreigner.

He closes the book and stares into the forest, at the mysterious spaces between the tall trunks of spruce. The sun slides in and out of clouds that have begun moving in from the sea. He lets the story go and feels light and grateful, anticipating the climb over the dunes, the rhythm of sea waves breaking on the sand.

The young men from the ferry are coming along the path, five or six of them. He hears their raucous voices. They have replenished their supply of beer at the landing and are making their way, slightly drunk and singing, to the sea. Should he hurry on ahead or let them pass? He hesitates, and his indecision allows them to come closer. He wonders later if he rose from the bench and moved willingly toward them, as though a meeting was inevitable. And they, as if in answer to that inevitability, or to some dark need of their own, rushed toward the meeting like gulls swooping down upon a tempting fish.

At the beginning everything happens in slow motion, he and the gang of young men gradually merging until they are all part of one mass, he somewhere in the middle,

uncertain but calm, one hand still holding Gita's book. The
first blow seems of no particular force or significance, but
then the half-dozen men become a mob, they turn into a
battering machine and there's no fending off the barrage of
blows from fists, elbows, shoulders more muscular than his.
A hard boot connects with his groin. His body slams down
on the gravel path under their trampling boots, his face
grinds into the stones. Another vicious kick sends the book
flying from his hand. He is still conscious, still able to think
that he is like the man who fell among thieves travelling
from Jerusalem to Jericho and there has to be a good
Samaritan somewhere. Jonas's repeated warning, *be careful*,
rings in his brain, a mocking echo. The anger that should
have come to his aid is absent; he feels nothing but stunned
amazement. The thought that he may not return home alive
flits through his head but he lets it go, knowing, and it is a
firm knowing, that this assault is not fatal. His attackers are
losing interest and he hasn't lost consciousness. He will
return to the room Gita tidies for him on the fifth floor.
And eventually he will return to Winnipeg, to the house
Carol has abandoned. One day he may see Carol again, it's
not an impossible thing to wish for. One day all visible
traces of this incident will be erased.

The anger that failed him flows now, belated and without force. It's of no use to him. His attackers are already disappearing around a bend in the path, and only now his
body explodes in a burst of searing pain. His voice keens
above the trees, above the wind. It rises, then subsides to a
whimper that the first passengers from the second ferry
can't hear until they are almost beside him.

ROGER IS SEATED AT HIS TABLE preparing lessons, a review
of verb tenses, past simple and present simple, though nothing's really simple, he thinks, not in the past, certainly not in
the present. For instance, Carol, who failed to return one
evening from the daycare centre where she was director. *You*

wouldn't understand, she explained in a note he found stuck to the microwave. And of course she was right; it was beyond comprehension. Their life together had settled into a denouement he had assumed they could draw out as long as they lived, each one giving in to the momentum that carried them both along. He had never, he realized, struggled much against that momentum, even though he had not been unaware of the slow splintering between them. He with his endless administrative duties at the school, the many committees he'd allowed himself to be appointed to. She with a heart always torn and bleeding over the plight of one or another of the children at the daycare. "Darcy came crying today. I'm positive that mark on her cheek didn't get there from playing." Or: "Honestly, the way parents drop off their kids, like stray animals they want to dump." It seemed that in Carol, compassion had transformed into perpetual, righteous outrage over which she had no control. The force of it swept her along like a twig on water. It claimed her completely and hurried her on. Long before either of them knew it, long before she left Roger, she had been sucked out of his life. He is afraid to think about it. He doesn't know how.

Roger's room is not tidy. He hasn't bothered to wash the dishes or straighten the papers on his desk. At the entrance there are muddy footprints, a consequence of this morning's rain. But it doesn't matter: Gita is coming to clean everything. Roger goes to the shelf and selects the book he'll take with him to the park to read while she works. He also takes paper and pen so he can write to Gail. Should he ask about Carol? When he returns to this room, Gita will have reestablished her order in it and she herself will be there, sitting on the kitchen chair, waiting for him to pay her the right number of *litas* for her work. Waiting for him and for his approval or disapproval.

When she first saw him after the attack on that Saturday, she gasped and, as in a novel, her hand flew involuntarily to her throat. "Why it happen?" she asked in anguish, as if she was taking all the trauma of the assault upon herself. He wanted to hold her then, comfort her. Or he wanted *her* to hold *him* in her sturdy, protecting arms. But instead he told her, "It could have been worse."

"An angel is with you maybe," she said.

"I was lucky," he told Jonas, who predicted the police would do nothing and he was right, though they did come around to ask questions.

"Because you are foreigner," Jonas said, his face innocent and earnest.

Roger is grateful for his concern and wants to acknowledge it. "Your father," he asks, "what did he really die of?"

Jonas does not immediately answer. He shrugs and fidgets in his chair, and the innocence vanishes from his face, though not the earnestness. Roger waits.

"My father's coffin," Jonas begins, "it should not be opened. Very strong order."

Roger waits for more, but Jonas is quiet.

"So of course it wasn't opened," Roger says.

Jonas lowers his head and his voice is the whisper of one afraid of being overheard. Afraid of surveillance.

"The coffin, it is opened. My mother wants that. She say me she has help, and they open it. At night."

"And?"

"Empty. It is empty."

"Empty." Roger echoes the words, foolishly, and when Jonas doesn't reply, "So then, what...what does that mean?"

There is no answer.

"Is your father still alive, then? Is that what you think?"

Jonas lifts his head. "Of course not alive," he says and his face is a mix of sorrowful amusement and pity for the foreigner who still doesn't understand.

Peter was sympathetic after the attack on Roger. "Take a couple of days," he said. "I'll cover for you. Sometimes there are things more important than teaching your classes."

Like the flood in Winnipeg this spring. When the swelling volume of the Red River moved inexorably up from the south, the principal cancelled classes at the collegiate and Roger found himself standing side by side with some of his worst grade eleven students, constructing a temporary bulwark around flood-threatened, three-car-garage homes next to the rising river. His students hoisted sandbags as if they were filled with nothing heavier than autumn leaves. Roger struggled to keep up.

"So now we get to save the king of the castle," one of them said, matter-of-factly. But the force of the flood was too great. The sandbag dike where they were working broke, and the water rushed in. With incredible speed it covered the concrete floors of garages, poured into basements and just kept rising. They were not, after all, destined to be saviours.

The flood that in May was all-powerful seems vague and distant now, as if it never happened. He was too busy afterwards with end-of-school duties, and preparing to come to Lithuania, to think about it much. There must be people in Winnipeg even now struggling with the effects of its violence.

Gita arrives, wearing the usual plain skirt and blouse. Her eyes move immediately to Roger's face, taking in every fading bruise.

"Would you mind dusting the top of the door frame?" Roger says, pointing, as he picks up his bag to leave. At the door he hesitates, then turns to where she's already running water at the sink. He removes the right number of *litas* from his pocket and brings them to her.

"You don't have to wait for me, Gita," he says, struggling against uncertainty as he holds the money out to her.

She takes the *litas* in her wet hand. Her face is inscrutable; Roger can't tell whether she's sorry or relieved. Then, remembering, he goes to the shelf for the book of Lithuanian legends. He's repaired it as much as possible. Before he gives it to Gita, he slides the flat of his hand one more time over the image of the blonde mermaid on its cover.

"Your book got battered," he says, "But the pages are all

there." And after a clumsy silence, "I read the one about Jurate twice. I'm sorry her beautiful palace got destroyed."

She protests, "You keep, please, this book," but he is already stepping through the door into the hallway. He wishes he had asked Gita which story *she* liked best. He is astonished how little he knows about her life outside of school. Nothing, really, except that she comes from the village Kintai, a place that has not stirred his curiosity.

When he moves from the building's poorly lit stairway into the summer street, he begins composing his letter to Gail. *Lithuania has a lot of ancient legends*, he will write. *I've been reading a book of them recently*. He considers this beginning, and then adds, *In one story, a man travelling to the sea falls among thieves*. He is surprised at this sentence, but pleased all the same with its possibilities. The assaulted man could be defeated. Or he could struggle with his attackers and prevail. He could walk away unhurt, continue on his way to the sea and spend a sun-filled morning on the sand. The outcome of the story, Roger thinks with satisfaction, is in his hands, and he is quite sure that when he reaches the serenity of the park he will find the next sentence.

JOURNEY TO PRAGUE

GRAHAM IS NOT THE LAST TO BOARD the bus when the group leaves Auschwitz. Bob Carr is still out there, in spite of the rain, panning his video camera in a slow arc across the barbed fence with its grey lookout towers and the wrought-iron sign: "*Arbeit Macht Frei.*" The Higginses are running across the parking lot with hot dogs in their hands. The sausages are smoked to perfection and Anne Higgins is filled with praise for the fine flavour added by the spoonful of sauerkraut topping. Graham moved with disgust past the snack counter where the others lined up after the tour. He has the bottled water he bought in Krakow and a sandwich he made from bread and cheese at the hotel breakfast. If only he had saved his orange too.

Graham doesn't get a window seat. Nanette, the fourteen-year-old daughter of the Higginses, has elbowed her way forward and slips into the last one just ahead of him. She is halfway through her hot dog and places the can of Coke between her denim knees. Graham takes the place beside her.

"Let's get this friggin' show on the road." Bob Carr

speaks and moves with a heartiness Graham finds offensive. Bob is a squarish man. Behind his sombre expression lurks an aspiring comedian, with a comedian's need for an audience. He moves grandly to the back of the bus.

Although the bleak stone barracks and barbed wire are within full sight, most of the women have put Auschwitz firmly behind them. They are pulling from plastic bags the hand-painted Easter eggs, embroidered linens, ceramic vases and candle holders they bought yesterday from vendors in Krakow's old town square. They exult over the good fortune of having found the perfect ashtray, a piece of genuine amber, a tablecloth that will complement a certain pattern of Royal Doulton china when it's spread over an oak or teak or cherrywood table somewhere in Canada. One woman worries about packing a costly cut-glass bowl so it can be flown across the Atlantic and arrive safely home. Another says, so loudly she can be heard to the front of the bus, "I only buy jew'lry. It don't take up any space at all and at customs, hey, you just shove it in your bra or someplace."

Someone wonders if her new possessions will pose a problem when she crosses the border from Poland into the Czech Republic.

Susan, a vague, middle-aged woman always humming in a breathy voice, always wearing an ankle-length, crinkly flowered dress, has bought a marionette, a dragon made of lime green and shocking pink felt. There's a little plastic device the vendor gave her to put in her mouth and when she whispers through it the dragon speaks. Or worse, sings. Her mind must be in terrible disarray, Graham thinks, watching her walk the dragon through the air in front of her down the narrow bus aisle.

One of the displays in the Auschwitz museum was a jumble of suitcases, names and addresses still readable, though the bags looked shabby and ready to disintegrate. Graham marvels that once those bags held the cherished possessions of still-living people, the hastily packed remnants of their dislocated lives. The guide pointed out the name on a particularly worn suitcase: M. Frank. The last text Graham read with his ninth-graders in June—the sun streaming through the east window, the students restless as caged animals—was *The Diary of Anne Frank*. Of course M. Frank couldn't possibly be from the same family, but he can't get rid of the idea that the black scuffed bag might have belonged once to a girl as young and unscarred as Nanette.

Graham isn't so much annoyed as peculiarly saddened to be sitting beside an adolescent who might be one of his ninth-graders. Or, for that matter, his daughter, if he'd married and fathered children. Something about her cool self-containment—a composure nothing on this trip has ruffled—depresses his spirits. Shouldn't he be the one with confidence born of experience and she looking to him for encouragement or wisdom? But it's clear Nanette needs nothing from him.

"She's stubborn, that one," her mother has told the other women. "Can't tell her anything."

John Higgins rarely speaks to his daughter.

Graham looks warily at Nanette. A kind of yearning springs up inside him, a desire hard to define. Will he get to know this young fellow traveller with her nonchalance and straight brown hair, as the bus takes them to Prague? He won't count on it. He takes out his *Lonely Planet Guidebook* and turns to the section on Prague.

In front of him Elise and Marge, also unmarried, are munching granola bars. Neither woman has spoken to him since he lingered too long in bookstores and kept the whole group waiting, once in Warsaw and again in Krakow. Elise is a nurse employed in the same Winnipeg hospital where Marge is a physiotherapist. Marge, in black Reebcks and faded navy sweatpants, can be counted on to give advice about the right kind of snack food for a day of sitting on a bus and the proper shoes for cobblestone and concrete. But Graham suspects that her concern with diet and posture and insteps arises not so much from professional interest as from deep-rooted misgivings about her own dumpy shapelessness.

"The most important thing is shoes," she says with authority, whenever she speaks of her travels. "I always take two pairs. Real comfortable ones. Forget about chic when you're travelling."

This is aimed at June Lewis, who steps onto the bus each morning crisp as a new page, jacket matched to skirt, a fresh blouse, a scarf that goes with the day's earrings. And narrow, tiny-heeled shoes of thin, soft leather not meant for cobblestone. Expensive. Her husband, Gerald, with whom she quarrels from time to time, is equally impeccable in pressed slacks and either a matching pullover or a coordinating sports jacket, a tie discreetly visible. It reminds Graham of the way he dressed for school until he discovered that his students were keeping a tally of how many ties he owned and laying bets on whether he had a system for shoe rotation. He became more casual then, like the other teachers, though he never wore jeans to class.

The Lewises are not popular with the group. June has a bladder the size of a peanut and asks for bathroom stops more often than any of the others. Afterwards she complains about the facilities, usually the squatting kind, and dirty.

"I'd rather use the bush," she whines. "Why can't we just stop near a bush?"

But although they pass plenty of forests, the driver says that's illegal. June's fastidiousness irritates everyone and Gerald can be heard muttering, "Can't you hold it, June? Everyone else does, you know," and Elise announces to no one in particular, "It's actually very good to hold it. Pinching the bladder muscles exercises them. It's very good." After that Bob Carr calls out periodically, "OK folks, time for pinching practice. Get those friggin' bladder muscles in shape. Ready, now, one two three pinch. Pinch, everybody. Pinch."

The bus explodes in laughter every time.

"Aren't we a bunch of crazies?" Marge calls out and Graham can't tell whether the enthusiasm in her voice is just unrestrained brashness or cynicism.

"Do us good to be silly," Susan says. "Do us lots of good."

Graham imagines Gerald cringing beside the fresh blouse and pointy heels of his wife.

Most of the shoes behind the window in the museum had no soles. Worn out, Graham thought, until the guide—she had been a good guide, grim, doling out just enough information and leading the group efficiently from building to building through the intermittent drizzle—told them the Nazi guards routinely tore away the soles to look for hidden money. He pictured a detachment of new arrivals stumbling like animals from the cattle car in which they have travelled God knows how many days. Released abruptly from the airless, stinking cage, their limbs numb, they are stunned by the sudden light and air surrounding them. Do they believe for a moment that they are not doomed after all? Do they shuffle forward with stupid hope, in shoes heavy with gold, holding tenaciously to some carefully conceived plan to save what they possess? In the end nothing is saved, not their shoes, not their lives. Graham escaped in haste from the crematorium, from the unbearable closeness in the cramped room, from his fellow travellers and the heavy, mute presence of the two ovens whose metal parts, the guide assured them, were original.

The bus is leaving the parking lot and Nanette turns her face to the rain-wet window. Graham wants to speak to her, to ask her something about what they have seen, to initiate a conversation, but he can't think of a good way to begin. In front of his class he always manages an air of good humour. He prepares anecdotes to go with his lessons and memorizes jokes, but alone with an adolescent he feels strangely shy. He believed earlier that this shyness would fade as he became experienced in the classroom, but that never happened. "I'm just not good at small talk," he would tell Lorraine, the English teacher in the room next to his. "Anyway, I think a teacher should teach. Popularity, well, that's actually overrated, don't you think?"

He can't remember whether Lorraine, whose students adore her, replied to that.

At the end of their tour of the barracks with those barbarous displays of old brushes—hair brushes, toothbrushes, clothes brushes—and human hair so faded it seemed artificial, hoary as the hair of ghosts, they were shown a film made by the Russians when they liberated Auschwitz. Sweat streamed down Graham's forehead and his hands grew clammy watching a team of doctors work over a young girl who had been forced to stand barefoot for hours in the snow-covered yard. When a doctor removed the bandages from the small feet, Graham had to take himself firmly in hand to keep from crying like a baby. Bewildered women, their grey heads sunk into filthy matresses or resting gauntly against the wooden edge of a bunk, turned their dull, uncomprehending eyes to the camera. He forced himself not to turn away from images of bodies tossed like refuse into burial pits. Their limbs, so thin they might be the limbs of birds or starved animals, reminded him of his mother, who lost flesh steadily in the months before she died.

Rain continues to fall on Poland. Fields and forests slide with easy leisure past the misted window. The driver seems always to find the narrow, slow roads, as if this country has no highways that permit speed. They pass rye crops, trees crowned with storks' nests, green meadows and, in the distance, groups of three or four small animals, deer or antelope, nibbling at the wet grass. John Higgins has a map which he disappears behind from time to time, and when he emerges, he claims the driver isn't following the best route to the border.

"We'll never get to Prague at this rate," he says, and Anne Higgins chimes in, "I think you're right, John. Absolutely." No one pays attention. Nanette keeps her face turned to the window, away from her father's childish complaints.

About an hour later the driver, shortly after navigating the bus through the single winding street of a small village with rundown, weather-beaten buildings, most of them fitted with satellite dishes, slows the bus and brings it to a stop. He pulls out a map and scrutinizes it.

"See? He's lost." John Higgins speaks with the satisfaction of one vindicated, but when he carries his own map to the front, the driver, whose English is tentative, waves him away and the bus moves on. "We should have told them in Warsaw we wanted a bus driver we can talk to," John says, disgruntled. "Not this Russian."

"That's right, John," his wife croons. "How can we be expected to understand Russian?" The travellers turn to the landscape or to the separate memories and dreams, pleasant or painful, that accompany them.

Graham unwraps his sandwich and withdraws into his own mind, where he is most at home. He wishes he had saved his orange. Given the time difference between eastern Europe and central Canada, yesterday must have been the day, one year ago, when the charge nurse at Donwood Manor called: "Mrs. Schwartz has taken a fall. We suspect a fracture and we've called an ambulance." Every life has to end somehow and Graham had long been wondering, not with impatience but with a kind of curiosity, how his mother's—she was eighty-six—would conclude. With attention that was almost academic, he had observed her slow fading during six years in the nursing home: her memory became unreliable. There was a perceptible diminishing of her body. Eyes and ears failed, and her hands, so busy all her life, lay motionless as dead birds in her narrow lap. But her spirit remained restless and resolute, as if readying itself for flight, aware of some event of significance still to come.

The fall had broken her hip, and although Graham protested, the doctor insisted on surgery to pin the crumbling bone. Graham was not surprised when his mother survived surgery. She had never been one to give in. The next day she lay serene and silent on the white hospital bed. Except for the tubes attached to her arm and nose, the catheter tube snaking out from under the bedcovers into a plastic bag filling up with yellow fluid, she reminded him of a saint. This surprised him. She had been a practical sort of person, a woman who proceeded with a certain tenacity to get what she wanted, not the sort anyone would have considered particularly spiritual. But standing beside her hospital bed, he wouldn't have been surprised to catch a glimpse of light spreading a faint glow around her sparse white hair.

"Look." Nanette is pointing to a roadside shrine, a blue and white painted plaster virgin housed in a small, plastic-windowed, wooden cage set on a pole. "That's number seven."

"In Manitoba you'd be counting grain elevators," Graham says.

Nanette turns to him. "Last year we flew to Vancouver," she says and Graham is about to ask does their family travel a lot, what does she think about Auschwitz, does she miss her school friends—she's the only teenager on the tour—but the driver has slowed the bus once again and is bringing it to a stop. The indistinct murmur that has filled the bus subsides and the whole group falls into uneasy expectation.

"Why did the Pole stop the bus in the middle of nowhere?" Bob Carr's question breaks the silence, but there are no takers and Graham is disgusted at Bob's boorishness. And ignorance. The driver is a Russian, not a Pole. This time when John Higgins carries his map forward, it is accepted reluctantly, studied to the accompaniment of grunts, folded neatly and returned to its owner. The bus moves on.

After twenty-four hours of lying quietly, asleep or semi-conscious, Graham's mother entered a state of delirium that he found appropriate for her. She insisted on sitting up in spite of the pain in her hip. "Jesus!" she called out, her voice amazingly firm for one so frail. "Jesus, Jesus!" The confinement of the raised bedrails irritated her and she would twist her gaunt body with its fragile limbs until a skinny leg found its way out between the metal rails and Graham would have to call the nurse.

Until it became necessary for her to be in the nursing home, Graham and his mother had lived together in her house. She always had meals ready for him—he particularly liked the way she prepared stew and dumplings —and he could count on his laundry being done, shirts and even socks pressed. Still, he wondered constantly what life would be like if they lived separately. He longed to try it. "Don't stay on my account," his mother said whenever he spoke of taking his own apartment. "I'll be fine." But he wasn't sure she meant it. "People would probably say we'd quarrelled if you moved out," she mused. He wondered if that really mattered, but made no move to leave, even though he felt the bungalow shrinking and the rooms growing stuffier each year, as if the windows were never opened, the fresh air kept resolutely out. There must be another way of living, he thought, but his mother's enduring presence barred that way.

The gas chamber at Auschwitz was surprisingly small. The guide pointed out the holes in the ceiling through which the lethal Zyklon-B gas had been injected when the room was filled with newly arrived, disoriented, doomed men or women. Had any of them realized with a sudden shock of comprehension that they had arrived at an absolute end? Graham imagines a mother standing thigh to naked thigh with her adolescent daughter whom she has managed to keep beside her until this moment. This very final moment. The daughter is embarrassed, awkward perhaps, standing naked like this, feeling her mother's warm flesh next to hers as she waits for the shower: the promised water that any moment now will rain down an extravagant blessing over her hot, grimed skin. The mother takes her daughter into her arms, presses the firm young breasts against her already sagging ones.

What really amazed Graham about his mother in those last days was the unexpected energy released in her frail body. Her hands began to move constantly, urgently, groping for something to grab and hold on to with amazing strength. When she was most frantic Graham had to grasp her hands tightly to keep them from yanking out the oxygen and intravenous tubes, and tearing away the bandages from the incision, pulling up the bedsheets, the blue hospital gown, leaving herself exposed. Graham hastily drew the curtain around her bed and wrestled to gain control of her hands, to restore her to decency.

The rain has stopped and for over an hour the bus has moved steadily, with more speed than usual, toward the border. The sun has followed its course and day has turned to dusk, dusk to night, when a new noise issues from the left rear of the bus. It increases and becomes a sharp clanging, a jarring counterpoint to the rhythm of the motor.

"Are we out of gas?" June asks, and Marge turns to Elise with, "Give me a break, already. That woman's going to drive me bananas."

Gerald says, "Shut up, June."

"Friggin' brakes are acting up." That's Bob Carr from his seat near the back, announcing his diagnosis with the smugness of a doomsday prophet.

All the travellers, some of whom have been sleeping, rouse themselves as the bus slows to a stop and the driver gets out, followed by Bob Carr. Gradually the others leave too.

"Better take the opportunity," Gerald tells June. "No matter if there's bush out there or not. It's getting dark, no one can see anyway."

"Want to stretch your legs, Nanette?" her mother asks on her way down the aisle.

"Nope. I'm fine here." The girl's voice is cool. Melodious but distant.

Wanting to align himself with that self-sufficiency, Graham thinks he'll stay too. He is aware of the movement of her warm body as she pulls on a sweater, jostling him with her elbow. He is appalled by the strength of the desire rising in him, the sudden need to hold her warmly in his arms. Touch the skin of her cheek. Stroke her straight brown hair. She turns again toward the window, away from him.

"I was hoping we'd get to Prague before midnight," he

says. He wants to dispel the silence, wants to bury his face in her hair, bury that longing that may be nothing more than a yearning for his own youth. "Who knows how long we'll be at the border," he says.

Nanette's "Uh-huh" sounds a lot like "Who cares?"

The bus is empty now except for the two of them. A wave of cool night air drifts in through the open door, carrying with it a flow of muted voices and a harsh clanging of tools as the driver works at the back.

And then Nanette turns deliberately toward Graham. "I know what those words mean, *Arbeit macht frei*," she says. "They mean work makes you free, but I think that's dumb. It doesn't. And all that hair they cut off the Jews. And kept it. Yuk. And those crutches and artificial legs. That grossed me out. I mean, do you think they were terribly afraid?" She pauses as if waiting for a response, but Graham is quiet. "I don't think so," she goes on. "I think they died like right away with that gas. They must have died right away." She looks at him, and there's a steadfast petition in her gaze. Or is it a challenge? Graham wants to reassure her, but he's not certain she wants reassurance. Maybe she'd prefer an argument.

"What are you looking forward to when we get to Prague?" he asks.

"The ghost tour."

"The ghost...?"

"Tour. I read about it. You meet like at the clock tower in the old town square and a guide takes you down all the dark and spooky streets and alleys and dead ends and every once in a while you stop and the guide tells a real scary ghost story. And sometimes, when you're not expecting anything, the ghost leaps out at you from a pitch-dark doorway or someplace and goes POW!" And here she contorts her face and swings a fist so close to Graham he flinches. "My dad says ghost tours are insane. A waste of money. But I'm going. It's cool."

Graham is baffled. He has been reading in *The Lonely*

Planet Guidebook about Franz Kafka, who lived and wrote in Prague and about John Hus, whose church he plans to visit. In 1969 Jan Palach immolated himself in the city, in the name of freedom. Graham has never heard of the ghost tours.

"Think I'll go out and stretch my legs," he says, thinking that he's never once heard John Higgins speak to his daughter.

When Graham steps from the cramped darkness of the bus into the larger darkness outside, he is stiff from sitting still so long and nearly bumps into Susan.

"Meet Franz," she says.

"Who?"

"Franz. I've christened my dragon."

Graham turns from her with a sigh.

"It's for Kafka," Susan calls after him, her voice resonant with plaintiveness. "He lived in Prague."

Moving away from the bus, Graham crosses the ditch, stumbling through the wet reeds and bumping his feet against rocks he can't see in the dark. The way Susan hangs on to that dragon disgusts him. As if it's the only creature she can count on. From the other side of the ditch, he observes the others milling around the door or bunched against the side of the bus for shelter from the night. In the window above them, he imagines Nanette's face, grey, indistinct. Her calm and fearless eyes peer into the darkness as she sips a Coke or apple juice. Does she see him? Is she watching her parents?

"Can't anybody in this godforsaken part of the world ever do anything right?" John Higgins asks as the driver fumbles with flashlight and tools. There is a kind of despair in his outburst as well a child's impatient petulance. His wife places a soothing arm around him. "John," she murmurs. "John."

Susan is walking her dragon through the air, making him sing, "The hills are alive with the sound of music." Thin and quavery, the song floats a while in the damp darkness and then dissipates.

Graham was with his mother when she died. After the delirium left her, she lay for two days, exhausted, curled like a cocoon under a hill of bedcovers, opening her lips obediently so he could inject tea from a dropper into her parched mouth. On the third day he had found her lying straight in the bed, her face almost transparent, eyes closed, her breathing so rapid he knew it couldn't possibly be sustained for long.

"Her feet are cold," the nurse said after checking under the covers. When he didn't reply she added, "It's a sign." The eyes had opened then in amazed protest, and the mouth moved stiffly, as if she was trying to tell him something. As if whatever was about to happen was completely unexpected and did not meet with her approval. Or perhaps she was already gone.

Graham crosses the ditch back to the road in front of the bus and begins walking in the direction of Prague. His thin jacket is no protection against the chill, his city shoes inadequate for the uneven pavement. As he gains distance, the voices behind him grow faint and then fall silent. He draws into himself, into that quiet, sheltered place where he feels safe. And free of the constant chatter, free of the nagging sense of obligation to be part of what's going on. On either side of the road pines tower, dark and ominous. They encourage his retreat. After a while he's walking on air, not asphalt.

He is aware, in this tranquility, that he has left behind him the group huddled around the bus. He pictures Bob Carr trying to advise the driver, June Lewis walking cautiously on her slim heels and clinging to Gerald. Anne Higgins consoling her husband. If the wait is long they will bring out snacks and pop, relieve themselves in the darkness. Maybe Nanette will leave her place at the window and come down to them. She might talk about the ghost tour. Marge will try to marshall everyone into a routine of rigorous bending and stretching that includes all the body's muscles. There is companionship in that small group on which he has deliberately turned his back.

Graham rejects the faint misgivings that appear like bubbles on the surface of his reverie. He walks on. Eventually the bus will chug to life, the headlights will once more cut a bright tunnel through the night landscape and if he hasn't walked too far or taken a wrong turn they will illuminate his solitary figure walking steadily along the dark road. Somehow or other, sooner or later, they will all reach Prague.

Graham considers it fortunate that he was at his mother's bedside when she died. It could easily have been otherwise. He believes if she had died alone, her loneliness would have been added to his. His guilt would have become unbearable. He harbours no illusions about having been a good son, but he remembers his hands touching her cold ones. He thinks he also remembers her last breath, but he's not certain.

Here, in the darkness, he is aware of his own breathing. The air is moist from the recent rain. The trees have become spectral shapes on the other side of the ditch. He isn't afraid that someone will leap out at him, but his steps slow down. He misses Nanette's body breathing beside him, even if it's turned purposefully away from him. He pictures, deliberately and without disdain, Susan and her outrageous dragon. Franz. If he should decide to turn back and return to the bus, he could tell her what Kafka is supposed to have said: that the true way goes over a rope stretched just above the ground, and the rope is more designed for stumbling than for moving along.

Graham walks more and more uncertainly and finally stops. He turns around. Ahead, as behind, there is only gloom, but somewhere near the stationary bus there is that murmur of voices, too distant for him to hear. He wills his feet into motion and begins retracing his steps, moving in the direction of the voices.

Before long, he feels the weariness. This has been more

exercise than he's used to. And he's cold, walking hasn't warmed him. When the dark shape of the bus finally looms at the roadside, Graham's fellow travellers are starting to push their way toward the door. The motor has rumbled to life and settled into a rough purr that sounds normal to his inexpert ear. And then the lights come on and he is dazzled, blinded by the sudden brightness. He walks faster, he begins to run, urging his body forward and swinging his arms in an effort to gain speed. Panic spreads to every limb, flows to his fingertips. He is too late. The last passenger has disappeared into the bus. There is the decisive sound of the bus door closing, an alteration in the engine's voice. He leans his body toward the bus and forces his legs and thighs forward, faster. Sweat pours down his forehead.

But the rumbling bus remains motionless. Waiting. Graham reaches the closed door and pounds his fist hard on the metal. It opens. He stumbles up the steps and moves down the aisle, not daring to look at the shadowed faces of the passengers. No one speaks. No one has claimed the place beside Nanette. He sits down, panting like a dog.

"Forty minutes," John Higgins whines. "Forty damn minutes."

Graham thinks for split second that everything is his fault, but then he realizes the driver is meant.

"Bet he can't get us to the proper border crossing," John continues. "Probably can't even find the border."

A murmur of comfort, almost inaudible, issues from Anne Higgins. A groan of disgust or embarrassment from Nanette.

"If you can't handle the stones, don't start on the journey," Marge grumbles for all to hear.

When the driver finally cajoles the bus into motion, there's an air of mixed relief and rebellion, a settling in for the last stretch, a before-sleep crankiness. Graham thinks that maybe no one has noticed his brief desertion until Nanette says, "Where were you? I thought you got lost. I was like thinking there'd have to be a search party."

She is part curious child, part accusing mother, Graham

thinks. Warm and grateful, he bends to undo the laces and ease his feet out of his shoes. His breath still comes in short, quick gasps.

"I wasn't lost," he says.

"Good thing." Nanette leans toward him so her arm touches his. "I could tell you some people in this bus who are," she whispers. "Lost and stupid too."

"Don't worry," Graham says, smiling into the darkness at his feet. "If I can find my way, anybody can."

He straightens up, fumbles for *The Lonely Planet Guidebook*. The word *Lonely* in the title stares at him. He pictures planet earth just hanging there, unattached to anything in the vast universe. But he knows the word refers to the people on the planet. They are lonely. But isn't that to be expected? And is it so bad? Kafka said the world will offer itself to the solitary. Graham is cheered by the thought. As Nanette turns once more to her window and the bus finally gathers speed, he closes his eyes and waits.